Munday

Munday

Hugh Zachary

Five Star • Waterville, Maine

Published in 2003 in conjunction with Tekno Books and Ed Gorman.

Set in 11 pt. Plantin by Christina S. Huff.

Printed in the United States on permanent paper.

Library of Congress Cataloging-in-Publication Data

Zachary, Hugh.
   Munday / by Hugh Zachary.
      p. cm.—(Five Star mystery)
    ISBN 0-7862-4323-6 (hc : alk. paper)
    ISBN 1-4104-0134-0 (sc : alk. paper)
    1. Police—North Carolina—Fiction. 2. Teenagers—Crimes against—Fiction. 3. North Carolina—Fiction.
    4. Policewomen—Fiction. I. Title. II. Series.
    PS3576.A23 M75 2003
    813'.54—dc21   2002043067

Munday

About the Author

Munday marks the welcome return of master author Hugh Zachary back to mystery fiction. The author of more than 100 novels, his books have appeared on many bestseller lists, including the *New York Times*. He has been a full-time author for more than thirty years, and has written mysteries, science fiction, and non-fiction.

1

On the day after Christmas, Clare Thomas was dispatching for all of Clarendon County. The communications room at the Sheriff's Department in Summerton was the only lighted area in the entire governmental complex other than the jail, where half a dozen unwilling guests of the county were being fed leftovers from the catered Christmas day turkey.

Everyone else in the world had a three-day holiday, but Clare had found a new home in the dispatcher's chair at the communications console. She was the newest deputy on Sheriff Jug Watson's staff, and it fell to the new kid on the block to pull holiday duty.

It made a girl think, spending twelve hours at a time watching for a blinking light on the telephone switchboard, exchanging occasional laconic, professionally bored chit-chat with the few patrolling deputies out in the field. It made her wonder if she'd been just a bit foolish to start a career in law enforcement at her age and, as a result, end up in a town of less than four thousand people in the middle of the bays, swamps, and timber farms of one of eastern North Carolina's largest, least populated, and poorest counties. For a lady of thirty who would never, no matter how much she watched her diet, be invited to participate in filming the *Sports Illustrated* swimsuit issue, the pickings were poor and the crop was lean in Clarendon. The best ones were married and in the months since she had become Deputy Clare Thomas she had assisted in apprehending a few of the rest.

She caught an incoming call on the first blink of the light.

"C.S.D., Deputy Thomas."

"Huh?"

She sighed. The call was coming from the eastern beaches exchange. The caller's reaction was predictable.

"This is the Clarendon Sheriff's Department, Deputy Thomas speaking."

"Uh, I was calling Fortier Beach Police."

"Yes. We answer their calls on holidays and at night. How can I help you?"

The voice on the telephone was male, and young. "What you do, you call Dan Munday and tell him he'd better come on up to the old machine gun emplacement."

"We can contact Fortier Beach Police, yes," Clare said patiently. "What is the nature of the emergency?"

"Just tell Chief Munday he'd better come on up here."

"Your name, please?"

"Huh?"

"Your name."

"Oh. Jimmy Small. Just tell Chief Munday it's Jimmy. He'll know. Tell him to come on up to the old machine gun nest."

"Jimmy, what's the matter? Is someone hurt?"

"Naw." There was a pause, then a muffled laugh. "Well, I guess you could say that."

"Who is hurt? What is the nature of the injury?"

"Well, there's this Afro-American moccasin we found in the surf, you know?"

"No, I don't know."

"A sneaker. You know. One of them you blow up by pushing on a little pump."

"A sneaker," Clare said. "Jimmy, why should I call Chief Munday because you found a sneaker in the surf?"

"Well, maybe because it's still got a foot in it."

Dan Munday rated his fireplace efforts on a scale of one to ten not for efficiency but by appearances. He had a class seven blaze going. A class seven was almost smokeless with flames about six to ten inches high above the stack of dried wood. It missed being a ten only by not having burned long enough to build up a bed of embers. It was one damned fine fire and it was a fine day to be indoors with a class seven going and a good movie ready on the VCR.

He made two trips to the kitchen for chips and dip, three Fig Newton cookies Jilly had overlooked, a steaming cup of coffee. He had a mouthful when the telephone rang. He lifted the instrument and managed to say, "Hold on a minute."

He was watching the store. He'd given his three-man force the day off. He chewed and the Fig Newton in his mouth seemed to expand. He tried to wash it down with coffee, burned his tongue, had to talk around the remainder of the cookie.

"Munday."

He listened with a pained expression, looked at his class seven fire with regret.

"All right, damnit," he said, at last. "Thanks, Clare."

"No problem," she said, "sorry to break into your day."

"Well," he said, "that's the name of the game, isn't it?"

"Have a nice Christmas?"

A bleakness came into his eyes. With Jilly gone the house was filled with ringing emptiness. "Fine. You?"

"If you call spending twelve hours in the communications room fine, fine."

"Stuck the duty to the new man, huh?"

"You got it. Sounds as if you've been there."

He laughed. "It's been a helluva long time since I was new at anything."

"Poor old fellow."

"Creak," he said.

Her voice took on a teasing tone. "Listen, if you need some help when it comes time to meet the new physical standards—"

He groaned. She was talking about the new state regulations for the physical fitness of all law enforcement officers. "Thank God I won't be around when that goes into full effect," he said.

He looked down at his copious spread. His uniform pants were too tight and his shirt was developing gaposis, but he had just a year and a half to go before he pulled the pin. It seemed economically counterproductive to invest in new uniforms to fit that part of Dan Munday hanging over his belt when he had such a short time to go. When he ceased being Chief Dan Munday and became a full time sales representative for McRae Realty he'd have to buy at least two changes of decent civilian clothes, and there was little enough slack in his budget on full salary. The retirement pay would give him a foundation, but he'd have to learn the real estate business damned fast when Jilly graduated from East Clarendon High School and was ready for college.

"Well, happy holidays, old man," Clare said.

"Same," Dan said.

"I'll be curious to know what you find up there with those kids," Clare said.

"I'll let you know."

She seemed reluctant to hang up. Dan could picture her. He'd trained himself over the years to remember faces and distinguishing features. She had a rectangular face with full cheek bones, large, corner-crinkled brown eyes, brown hair tapered up at the back and flared at the sides like a 1920's flapper, a full mouth with corners twisting interestingly when she smiled. Although she was pleasingly shapely, she was a solid, sturdily built girl.

"I'll be here," she said.

"Hey, Clare—" He almost said it, almost asked her if she'd like to help him finish off a butt of honey-cured ham and a six pack of Coors when she came off duty, but he was forty-five years old and he hung over at the belt and she was, what? Maybe twenty-five, twenty-six?

"Yeah?"

"Thanks for the call."

"See you, Dan."

He girded himself with his belt, beeper, cuffs, the new 9 mm automatic that had cost Fortier Beach more than the Board of Commissioners wanted to pay. Had she sounded a little put off there at the end? She always had a smile for him, but then she had a smile for most everyone, didn't she?

He went out into a chill northwest wind drifting down from dark, rain-promising clouds. The temperature had dropped twenty degrees from Christmas Day when there had been players in shirtsleeves on the fairways of the Fortier Beach Golf Club.

The city purchased its police cars, three of them, from the North Carolina Highway Patrol. By the time Dan Munday and his three-man force began to use them to patrol the eight miles of narrow, barrier island, each of them had been ridden hard and put up wet with a hundred thousand miles on the odometer. They were fitted with new radio equipment, but there were no computers. It wasn't for Fortier Beach Police to push a few buttons and have a complete rundown on the license tag of a suspicious automobile. The Kid, Munday's policeman, was ashamed of the cars. He said the town Board of Commissioners strictly forbade high speed pursuit not because there was only one road off the island and one had only to call the Clarendon Sheriff's Department or the highway patrol to have roadblocks put in place, but to keep the weary F.B.P.D. Fords from being embarrassed by a kid in a recycled Volkswagen bug. The logic was that radio was faster than the F.B.P.D. cars, but, the Kid said, so was a twelve-year-old asthmatic girl on a bicycle.

When Dan turned the key the old Ford groaned and strained. Unnnnnn-unnnnn-unnnnn. To his relief the motor caught. He let her warm up for a full minute before easing out of the drive.

Jimmy Small and a visiting cousin met Munday on the roadside in front of a cement box with machine gun slits half covered by drifted sand. The box dated back to World War I when it and the old army camp on the eastern tip of the island successfully prevented an invasion of the United States by Kaiser Bill's Huns.

"Chief, this is Cuz," Jimmy said. The boys were sleek as seals in black wetsuits.

"Does Cuz have a real name?" Munday asked.

"Skip," Cuz said.

"Hi, Skip," Dan said. "Good surf?"

"Well, you know," Skip said.

"No," Dan said.

"Huh?"

"No, I don't know," Dan said.

"Did you and Jilly have a nice Christmas?" Jimmy asked.

"She was with her mother," Dan said. "She'll be flying into Worthing on Sunday before school starts."

"Wow, Florida," Jimmy said.

"Yeah, wow," Dan said.

"Well, we found this thing," Jimmy said.

"Let's have a look."

Dan followed the boys down a sandy path through the seaside growth. The developers had not yet stripped that section of beach of the protective yaupons, wind-bent oaks, and dense vines on and behind the dunes because there was not enough land between high water and the road to build cracker-box-on-stilts cottages to match those along most of the ocean front.

A spatter of rain hit Dan in the face as he trudged through loose sand. There was no surf at all. A smooth swell lifted lazily to plop onto the dark, wet sand from a height of inches. Fortier Beach was an East Coast anomaly, running west from the Cape. The pale winter sun was low to the south out over the water and would set in the sea.

The sneaker lay on its side near two colorful surfboards. It had been washed up by a full moon high tide. Dan turned it with a stick. Shreds of flesh were bleached white. Jagged bone protruded just past the waterlogged top of the footwear. He stood and looked out over the glassy sea. Two shrimp boats were trawling about a half-mile offshore. If the owner of the sneaker and the foot inside it had gone overboard from a legitimately operating vessel, the Coast Guard would have been notified, and, in due course, the appropriate law enforcement agencies would have been contacted.

To the east, marked by a range of black buoys, was the shipping channel into the Blue River. A variety of vessels came and went through the mouth of the river and the port at Worthing. Foreign flag ships sailed from the Blue toward Germany, Israel, Taiwan, Japan, the Gulf Coast, the Arab states, South America. To the west and south unlit, isolated inlets and estuaries had been the destination for more than one fast, night-running boat with a cargo of Jamaican *ganja* or worse.

2

Three days after Christmas Bubba Dean decided to have a birthday. In the old days, when Munday first came to work for the F.B.P.D. and everyone on the island knew everyone else, Bubba had at least three birthdays per winter. The back dining room at Sellers Harbor Fine Seafood could seat most of the permanent population of Fortier Beach then, and Bubba's famous birthday parties were open to all. There hadn't been as many celebrations since the nationwide seaward migration, the chemical plant, and the smaller industries associated with it brought a measure of prosperity and a growing accumulation of strangers to Clarendon County; but three days after Christmas cold, Canadian air collided with Atlantic moisture to create huge, floating snowflakes that dissolved as soon as they hit the ground. Snow made Bubba sentimental and lonely. He put his office girls to work calling everyone on his birthday list with the usual no-presents-required-bring-your-own-bottle invitation. By nine o'clock sixty plus people were gathered in John Sellers' back dining room and Bubba was so drunk that he had to hold onto the tablecloth to stay on the world.

For music there was a mixture of rock and country on the jukebox. Someone had turned the volume to maximum. The monotonous boom of a drum punctuated the babble of voices. A few of the younger ones pushed tables aside in the front dining room to make room for dancing. Dan Munday stood behind the swinging door leading into the kitchen. He knew all but three or four of the people in the two dining rooms. A few of the pioneers who had moved to the island when it was nothing but twice-cut piney woodlands were still around, and most of the others were residents of at least a decade's standing, which made them honorary natives.

Bubba Dean saw Munday peering over the top of the swinging door and bellowed out a greeting. Munday obeyed Bubba's commanding but wobbly beckoning.

"Buddy, have a drink," Bubba yelled.

"Someone's going to have to drive you home, Bubba," Dan said.

"Oh-hell-yeah," Bubba chortled. "Ain't this a fine party?"

"Abso-damned-lutely," Dan said.

"Makes me feel right humble, so many folks here to honor my birthday."

"At the rate of two or three a year, how old does that make you?" Munday asked.

Bubba roared laughter. "Who's counting?"

From the jukebox, a rock band screeched distorted electric guitars at tooth-vibrating volume.

"Bubba, when they started to put amplifiers on drums I knew the world was in trouble," Munday said.

"Huh?" Bubba asked.

"Have yourself a ball," Munday said, turning to almost bump into Evie Baugh.

"Hi, Dan."

"You're looking super, Evie."

"You lie so nicely." She was a maturely plush woman. The top of her head came to Munday's chin so that she was looking up at him from behind the jeweled rims of her glasses. Her hair was cut short and permed into a tight, wiry mass.

"No lie, just fact," Munday said, taking Evie's hand in his. "Who are you with?"

"I'm alone," she said. "I came hoping to snag myself a handsome young man, but I'll settle for you. I have a table over in the corner."

Munday followed Evie to a table slightly removed from the others. She was drinking bourbon and ginger ale. He accepted a glass of mix without the sweetener.

"So, how are things in town?" Munday asked.

"Well, you know."

"No."

"Summerton is Summerton."

"The only cemetery in the western world with a sewage disposal system."

She laughed. "Well, it's quiet." She sipped, trained her brown eyes on his face over the rim of the glass. "I hate holidays."

He nodded.

"I picked up the telephone to call you Christmas Eve," she said.

"I wish to hell you had."

"Well, I knew that you'd want to spend such a special time with your daughter."

"Jilly's in Florida."

"Oh." She toyed with her drink. "How is Elaine?"

"Fat, rich, and sassy," he said. "I spoke with her on the telephone while we were making the arrangements for Jilly to spend Christmas with her."

Evie reached out, placed her hand atop his. "Still hurts? After all this time?"

He shrugged. "Why didn't you call on Christmas Eve?"

"The telephone lines between Summerton and the beach work both ways."

Evie Baugh had moved to Fortier Beach a few months before Elaine McWhorter Munday annihilated all of the romance in Dan Munday's life and proved once again that money is everything by announcing quite calmly she was deathly tired of living on the pittance Fortier Beach paid its chief law enforcement officer. Elaine was a petite woman, as tidy and trim as a Barbie doll. She was dressed in white when she came into the study where Munday was reading a law enforcement journal to tell him that she was leaving him to marry Jason Flowers.

"Jason Flowers? My God, he's old enough—"

"The matter is not open for discussion, Dan."

"You waltz in here and tell me that you want a divorce and it's not something we can talk about?"

"I didn't make my decision lightly."

"Just independently," he said. "At least I don't recall being consulted."

"I'm sorry that I had to hurt you, Dan."

"Hurt? Me? By the way, since Jason Flowers has a pot full of money and some on the handle I wonder if yawl would mind paying me alimony?"

"No, Dan, we can't laugh it off this time."

Hell.

Evie Baugh's hand was warm on his. He turned his hand to clasp hers and squeezed. Evie had kept him alive during the first terrible month after Elaine left the cottage carrying only one small case—her way of getting in one last jab to his solar plexus by telling him the clothes he bought for her out of his salary were not worth carrying off. Evie had moved to North Carolina to escape her own bad marriage and in that torrid month of their mutual anguish she exhibited as much need as he.

But even death heals, in all but the dead. Evie landed a job teaching at East Clarendon High School and moved into town to be closer to her work. Dan assumed she felt the same pangs of guilt that he felt, although Evie had no daughter to be left alone when they met to cling and share a few tears and use sex as a drug to deaden memories.

"You asked me if it still hurts," he said.

She nodded.

"It does, but I don't let it bother me. You wanta get out of here?"

She shook her head. "We've traveled that road, Dan."

"Not lately. I figure we were both like kids trying to learn to drive again after having our heads bashed in a very loud smash-up. We were both thinking more about the accident and the pain of it than what we were doing. I think we deserve a second chance, don't you?"

She looked away. Light reflected on the lens of her glasses. She had the softest brown eyes, long lashes, a perky little nose and a full mouth. Her upper lip was flat, and spread to a pleasing wideness when she smiled. After a long pause she nodded her head slowly.

For a full thirty seconds it sounded—unnnnnnnn, unnnnnn, unnnnnn—as if the pride of the F.B.P.D.'s automotive fleet had been bested by the December cold.

"Good Lord," Evie said, "what's that smell?"

The motor caught, coughed, rattled, smoothed down as well as a police interceptor rig could after being driven almost one-hundred-fifty-thousand miles.

"Evie, I don't think you really want to know."

"Smells like something dead."

"One time when Jilly was just six we found a bed of live sand dollars in the inlet. Several of them fell out of the container and stayed in the trunk of the car over a long weekend in August. We scrubbed and sprayed and aired and the smell still stayed with us for weeks."

"You haven't been out gathering sand dollars in December."

"Nope. I learned my lesson. About sand dollars, at least."

The sneaker with its contents had been so saturated with salt water when he put it into the trunk for an overnight stay there'd been almost no smell. He left it in the trunk because he couldn't very well take it into the little office in City Hall to edify the Town Clerk and the Budget Officer. He considered putting it in the freezer of his refrigerator, but it was full of frozen trout. Fall fishing had been good. Now the sneaker and contents were on the way to the medical officer in Raleigh packed in dry ice, leaving behind a stench in the trunk of F.B.P.D. Number One and questions in the mind of Dan Munday.

"I'm not going to ask you again," Evie said.

"Good."

"Bastard," she said

He grinned and said, "Guilty."

He was glad he had spent a portion of the afternoon cleaning the cottage. He turned the heat down before leaving for Bubba's party. It was sixty-five degrees in the bedroom, cool at first. Exposed, she shivered. He covered her with his body, pulled a blanket atop them.

She peaked with a ladylike little moan, opened her eyes, kissed him lightly, smiled. "You haven't forgotten how."

"You did pretty well yourself."

"For an old woman."

"Old, hell. I'm older than you. Don't lay that *old* jazz on me."

"Mature, then."

"I'll accept that."

She waited until he finished in the bathroom and was lying beside her again before she went to freshen herself. He watched her buttocks move up and down enticingly, felt a sense of loss when she disappeared into the bath. He heard water running. The john flushed. She ran to the bed, crawled under the blanket.

"Damn, woman, how'd your feet get so cold so quick?"

"Why do you keep it so damned cold in the house?" she countered.

She turned, pressed her rump into him. He put his arm around her.

"Don't let me go to sleep," she said. "Even in this day and time a maiden lady schoolteacher has to watch her reputation."

" 'Kay," he said.

"Don't you go to sleep, either."

"Ummm."

"Dannnnnnn."

"All right. Know why women have legs?"

"No, and I'm not sure I want to."

"So their feet won't smell like pussy."

"You're terrible."

"You always used to ask me about my work."

"And you were always closemouthed about it."

"We had an interesting case just this week."

"Ummmm?"

"Woman was assaulted by two gay fellows on the beach."

"Really?"

"One of them held her down while the other did her hair."

She punched him in the stomach with her elbow. He grunted.

"You're going to sleep," he said, a few minutes later.

"No, just thinking."

"I'm fresh out of pennies."

"I was just dreading going back to the grind next week," she said. "Back to the zoo."

"I thought you loved your work."

"The work I love. It's the bullshit that keeps me from doing my work that bothers me." She turned onto her back. "I'm a good teacher, Dan. I like teaching. I like introducing young people to the beauty of our language. It's true that most of them read Shakespeare because if they don't they won't pass English and, therefore, won't be able to graduate, but every now and then one comes along who not only understands the words, but hears the music. One out of each class, that's all I ask. I can put up with the gigglers, the note passers, the chronically late, the profane, the threat of violence that hangs over every teacher just as long as there's one student who sits there with his or her eyes wide taking in every word, every nuance, reveling in the thunder and passion of it."

"I'm afraid my Jilly might be one of those who reads old Will simply because of the threat involved in not doing it."

"Oh, Jilly's all right. Sometimes preoccupied with other things—" She paused. "Sorry, let's not bring up that subject again."

"No problem, but I take it Jilly's not the one who sits there wideeyed and sponge-like."

"No. Sorry. This year's teacher's pet is little Hillary Aycock."

"Tom and Fran Aycock's girl. She's a cutie."

"But I'm worried about her."

Munday raised himself to one elbow, looked down at Evie. In the dim light of the bedside lamp she looked years younger. If you want to see how a woman's face would accept cosmetic surgery, look at her from above while she's lying on her back.

"In the last reporting period her grades have fallen startlingly," Evie said. "She's a straight A student. A shoo-in for top honors, in line for her choice of the two best scholarships in the state, and if I grade her on performance alone I'm going to have to give her a D in English this time. Her counselor tells me that it's even worse in her other classes."

"Does she seem remote and detached?" Munday asked. "Sleepy in class?"

"Yes, but I know where you're going. Dope. That was the first thing I thought of. Her counselor had a talk with her parents. They said she hasn't been sleeping well. They had no clue as to what was going on with her, but they did state vehemently that, of course, their little darling was not on drugs."

"Any way you can convince her parents to have her see a doctor?"

"Oh, she has. The school nurse had a look at her files. Blood test clean. The doctor said stress, fatigue. Suggested that Hillary get more rest."

"Well, she'll come out of it," Munday said, reaching out with thumb and finger to massage Evie's right nipple into proud erectness.

"Do you have further evil designs on my maidenly bod, sir?" she asked.

"Yep," he said.

"My, you sound so excited about it."

"Doesn't pay to get excited. When I graduated from the third grade I got excited and cut myself while shaving."

She rolled atop him, felt evidence that he was not exactly unaware of her, after all, smothered his mouth with hers. He gasped for breath, broke the kiss.

"What in hell is wrong with you?" she asked, as she felt smooth entry.

"I just wanted to tell you that if I get excited and call you Bruce not to think too much about it."

"Shut up," she whispered, pushing down, down, down.

3

Standing behind the wire mesh barrier at the Worthing airport, Munday saw a slim young girl in a fashionably cut peachglow jacket framed for a moment in the exit door of one of U.S. Air's small jets. Her long, slender legs flashed knees at him as she came down the mobile ramp. White lace showed at her throat.

Munday glanced away, watching others take their turn in the door, let his eyes jerk back to the girl in the peach-colored suit, for it was indeed Jilly. Her hair was different. When he put her on the plane for Florida it touched her shoulders. Now it was curled into a tight mass accenting the good shape of her head. The late afternoon December sun sparked on auburn highlights. Modified heels added an inch to her height. She was a dainty girl, even more petite than her mother had been the first time Munday met her.

She saw him, lifted one arm in a graceful gesture, called out, "Dad, hey, Dad."

The love in her voice caused his vision to blur for a moment. He wiped his eyes with the back of his hand and moved down the wire barrier to the waiting room. Through the windows he saw Jilly running, met her just inside the doors. She smelled of burned jet fuel and the same expensive perfume Elaine had favored.

Such a small weight in his arms. Her feet clear of the floor.

24

She was laughing. "Old bear, you haven't shaved since morning." Her cheek smooth on his.

"Hey, I'm glad to see *you*," he said

"Me too."

Other deplaning passengers milled past. Munday held both her hands in his. "Look at you."

"Like it?" She pirouetted, looked up at him, pouting her lips like a fashion model.

"Well, a good-looking girl looks good in anything she throws on."

"Elaine had me color coded," she said, taking his hand to lead him toward the baggage claim area. "I can't remember whether I'm summer or spring but this is one of my colors— or so they told me."

"It's definitely one of your colors," Munday said. "And your hair looks great."

She beamed. "Do you like it, really?"

"I like it, really."

"I was so afraid you wouldn't."

"I didn't recognize you, but I like it."

Her face fell. "I knew I shouldn't have cut it. You hate it."

He laughed and squeezed her hand. "Honey, I like it very much. It makes you look older."

Pleased, she smiled. "Does it really?"

Munday waded into the crush around the baggage conveyor looking for the one battered suitcase belonging to the Munday family of father and daughter.

Jilly pointed. "There's one of them."

He wasn't quick enough. Jilly stepped forward, seized a leather case, was pulled off balance by the weight. Munday took it from her. "My God, what's in here?"

"A thong bikini, among other things," Jilly said. Her quick giggle belied the sophistication of her suit, her hair. The sound spoke of what she was, a girl just turned fifteen, a child on the brink of young womanhood.

"Not likely," Munday said, as Jilly dived to catch a second leather case only slightly smaller than the first. She leaned far out of plumb to compensate for its weight until Munday took it in his other hand.

"Is there more?"

She giggled again. "That's it. The rest is being shipped U.P.S."

"The rest? My God."

Jilly lifted her nose, affected an odd accent that was not recognizable as anything but an attempt by a soft speaking southern girl to sound haughty. "Elaine and Jason are ever so rich, you know."

"No," Munday said.

"Don't pull that on me." She punched him in the side with her elbow. "They're rich and they're damned well going to prove it to everyone, especially you."

"Language, girl."

She went ahead of him, opened the outside door. After the heat of the terminal the north wind was a shock. She shivered. "It was in the seventies in Palm Beach this morning. Elaine and I had a quick dip in the swimming pool. The heated swimming pool."

"Hummm," Munday said.

"In my new thong bikini."

They had arrived at the car. "Oh, no," Jilly moaned, "not the wreck of Old Number One."

"The Rolls is in the garage."

He put the bags in back. Jilly huddled against the chill in the passenger's seat. Old Number One cranked on the first try.

"What's that smell?" Jilly asked.

"What smell?" The lingering aroma of Munday's mistake was faint, but still detectable now and then.

"Like the time we left the sand dollars in the trunk in the summertime."

"Well, while you were gone I got lonely and rented myself a small girl and we went hunting for sand dollars."

"Surrre," Jilly said. "Aside from that, what else have you been up to while I was gone?"

"My social obligations were overwhelming."

"Daaaaad!"

"Bubba Dean had a birthday party."

She laughed.

"Aside from buying out all the shops in Palm Beach, what about you?"

"Elaine and Jason had a party."

"And?"

"She insisted that I wear a long dress."

"Nice, huh?"

"I told her I didn't want it. I left it there."

He was remembering. Elaine had wanted to buy Jilly an evening gown for the dance celebrating her graduation from middle school and Jilly had said no. Solid-minded girl, his daughter.

"Mother," she had said firmly. "I don't want an evening dress. I don't want a long gown until my junior prom. I want to have something to look forward to."

The police radio sputtered. With the holidays past, the regular Sheriff's Department dispatcher was back on duty.

"Can we turn that off?" Jilly asked.

"At your service, lady," Munday said, cranking the volume down to nothing.

"They have four cars," she said.

"Lucky them."

"And a big, fuel-guzzling cabin cruiser. That's not to mention the ski-boat, although she never skis anymore and I had to get the Cuban gardener to drive the boat for me."

"A gardener, too."

"And a cook and two maids."

"I guess she's happy, your mother."

Jilly looked away. The sun was a red glow behind the pine trees lining the road. When she spoke her voice was soft. "Dad, why did she leave us?"

He had never tried to influence Jilly against her mother. "Well, honey, I guess some people just are not meant to live the quiet life."

"I know you two—ah—had your differences. I remember that much."

"It was good for a long time," he said.

"I remember the night you came home—"

She fell silent. Munday's face flushed with the residue of old, remembered anger. He knew without asking which particular night she meant. The incident was fresh in his mind although it was years in the past, when Jilly was only five.

He had had a tussle with a loud drunk in the parking lot of the convenience store and gone home to change out of ripped pants. The car was not in the drive and the house was dark. He let himself in and immediately heard Jilly's sobbing, whimpering. He turned on lights. She was not in her bed. She was sitting on the carpet in the corner of his and Elaine's bedroom.

"Daddy, it's all dark," she said as she ran into his arms.

Elaine came in at eleven-thirty to find him waiting in the living room, rigid with anger.

"You can't expect me to sit home alone night after night," Elaine said. "I didn't leave until she was asleep and Mrs. Jones next door was watching out for her."

28

Yes, they had their differences, but she had the last word, a simple *"Take care of yourself, Dan,"* as she was leaving behind her all evidence of twelve years of marriage, including her daughter.

A deer leaped across the road directly in front of the car.

"A bambi," Jilly said.

Munday touched the brakes, but the moment of danger had passed.

"Jilly, she loved you in her own way," he said.

"I was so scared when I woke up and the house was empty and there were no lights."

"I know, honey."

"I remember when she left. She kissed me on the cheek and said, 'now you be a good girl.' Just as if she was going shopping, or to a party."

"Well, kid, we've done all right, haven't we?"

She moved close to him, took his arm. "Aside from my having to put up with an old bear it's been all right."

Jilly cracked the window on her side as Number One climbed the rise of the bridge over the Intracoastal Waterway. "Salt water doesn't smell the same in Florida," she said. "I'm really glad to be home."

He put the bags in her room and waited for her in the living room. He had the beginnings of a class five going in the fireplace when she came out wearing nothing but a large band over her young breasts and a triangle of gold lamé cloth over her pubic mound.

"Ta-dah," she said, spreading her arms.

"Jumpin' Jesus," Munday said.

"You didn't believe me."

"Don't turn around," he said, as she moved.

"You turned around," he said, as he was mooned by bare girl rump broken only by an almost non-existent thong

29

buried in an uncomfortable looking way into the crevice between her taut buttocks.

She whirled to face him again, her face flushing.

"You didn't wear that thing in public?"

"Just in the swimming pool."

"You picked it out?"

"Elaine. She said you wouldn't like it. Said you always
were a stuffy old bear."

"Well, I guess it's all right if you sleep in it," Munday
said, "but if I catch you on the beach with it I'll have to run
you in."

She giggled. "You would arrest your own darling
daughter?"

Munday grinned wryly. "I think I'm having my leg
pulled."

"A little bit," she admitted. "Elaine wanted me to call her
and tell her about your reaction."

Munday knew about the cost of things like fashionable
swim suits for teenagers. Elaine had reached all the way up
from Florida to punch him in the gut again with a joke that,
depending on the exclusivity of the shop, cost somewhere between thirty-five and one hundred and thirty-five dollars.

"Does she wear those things?"

"Very, very well."

"Yeah."

"I feel naked. I'm going to put on some clothes. Want me
to model the rest of my wardrobe for you?"

One by one she posed for him in surprisingly sensible
clothing, things suitable for school wear, a couple of dressy
outfits for church and occasions. She had picked most of
them herself.

He made popcorn and hot chocolate. The fire developed
into a classic ten with a heat-radiating bed of embers and

crackling blazes. Sleet rattled on the windows. A fitful wind caused the cottage to sway on its creosoted pilings. Over the dry chatter of the sleet on glass and roof came the soft whisper of a surf tamed by the northerly wind. Jilly wanted to hear all about Bubba's latest birthday party and about her friends. He told her about seeing Jimmy Small trying to get in some cold season surfing.

"Jimmy's a yo-yo," she said.

"You're waiting for me to mention a certain good-looking young lad who works evenings at the service station," he said.

"Not particularly," she said, feigning indifference.

"O.K."

"Daaaaaaad."

"He inquired about you twice."

"What did he say?" Her indifference had changed to avid interest.

"Oh, you know."

"No, I don't."

"Asked if you had the braces off your teeth yet."

"He did not," she cried.

"Just asked about you, that's all. Like 'when's Jilly coming home, Chief.' Things like that."

"He wanted me to call him when I got home. Is that all right?"

"No. Ladies do not call gentlemen."

"All my friends say you're hopelessly old-fashioned."

"In an emergency, such as this one, I guess we could allow one exception."

She leaped to kiss him on the cheek, ran into her room. He heard her voice rise with excitement as she told Chad Lacewell, a tall, fifteen-year-old boy-going-on-man things she had not mentioned to her father about her stay in Florida. She was telling Chad details of her visit to Sea World when she closed the door, leaving Munday to watch his fire die slowly to embers.

Jilly came out an hour later to kiss him goodnight. She was already dressed for sleep, that garment, too, new and expensive. He followed her example and was getting ready to turn out his bedside lamp when she knocked on his door. She sat on the side of bed.

"Dad, she wants me to spend the summer with her."

"It gets damned hot in south Florida in the summertime."

"In the French Alps."

He could manage nothing more intelligent than, "Well."

"That's all you have to say?"

"Jilly, I've always given you guidelines to follow, haven't I?"

"I'll say."

"I haven't drawn up the rules for this one yet," he said. "She's your mother. You're fifteen years old." He held up his hand quickly. "That doesn't mean you're an adult."

"Meaning I can't decide whether or not to drink beer and mess around." She was teasing him.

"Meaning that—"

"I know, I know," she said. "I'm not *in* life. I'm just teetering on the brink of it."

"Why can't you remember your math that well?"

"I don't want to spend the whole summer with her," she said, looking down at her hands folded in her lap.

"Then you've just defined the parameters of the situation," he said.

"But, wow! Paris!"

"I want to go to New York," Elaine said, her voice harsh. *"I want to go to New Orleans, and the Bahamas, and London, and Paris."*

"Hell, I took you to the shopping mall in Worthing just last month," Munday said.

"Honey, you've got time to think about it," he told Jilly.

"No," she said, shaking her head. "I've made up my mind. My friends are here. My home is here."

"Your old dad is here."

She grinned and stuck out her tongue at him. "Oh, that old bear. Well, that, too."

She bent, kissed him on the forehead. "Night again."

"Night, honey."

Jesus, he felt good. He felt like he imagined it would feel if he held the winning ticket in a sixty-million-dollar lottery. He had never been a betting man, but he figured that laying out a couple of bucks in exchange for a shot at a sixty-million-dollar dream wasn't a bad deal.

Outside the sleet turned to snow. The wind died and the ocean calmed. There was only shattered silence when Munday was awakened. He sat up, startled, puzzled until the telephone rang again.

"Munday."

"Yeah, Chief, C.S.D. here. You've got a ten-sixty-seven at 23 Holly Street."

Munday's mind was blank. "What the hell's a ten-sixty-seven?"

"Investigate a report of a fatality, Chief. What's the matter, you asleep?"

"Jesus," Munday groaned. "Time is it?"

"Let's say, depending on your point of view, you're getting a late start on the night or an early start on the morning. It's three-ten."

"Jesus."

"You awake?"

"Yeah, thanks. I'm rolling."

He turned on the bedside light in Jilly's room, put his hand on her shoulder. Her eyes opened wide and wild for a moment, then she took a deep breath.

"Honey, I've got to go out. I'll leave on some lights and lock the door."

"So'kay, Dad," she mumbled.

"Go back to sleep."

"I'm fine, Dad. I'm not a little girl any more."

Arctic air bit into Munday's face as he opened the outside door. Snowflakes, big, fat, silent, touched his nose and his lips. The ground was covered to a depth of half an inch and snow had blown onto the concrete pad under the cottage. The engine of good Old Number One growled, moaned in helplessness, and became stubbornly inert. With his hands going numb from the cold he opened the storage closet and hooked up the electric battery charger. A few minutes later Number One grudgingly said "unnnnn-unnnnnn-grrrrrr." She backfired to show her displeasure at being awakened in the middle of the night and then complained with chattering valves. It wasn't supposed to get that cold in southeastern North Carolina. Hell, there were palm trees growing on the island.

The house at 23 Holly Street leaked light from every window. The garage door was closed. There were no cars parked out front in the driveway.

In the summertime, when the population of the island was swollen by owners and renters in the oceanfront and second row cottages, the sheriff's dispatcher would have radioed the Fortier Beach policeman on duty. In the winter Munday stood down his auxiliary men and kept one member of his permanent force on night duty two random nights each week.

His mind was numbed by the cold and by old Number One's balkiness in a time of need. He didn't recognize the house as that of Tom and Fran Aycock until he was getting out of the car. Tom Aycock, striped pajamas showing under the hem of a ratty terrycloth robe, opened the front door as Munday made his way gingerly up the snow-covered steps to the porch. Big, fluffy flakes swirled in to melt on the living room carpet.

"What is it, Tom?" Munday asked.

Aycock's eyes and nose were red. "It's Hillary."

"What about Hillary?"

"She's dead."

Munday's stomach flipped. "Where?"

"Out here." Aycock led the way out the side door of the kitchen into the garage. A bare hundred-watt light bulb suspended by a single wire lit cluttered shelves, boxes stacked against the walls, and a late model rice burner sedan.

Munday's breath made clouds in the cold air. Hillary Aycock dangled motionless from a nylon ski rope looped over an open rafter and tied below to the bumper of the Japanese car. She stank.

"He wouldn't cut her down," Fran Aycock said from behind Munday. "I said, 'Tom, you've got to get her down. You've just got to.' But he wouldn't do it."

Munday touched the girl's leg. Her flesh was as cold as the air in the garage and there was a stiffness in her knee joint when Munday tried to move the leg. She wore a baby doll gown with matching panties. Both garments were soiled.

"He just left her hanging there," Fran said. She was dry-eyed, but the evidence of weeping was on her face.

"Tom," Munday said, "can you go in and call the Sheriff's department and have them send out the coroner and the rescue squad ambulance?"

Aycock nodded and went into the house. Fran Aycock looked up at the purple, distorted face of her only daughter, her brows knitted quizzically. The girl's tongue protruded in a swollen mass between lips drawn back in a snarl.

"I don't understand," Fran said. "I knew she was upset about her grades, but—"

"Fran, do you think that was the only thing bothering her, her grades falling?"

"That's all I can figure," Fran said. "Can you please get her down from there, Dan?"

"Soon as Tom gets back to help me."

Aycock appeared in the doorway. "They said it would be a while."

"Yeah," Dan said. "Damned weather. Tom, you stand down here and catch her while I lower her."

Munday stood on the hood of the car, just as fourteen-year-old Hillary Aycock had stood before stepping off into the big nothing. He used his pocketknife to saw through the thin nylon ski rope. The line slipped through his chilled fingers. Tom, surprised by the stiffness of his daughter's body, let her slide through his arms. Her head hit the bumper of the car with a thud. She toppled rigidly. Fran Aycock screamed and fell to her knees on the cold cement floor beside her daughter, her voice hoarse as she screamed out hysterical tears.

4

In Clarendon County the coroner was, like District Judges, an elected official. In theory the town drunk could run for and be chosen by the informed electorate to fill either office. A man without medical training could look down into the discolored, distorted face of a pretty little fourteen-year-old girl and say, "Yep, she's dead, all right." In practice it usually worked out that no one ran for a judgeship without a law degree and no one wanted the job of coroner except one of the county's several undertakers. Cynics said the only reason the morticians wanted the bother of the job was to get a head start on the competition in the matter of the final disposal of the results of accidental or criminal violence; but since there were not all that many fatal crashes or crimes of passion in peaceful Clarendon, Dan Munday gave Coroner Clef Burns credit for being a responsible citizen interested in doing his civic duty. Actually, Clef was better qualified than anyone who had held the office in the recent past. He had finished his second year of medical school before being kicked out.

Clef was a dapper, cigar-smoking, fancy-dressing little man who seemed to be not at all bothered by the rankness of the bodily discharges soiling the pink baby-doll nightie worn by Hillary Aycock when she stepped off the hood of her father's car on a very short trip to an uncertain destination.

"That is a terrible shame," Clef said calmly. "A terrible waste."

"Clef," Munday said, "I thought it best, for Fran's sake, that we cut the body down. You can see how the girl did it. She threw the tow handle of the ski rope over the rafter and pulled it down until the rope was doubled."

The rope was still around the dead girl's neck. Swelling had indented the two narrow, nylon strands into her flesh.

"What she did was just throw a simple boat hitch over her head," Munday said.

"Not a very efficient way to hang oneself," Clef said.

"It doesn't look as if her neck is broken," Munday said.

The coroner pulled the zipper of his leather jacket higher. It was cold in the garage. Tom Aycock had taken his wife back into the house.

"Clef, we need a cause of death," Munday said.

Burns lowered himself to one knee beside the body. "I agree with you that the neck does not appear to be broken," he said. He lifted one of the girl's hands. "Look here, Dan."

Two of the slim, girlish fingers had long, gracefully kept nails. On the index and middle finger the nails were freshly broken.

"Changed her mind," Burns said. "Tried to get the rope loose, or pull herself up."

Munday's face twisted in pain. He lifted his eyes to the harsh, exposed light bulb, looked away quickly with the image of the bulb burned into his vision.

"Death by strangulation," Burns said. "A long and agonizing way to go."

The distant wail of a siren gave Munday an excuse to turn away from the body of a girl who was only slightly younger than his own daughter. He threw the catch and rolled up the garage door. The siren screamed closer until a square-bodied ambulance careened around the corner a block away with all lights flashing.

"That's it, assholes," Munday said, "wake up everyone in town."

The Summerton Rescue Squad ambulance slowed, turned into the driveway. The siren died away to a growl as half a dozen volunteers, male and female, poured out of the vehicle like clowns in a circus act.

"What's happening, Chief?" yelled one of the newcomers.

"You think you can find room in that thing for a passenger?" Munday asked, as the rescue squad volunteers rushed past him.

The sarcasm was lost. In the garage a woman moaned loudly. A man cursed. Munday let the volunteers have their moment. They performed a service neither the town nor the county could afford to provide. Both Summerton and Fortier Beach contributed to the rescue squad, but most of their operating money came from public contributions through bake sales and yard sales and their own solicitation of local businesses and individuals.

Munday went into the living room. Fran Aycock was huddled on the couch, her feet drawn up under her. Tom sat on the edge of a chair, hands dangling between his spread knees.

"Tom, we're going to take her into town now," Munday said.

"They're not going to have to cut her up, are they?" Tom asked.

"No, I don't think so." An autopsy would be performed only if there was strong evidence, or suspicion, contrary to his first impression that Hillary's death was suicide.

"I wouldn't want them to do that."

"All right, Tom. She'll be at Burns Funeral Home, if that's all right with you and Fran."

"Yes. Yes."

"I imagine Clef will be contacting you later about the arrangements."

"All right."

Low voices and sounds of movement came from the garage. Tom Aycock and Munday watched through the living room windows as more male volunteers than were needed for the job rolled a gurney to the ambulance. Hillary had been put into a body bag. After the gurney was folded and loaded the volunteers poured into the ambulance, the reverse of circus clowns emerging from a mini-car. The siren growled into life and the rescue squad went flashing and blinking and howling away into the night.

"Jumpin' Jesus," Munday whispered.

Tom was still sitting on the edge of the chair, head down.

"Tom, we're going to have to talk a little bit about this. I'll come back later tomorrow—today, that is, if that's all right."

"What do you want to know?" Tom asked.

"I'll come back later."

"I won't be doing any sleeping," Tom said.

Munday nodded toward Fran. She opened her eyes and said, "It's all right, Dan."

"You mentioned that Hillary was upset because her grades were down," Munday said. "Was there any other reason that you know of why she might have been depressed or worried?"

"We thought she was just going through a stage," Fran said. "She was such a good girl. Not like our oldest daughter."

Munday nodded. The older Aycock girl had been a wild one, totally irresponsible, especially when she was behind the wheel of the sleek, reconditioned Datsun 300ZX Tom Aycock had bought for her.

"You may have heard me say everyone should have a daughter like Hillary," Fran said.

"No, but I know she was a good kid," Munday said.

"I didn't have to tell her, Hillary, clean up your room," Fran said. "I never had to say, Hillary, do your homework." She wiped her eyes with the back of her hand. "At least not until just the past few weeks."

"When did you notice a change in her?"

"I can't name an actual date. The first thing that struck me, I guess, was her complaining about what I served for dinner."

"She wasn't eating well?"

"Nothing pleased her. If I had chicken she asked why it wasn't ham."

"Did she lose weight?"

Fran looked disturbed. "I—I don't know. She was such a slim, graceful girl."

"What else did you notice about her that was not in character?"

"She didn't want to go to sleep at night. I'd look into her room and she'd be just lying there staring at the ceiling with the bedside light on. And then she wouldn't want to get out of bed. She was such a solid-minded girl. When she said she didn't feel like going to school I knew she was really feeling badly. She loved school. I knew she wouldn't stay at home unless she had a darned good reason. Then—"

"Then?" Munday prompted.

"Then she began to want to stay at home one, two days a week."

"Was she irritable, fretful?"

"Oh, yes, and that wasn't like her at all."

41

"Fran, I know this is a hard thing for you to hear, but you've just described the classic symptoms of a teenager on drugs."

"Not Hillary," Tom said forcefully.

"I thought of that," Fran said. "You know our oldest daughter drank—"

Munday knew the oldest Aycock girl drank. Twice Fortier Beach Police could have charged her with Driving Under the Influence, but it was a small, friendly town and the permanent residents looked out for each other. He talked the problem over with Tom and Fran and, in the end, just before Toni Aycock dropped out of school to marry a boy from Greensboro, Tom took the keys to the car.

"—so we looked for the signs in Hillary," Fran continued.

"Hillary doesn't drink and she doesn't do drugs," Tom said in indignation.

Munday directed his next question to Tom. "Did you allow Hillary to date?"

"No real dates," Tom said. "Fran would take her to the skating rink or to the movie and she'd meet some of her friends there. No car dates. No single dates. She had this little boyfriend. They'd talk on the telephone and sit together in a group at the movies, things like that."

"What's his name?" Munday asked.

"You know him, Dan," Tom said. "Works at the service station after school and on weekends."

"Chad Lacewell?"

"Yes."

Munday found himself thinking like a father instead of an investigating officer. Chad Lacewell was Jilly's boyfriend. Then, with an inner chuckle, he was thinking like a chauvinist, saying, "Well, well, kid, good for you." Jilly Munday and Hillary Aycock were two of the most attractive girls in East Clarendon High's freshman class. Chad was a good-looking kid, even if—because of the male child's slower growth pattern— he and Jilly were almost exactly equal in height.

Munday understood but could not agree with the younger generation's method of pre-courtship. The mating dance of the juveniles was eternally the same in purpose. The fruit ripened and the fruit pickers gathered around snorting and pawing the ground; but aside from the underlying hormonal drive the rules changed with the times. Boys and girls started "going together" in the sixth grade. In most cases the relationship consisted of telling others about the mutual agreement, of telephone calls, shy encounters in the crowded halls of the school, and meeting in a group at the skating rink or the movie theater. By the seventh grade some parents were allowing their daughters to date; and single-dating began for many in the ninth grade. Jilly Munday was the exception. She was allowed the telephone calls and now and then Munday transported her to the theater where, no doubt, she held hands with Chad, but there was no real dating allowed. Knowing the Aycocks to be good, solid, church-going people, Munday assumed their rules for Hillary were much the same as his for Jilly.

Hearing that his Jilly was not the only girl who was "going with" Chad Lacewell reminded Munday of the innate slyness of the young. If Chad could so skillfully manage relationships with two girls, was it logical that a girl was less clever? Munday wondered if, after all, he shouldn't order an autopsy. Fourteen-year-old girls do get pregnant, and there were still a few girls left in the country, he imagined, who just might be upset by such an event.

"Did she ever spend the night with friends?" he asked.

"Every now and then," Fran said.

"Who?"

"Baby Lowman," Fran said. "Baby mainly. They're best friends, although for the life of me I can't see why Hillary ties herself to a girl like Baby. Once with a new girl, Julie Adams. Father works at the chemical plant. Nice family. I talked with the girl's mother before I agreed to let Hillary stay over."

"Where does the Adams family live?"

"Out on the Worthing highway in the Charlestown area."

"Dan," Tom said, "I wish you wouldn't stir this around too much. She's gone, and there's nothing we can do about that. I can blame myself for not realizing how upset she was about whatever it was that was going on with her in school, but I see no reason to go bothering her friends and their parents."

"What was going on in school, Tom?" Munday asked.

Tom shrugged. "I don't know."

Munday wasn't willing to write off one pretty little girl by saying, well, she was upset because her grades had been falling. It seemed logical to him that worry, concern, upset would have come first, and then the falling grades; but shortly before dawn on a cold winter morning with big, fat snowflakes still drifting down to add to the one inch cover was not the right time to probe further into the minds of two bereaved parents.

Jilly was in the kitchen making wonderful smells when Dan walked into pleasant warmth, the aroma of coffee, the hungry tang of frying bacon.

"Whee," she said. "No school today."

"Figured not," Munday said. Snow was rare enough to be a curiosity in coastal Clarendon. Both Summerton and Fortier Beach, on those odd and festive times when snow fell and did not melt immediately, relied on the most efficient snow removal system in the world, the sun. School buses had no snow tires. Actually, the inch of snow that lay on the streets offered no real obstacle to getting about, except to Southerners who had no conception of how to drive on a snow-slick surface. There'd be a few fender-benders to check out as the morning progressed.

"So, Father dear," Jilly said, "I am yours for the day. Let's build a snowman."

"Brrr," Munday said.

"It is my duty to keep you young and vigorous," she said. "It would be great exercise. How long has it been since you built a snowman?"

"I seem to remember something about the *Titanic* that year."

"You're not *that* old."

"Jilly, there are things I have to do."

"There are always things you have to do."

"Something bad has happened."

She turned away from her cooking to look at him, her green eyes wide, frightened.

"It's Hillary Aycock," he said.

Relief caused her to slump slightly. She picked up a spatula and turned eggs in the pan. "What about Hillary?"

"She's dead."

"That's awful, Dad. How?"

"She hanged herself, honey."

"Jumpin' Jesus," she said.

"Language," he said.

"God, I knew Hillary went off to la-la land now and then—"

"What do you mean?"

"Oh, you know."

"No."

"She was a little boy crazy, that's all."

"Hmm. Do you know a girl named Julie Adams, maybe new here?"

"Yes. She's a cheerleader. Nice girl. She and I have math together."

"You and Hillary were not especially close."

"No. She was so *young*."

"Almost a year younger than you."

"She acted younger than that."

"Her mother said she didn't date."

"Ha."

"Would you care to expand on that articulate comment?"

"Did Mrs. Aycock tell you Hillary spent about one night a week at Baby Lowman's house?"

"She did."

"But she didn't tell you that Hillary and Baby climbed out the window of Baby's bedroom to meet boys, I'll bet."

"No, she didn't. What boys, do you know?"

"Daaaad."

"Look, I know the code. You don't rat on your fellow teeners. But I give you more credit than that, Jilly. It's not you and the likes of Baby Lowman and Hillary Aycock against the world, meaning all parents, is it?"

"Glenn Schul and Al Hill."

He recognized the names. "Football players?"

"Riiiiiight."

"Seniors?"

"Glenn is. Al is a junior."

"Which one was for which girl?"

"Glenn was Hillary's."

"A bit old for her, wasn't he?"

"Hummph."

"You just told me that she acted so young."

"In some ways she was very mature," she said, emphasizing the word very. She put his plate on the table. Two eggs,

46

four pieces of bacon. When she opened the oven door the hot, yeasty smell of canned supermarket biscuits came wafting out. He buttered two.

"Next week I'm going to start a diet," he said.

"Surrrrrre," she said.

"Jilly, why would a girl like Hillary hang herself?" he asked around a mouthful.

"I don't know, Dad. Maybe she got knocked up. Mr. and Mrs. Aycock are pretty strict. Maybe too strict, what with making Hillary go to that fundamentalist church all the time. Maybe that's why she is—was—best buddies with the school whore."

"Baby Lowman?"

She nodded. "Eat your eggs before they get cold."

"Yes'um."

He took his plate to the sink and rinsed it. Jilly was still at the table. He went into the living room and dialed Evie Baugh's number. She answered on the second ring.

"No school today," he said.

"Whee," she said. "A day of freedom. Wanta help me cele-brate it?"

"Matter of fact, Evie, I want to come over in a few min-utes."

"All *right,* tiger."

"So get decent and I'll see you in about forty-five minutes if I can make it over the bridge."

"Get a running start."

"I'll do that."

He looked up another number. It took several rings for Clef Burns to answer. "Clef, Munday. Listen, there's some-thing I want you to do for me. Have you started on the Aycock girl yet?"

"I thought," Clef said primly, "that she would not be

47

upset if I left her alone until I'd had my breakfast. What is it you want?"

"Do you remember enough of your medical training to be able to tell me, just between the two of us, if she's pregnant?"

"That's a fairly simple procedure if the pregnancy is developed past, oh, say two months."

Munday nodded to himself. If Hillary had been pregnant and concerned enough about it to kill herself she would have been well past two months. "Will you do it, then? And keep the result just between us for the time being?"

"I'd feel better if you'd make an official request for an autopsy and let the state people do it."

"Clef, there's no doubt in my mind that the girl hanged herself," Munday said. "I'd like to know why, but I'm not sure the knowledge would be important enough to add to the pain her parents already are experiencing. You can go in and find out without really messing her up, can't you?"

"As I said, it's a fairly simple procedure."

"I'll check with you later today, Clef."

"Have a nice day," Clef said with dainty sarcasm.

5

It was snowing harder when Munday coaxed old Number One carefully onto the approach to the high bridge over the Waterway. A low-slung muscle car zoomed up behind and pulled out into the oncoming lane to pass before seeing the markings on the police car. When the driver of the hot car slammed on brakes and began to skid Munday had to pull over close to the low rail of the bridge to keep from being sideswiped.

"You can fair drive 'er," Munday said.

A Department of Transportation crew was spreading sand on the steepest slope of the bridge, making for one-lane passage. Munday stopped, leaned out the window, and motioned the impatient driver past.

"If you're going to kill someone, asshole," he said, "I don't want it to be me."

There had been enough traffic on the highway past the bridge to make wet, black ruts in the snow covering. Only a few vehicles were moving. It was a good morning to be in bed with a comforter tucked up under your chin.

The black muscle car had skidded off the road at the bottom of a slope where the slush made by passing vehicles was refreezing. Munday put on all his lights and stopped in the road. The black car was nose down in the grade ditch. The driver was standing on the shoulder of the road.

"You all right?" Munday asked.

"Yes." He was, of course, a young man. The young have so many important things to do, and are always in such a hurry to get to them, especially when they're behind the wheel of a car. "Can you call a wrecker for me, sir?"

"I imagine it'll be a while," Munday said. "I'll give you a lift into town."

"I don't want to leave my car. I'll wait here."

Munday shrugged, rolled up the window. The heater was blowing at top speed, making such a noise that he had to turn it off while he was trying to reach the dispatcher at C.S.D.

"C.S.D., this is Fortier Police oh-one. I need a wrecker one mile south of the junction on the beach road."

"Ten-four, Fortier oh-one. But they're running more than an hour behind. Every wrecker in the area is out."

"Ten-four."

"That you, Dan?"

"How you doing, Clare? They picking on the new man again?"

"I'm a volunteer. We have two dispatchers out with the flu."

"The world loves a volunteer."

"You and the horse you rode in on," Clare Thomas said. "The wrecker, I hope, is not for you."

"Nope. Young hot-rod hit a patch of ice and went into the ditch. No injuries."

"Keep it cool, Dan."

"Today I can do that without any effort at all."

"Think I'll have any problem getting to the beach when I'm relieved at seven?"

"Not if you take it easy."

"I roger that. Bye."

"Love your radio technique," Dan said with a wide grin, as

he put the mike back on its rack. Clare Thomas' voice had not erased the memory of Hillary Aycock's bloated face, nor the smell of her, but now the roar of the heater fan was not quite as annoying. He drove the rest of the way into Summerton with the wet slush making a hissing, sawing noise as Old Number One's tires threw it against the floorboards.

Evie Baugh had used her settlement money to buy an ancient two-story house overlooking the marina and the Blue River. She rented the lower floor. The front steps to the porch were two inches deep in snow and sleet. Munday eased himself up them carefully, stepped into the hallway. Evie, in a colorful, clinging robe, came out onto the landing at the top of the stairs. She had neatened her hair and applied lipstick.

"Hi," she said, as Munday halted at the top of the stairs to get a good, deep breath. She stepped forward, put her arms around his neck, lifted her lips to his.

"You're cold," she said, shivering. There was nothing under the silken gown but Evie, soft and warm.

She took his hand and led him into her apartment. She had done the main room in blues and whites. The effect was quite feminine.

"Want coffee?" she asked.

"Is the Pope a Catholic?"

The kitchen, blacks and wood-tones, was toasty and aromatic of freshly brewed coffee. Munday shed a few pounds of clothing and sat at the glass and lacquered wood dinette. Evie didn't have to ask him how he liked his coffee. She sat opposite him. Her smile faded as she looked into his face.

"Something has happened," she said.

"Yes."

"Not to your Jilly?"

"No," he said. "It's Hillary Aycock."

"Oh, no." She was wounded without yet knowing why.

There was an acceptance of finality in her two words.

"She committed suicide."

Evie turned her face away, giving Munday her profile. She was developing the first hint of drooping flesh under her chin. A tear rolled down over her high cheekbone.

"How?" she whispered.

"She hanged herself in the garage."

"That poor child." She rose quickly, tore off a paper towel from a standing holder, daubed at her eyes. "Sorry."

"No problem."

She blew her nose into the towel, tossed it into the kitchen garbage can. Her eyes were red when she turned to face him.

"Was it cold in the garage?"

"Yes."

Silent tears wet her face again. "You watch them come and go. Year after year. Some years you get a bad bunch and it's a struggle all the way. They told me this class was the worst eighth grade they ever had at Middle School, said they'd been hell on wheels, that I'd better batten down the hatches and prepare for rough seas. A bad class. Over a third of them in the at-risk category. Then Hillary came into my room and sat down on the front row and smiled at me. I knew when I read her first paper she was special. The words and the music. She was a super kid. Stayed after school to help me grade true-false exams. Tutored some of the slow ones and actually helped a couple of them to make passing grades."

She was overcome for a moment, reached for a new paper towel. Big, racking sobs. An explosive blowing of the nose, a weak, teary smile. "She wanted to be a teacher."

Munday went to her and took her in his arms.

"Yes," she whispered. "I need to be held, if you don't mind, sir."

"Good duty if you can get it."

"She reminded me very much of my daughter."

He drew back, startled. "You've never mentioned a daughter."

"No, I haven't, have I?" She pulled away, sat down. "In the mood for sordid confessions?"

"You don't have to, Evie."

"I had—have—two daughters. One of them is twenty-two now, the other twenty. I haven't heard directly from them since—." She paused, picked up her cup, sipped. "I married the son of the town millionaire, Dan. They said, oh, lucky Evie. We lived in the house on the top of the hill. I had a Jaguar. I had two lovely daughters. My husband caught me in our marital bed with the delivery boy from the grocery store."

"Evie, you don't have to do this."

"It's just that I want you to understand," she said. "You've asked me once or twice why I don't drink. Now you know. I might be able to handle it now, but I don't want to take that chance. I couldn't handle it then. I'd get the girls off to school and my husband off to work and I could hardly wait to close the door behind him so that I could have my morning coffee—with a couple of ounces of brandy to sweeten it. The marriage would have self-destructed sooner or later, but I think deep down in my subconscious I wanted to make it sooner. In a way, I guess, I felt somewhat like Hillary must have felt, although I lived."

"What happened?"

"My husband and his family were philanthropists. My husband had a pet project, to improve living conditions in the inner city. He poured millions into the project and seemed not to be too upset when they trashed his fine, new and recon-ditioned apartments and houses immediately. He said you have to understand those people had been victimized for centuries. But when he found me in bed with the delivery boy—"

She drank from her cup again.

"The boy was black," she said, looking at Dan in challenge.

He made a carefully neutral comment. "Uh huh."

"My husband hired the finest lawyers money could buy. They took my children. Oh, they sent me off with enough money to pay for drinking myself into oblivion several times over, and I tried it for a while. Woke up in a detox unit. They thought I'd suffered brain damage." She laughed. "Maybe I did, but I had enough brain left to get the right sort of help, enough to go back to school for a year to get my teaching certificate. They said I was not a classic alcoholic, that I drank not because my body craved the drug but because of a desire to escape. Do you see why I say I was feeling much as Hillary must have felt?"

"But you didn't hang yourself."

"No, but when I took that young boy to bed I was committing marital suicide."

He cleared his throat. "Well," he said.

"Disgusted with me?"

"No."

"I wanted you to know why Hillary's death hit me so hard. She was this year's daughter."

"I can understand that."

"They're so rare, the good ones. The problem is there are too few genuine adults in the world. They may be mature in body, but what we have is the pitifully incompetent in charge of the only natural resource that is absolutely irreplaceable, the children. Or we have those who don't give a damn. Even though they didn't attend school functions I thought, judging from the fact that Hillary was one fine little girl, she had responsible parents."

"Tom and Fran Aycock are good people. Church people."

"Then what went wrong?"

"I thought you might help me answer that question, Evie. Fran and Tom think that something was going on in school to upset Hillary."

"Just the usual crap."

"Such as?"

"Oh, what would be called extreme sexual harassment in Anita Hill's workplace. In high school they call it youthful exuberance. They say things like, and I quote, did you suck any dick last night, baby? If a girl complains to the administration the answer is, well, we didn't hear him say that, did we? The attitude is that boys will be boys. Then there's the ever-present threat of violence. Do you have any idea how many weapons are confiscated each year in good old East Clarendon High? Let me give you a clue. It might not quite be four digits, but it's damned sure three. And I'm not talking about Boy Scout knives. I'm talking brass knuckles, switchblades, guns."

"I get a little of that from Jilly," Munday said. "But she doesn't seem to be frightened."

"My guess is that she is frightened, deep down," Evie said. "I know I am. The other day I saw a junior boy—six feet tall and one-hundred-ninety pounds—cleaning his nails in the hall with a knife. I swear the blade was a foot long. I marched my little self up to him and held out my hand and told him to give me the knife. I still remember the look in his eyes. He told me it was his and he wasn't, and I quote, fucking well gonna give it to me. I told him if he didn't I'd see, and again I quote, his ass kicked out of school. He gave me the knife. I went to the office and turned it in to the principal. I shook all the way there, because that boy—that boy-man—could have picked me up and broken me in two like a twig. Or he could have cut me."

"I don't think you had any real worry about that."

"No? Did you hear about the knife fight on the school bus?"

"When?"

"A week before the Christmas break." She smiled. "No, you didn't hear, even though you're a policeman. And I don't suppose you heard about three tenth grade boys assaulting a freshman girl. Not sexually. Physically. They had her on the floor holding her down while they beat her."

Munday shook his head.

"Or about the attempted rape in the girls' restroom?"

"Jilly told me about the attempted rape."

"But not about the others? Maybe she didn't know, or maybe she was sticking to the code. You don't rat on your peers, not if you're a teen in this somewhat messed up world. And you don't tell tales about certain people lest they come and break your bones. If you're in administration, either in the school or in the county offices, you don't allow incidents of violence to be publicized. You keep it in house, because, and again I quote, things are not really that bad. When a girl masturbates a boy to ejaculation in the back corner while the teacher is out of the room for five minutes you don't expel the culprits, because children will be children, and if you kick their asses out of school they'll show up later on the welfare rolls or the police blotters. They did call in the sheriff's people on that one, and after an investigation that lasted maybe fifteen minutes the deputies said that there was no evidence to prove that a sexual act had occurred. They said that white, slippery stuff on the floor was lotion the boy used because his skin got dry from all of his outdoor activity. Naturally, the kids were not going to talk, because the boy involved was a football player, big, mean. And, of course, it isn't the function of the school to teach morality. The Supreme Court of this land said that several years ago. You just accept the so-called fact that kids are going to be sexually active and start handing out free condoms, using the excuse that AIDS is increasing in the teenage population."

"You make it sound pretty grim," Munday said.

"You suggest it might be a good idea to bring back morality, to teach values, and they look at you and say, and once more I quote, you don't understand. The world has changed. Well, damnit, I agree that the world has changed. I fail to see, however, why we can't change it again, for the better."

"And you think Hillary was sensitive to all the tensions in the school?"

"I don't know. She didn't come to me for counseling. We talked books and poetry. She was interested in how I became a teacher. She asked if I thought that college in Worthing was a good one. Things like that."

"Jilly says she ran with a girl of doubtful reputation, to say the least."

"Baby Lowman," Evie said, nodding. "I'm not sure I understand that particular friendship, but I suppose it came about because Hillary, in spite of being a good generation crosser and quite at ease with an adult—at least with me and the other teachers—was lacking in self image. Often you'll see very pretty girls who are insecure or shy make alliances with girls who are overweight, or not attractive, or, as in Baby's case, of, as you said, dubious reputation."

She wiped her eyes with the back of her hand. "They're so inconsistent, our children. Some large percentage of them are sexually active, if you believe the surveys. I've overheard girls state with evident conviction that if one hasn't lost one's virginity before junior-senior night that's the time to do it.

That's what junior-senior night is for. The parents cooperate with that ambition by allowing what a lot of them have guarded against for seventeen or eighteen years. They let their little sweet pants daughters stay out all night, because they've earned the right by enduring twelve years of school. What I'm saying is—I got off the point—a lot of girls are covertly sexually experienced, but they still condemn girls like Baby Lowman."

"Because girls like Baby are open about their sexual doings?"

"Or they just don't give a damn. Baby was caught in the parking lot after school taking turns with four members of the basketball team. It didn't seem to bother her at all. Incidentally, one of the players was the school's leading scorer. He's still playing."

"What if Hillary was pregnant?"

Evie looked at him quickly. "Was she?"

"I don't know yet."

"That might explain it," she said. "Yes, that would explain it."

"I've got to go," Munday said, standing.

She came around the table and pressed against him. "Wouldn't you like me to raise your body temperature as a defense against the cold, cold outside world?"

He kissed her. "Nothing I'd like better, but I've got to go."

"Leaving me spurned and rejected."

"Sorry," he said, grinning. "Rain check?"

"Sure thing, sailor."

Outside was a gray, forbidding twilight. Dawn had come while Munday was in Evie's apartment. Summerton was coming to life, cars steaming trails of white vapor, a man trying vainly to push a car with wildly spinning wheels out of his driveway, a minor fender-bender at the intersection of

Water Street and Main. Munday waved at the policeman who was directing traffic, was answered with a wink and a grin. Traffic on the streets had melted wide, wet-black tracks in the snow.

There were no lights on the ground floor or in the living quarters upstairs over the Burns Funeral Home. Munday went around to the side door where a cement ramp led down into Clef's basement work area. The door was unlocked. He stepped into odd, chemical smells leavened with the lingering odor of body wastes. Under a bright, covered, white light Clef was bending over the naked body of Hillary Aycock. He looked up at the sound of the opening door and nodded to Munday.

Munday averted his eyes, but they were drawn back to the slim, shapely body on the slab. Small, taut breasts, a pale bush of pubic hair, shapely hips. And a swollen, purple tongue protruding from a dead, agonized face.

"I'd just finished cleaning her," Clef said.

The smell of body waste came from the wet gutters on the side of the work slab. Clef turned on a hose and rinsed them down and the smell was replaced by a chemical tang.

"Well, I had to come into town," Munday said.

"I'll give you a call in about an hour."

"Great."

The snow stopped as Munday crossed the Waterway onto the island. The town's Superintendent of Public Works had his two-man department at work pushing slush off the streets with the road grader. It was still early. City Hall was dark. Munday drove to the Sellers Harbor Fine Seafood restaurant, joined a group of locals at the redneck table at the back near the entrance to the kitchen, exchanged weather talk with John Sellers and half a dozen early risers, drank two cups of coffee, declined still another on the grounds that his tonsils were floating. He called Jilly from the telephone beside John Sellers' cash register.

"How's it going, honey?"

"Fine."

"Listen, I'll pick you up about eleven-thirty and we'll have lunch."

"That's great, Dad."

"See you then."

"See you."

He was alone in City Hall for a full hour before the Town Clerk and the Budget Officer showed up. The Kid, his youngest policeman, came in shortly after nine o'clock to report no less than six single vehicle accidents on the island and two fender-benders.

Munday was completing his notes on the death of one Hillary Aycock, fourteen years old, when the clerk yelled back that he was wanted on the telephone.

"Chief Munday."

"Hey, Dan. Lance Carver here."

"Hey, Lance. How're they hanging?"

Lance Carver was young Jug Watson's chief deputy. He was pushing retirement, having been the first black to be hired as a law enforcement officer in Clarendon County by the present sheriff's father, old Jug.

"Freeze 'em off today, you don't watch out," Carver said. "When you people over there gonna invest in a fax machine?"

"I'll ask the city commissioners at the next budget planning session, and then you can collect my picked and bleached bones after they finish chewing on me," Munday said.

"Got a fax here from the medical officer in Raleigh. You wanta pick it up?"

"Lance, there are a lot of nuts on the road today, and I just got back from Summerton. Read it to me and put it in the mail."

"Says that foot you found on the beach belongs to a white male, age fifteen to twenty. Says it was probably in the water four days."

"O.K. Thanks, Lance."

"You found the rest of that body yet?"

"To tell the truth, I haven't been looking for it."

"What about that girl on the beach last night? I hear she called her own number."

"I'm saying it's suicide."

"Too bad," Carver said. "Well, don't be a stranger, Dan."

"See you," Munday said.

"Stay warm."

Clef Burns called at ten-thirty.

"Yeah, Clef, what did you find?"

"She was menstruating when she died."

"Definitely not pregnant, then?"

"I would say definitely not. Of course I have no equipment to examine things on a microscopic level—"

"If she was menstruating it's a pretty good bet though?"

"I'd say, definitely, that she was not pregnant."

"Clef, in your opinion—is there any way you could tell—"

"Yes?"

"Was she sexually active?"

"I'm not qualified to make that determination," Burns said. "There was no hymen, but these days girls are just about as athletic as boys and I'd guess it would be a rarity to find a fourteen-year-old with the membrane intact."

"All right, Clef. Thanks. No need to mention this to anyone else."

Clef's voice was dry, acid. "It would not be exactly favorable to my reputation as a mortician to have it generally known that I made an unauthorized exploration of the sexual and reproductive apparatus of a fourteen-year-old girl left in my care."

Munday suited up for the cold, drove up the beach to the service station. Both wreckers were missing and Chad Lacewell was gassing up a minivan. Munday waited until Chad was finished and motioned him over to the car.

"Get in, Chad," he said.

"Some stuff, huh, Chief?" Chad asked, sliding in and slamming the door. "Not that I'm complaining. I'll get a full day's wages. My dad says I'm going to have to pay the insurance on my car when I'm sixteen."

Chad already had his car, a low-slung, three-year-old Camaro. Munday knew Chad drove it on the back streets without an adult in the car in violation of his learner's permit, but he was easy about things like that as long as Chad wasn't one of those who spun around corners and tore up the dirt roads on the back side of the island.

"Chad, have you heard about Hillary Aycock?"

For a moment the boy's eyes met Munday's, then shifted away. "Gee, yes. What about that?"

"I understand you were friendly with her."

"Sure, I knew her. We rode the same bus."

"Mrs. Aycock said you were Hillary's little boyfriend."

Chad bristled. He detested being called little, or short, or small. "She was always calling me, Mr. Munday." He shifted uncomfortably. "I wouldn't want Jilly to think—"

"Chad, what I'm wondering is if you have any idea what might have been so terrible in Hillary's life that she became desperate enough to kill herself."

The boy shook his head. "Mr. Munday, I have no idea. She was off in la-la land sometimes, but—"

"But?"

"I just don't know why she would do a radical thing like that."

A red Cadillac pulled up to the pumps. The driver blew the horn impatiently. Chad gave the Caddy the finger, but at a level below the dashboard so that the driver didn't see.

"You two hadn't had a spat?" Munday asked.

"No, sir." He turned to face Munday and said in a serious voice, "I never gave her any encouragement, Chief. I told her that I was going with Jilly."

"When was that?"

"Several times."

"The last time?"

"Oh, about Thanksgiving."

"Do you think she was upset about that?"

"She didn't seem to be. If so she didn't act like it. She had her football player, after all."

The driver of the Cadillac blew his horn loudly. Chad opened the door. "Chief, I don't think she did it out of un-dying love for me." He grinned. "Remember that old T.V. show where Flip Wilson dressed up like a woman?"

Munday nodded.

"Maybe, like Flip was always saying, the devil made her do it."

"Maybe," Munday said.

The driver of the Cadillac blew his horn again. "Go take care of that jerk before he has a coronary," Munday said.

The snow stopped completely before noon. Munday and Jilly had lunch at Sellers Harbor Fine Seafood. John Sellers served a monster plate of shrimp for under four dollars. He could afford to because he imported frozen shrimp all the way from Australia. The Atlantic coast catch was gobbled up by the Japanese at a price that made homegrown shrimp too expensive for the likes of John Sellers.

63

By mid-afternoon Fortier Beach's snow removal system was working full time, the sun beaming down from a blindingly brilliant blue sky. Munday drove out the river road to a new development on a high bank overlooking the water. The Adams house had pseudo-antebellum columns on a narrow, bricked porch. The woman who answered the doorbell wore a woolen skirt with a cashmere sweater. She was traveling toward forty with dignity and grace, a handsome woman.

"Mrs. Adams?"

"Yes?"

"I'm Dan Munday, Chief of Police at Fortier Beach. Is your daughter, Julie, at home?"

"May I ask why?"

"I understand that she was a friend of Hillary Aycock."

"No, she was not," Mrs. Adams said.

"Hillary's mother told me that she once spent the night with Julie."

"Then she told you a flat lie."

"She didn't spend the night with Julie?"

"My daughter does not associate with girls like that."

"Just what sort of girl is Hillary, Mrs. Adams?"

"Who is it, Mother?" asked a teenage girl in slacks and sweater from behind Mrs. Adams.

"Are you Julie?" Munday asked.

"Yes."

Julie Adams was painfully thin. She had lifeless blond hair that lanked to her shoulder. Her blue eyes were weak and washed out under almost colorless eyebrows.

"This policeman was asking about Hillary Aycock," Mrs. Adams said.

"Mrs. Adams, wouldn't you like to ask me in so that we won't let out all the warm air?"

"I think, Mr. Munday, that our conversation is over," Mrs. Adams said.

"Mother," Julie said in reprimand. "What did you want to know about Hillary?" she asked Munday.

"Your mother says she did not spend the night with you."

"No." There was something furtive in the girl's pale eyes.

"Why would she tell her mother that she did, Julie?"

"I don't know."

"Did you know she was going to tell her mother she was spending the night with you?"

"Mr. Munday," Mrs. Adams said, "I think that's quite enough."

"She asked me if I'd cover for her," Julie said. "I told her I didn't lie to my parents. She said I didn't have to lie to my parents, just to hers if one of them called."

"Julie!" Mrs. Adams gasped.

"Don't have a cow, Mom. I told her I didn't play games like that."

"You were not especially close to Hillary, I take it."

"Not really." The girl seemed to be telling the truth. "What has Hillary done?"

"She's dead," Munday said.

"Oh, wow," Julie Adams said.

"I don't see that that is any concern of ours," Mrs. Adams said.

"Got your own island, huh?" Munday asked.

"I beg your pardon?"

"Nothing," he said. "Thank you, Mrs. Adams. Thank you, Julie."

Baby Lowman had already heard of Hillary's death. It often amazed Munday how news traveled in a community that had no radio station of its own and nothing more than a weekly newspaper. Baby was a softly obese, pale-skinned redhead. Her full, rounded face gave a hint of prettiness through the surplus flesh. Her eyes were blue, but not the weak blue of Julie Adams' eyes. She'd been crying. Her mother worked. She was home alone.

"I don't know why she did such an awful thing," Baby said. "She was so much fun. God, if it hadn't been for her I'd be flunking most of my subjects."

"When did you see her last?" Munday asked.

"Oh, the last day of school before the Christmas break. We exchanged gifts. She was supposed to spend the night with me on New Year's Eve."

"You and Hillary were very close?"

"Really. Like sisters."

"So if something had been bothering her she would have talked about it with you?"

"I think so. We didn't have any secrets from each other."

"Was something bothering her?"

"No. Not really."

"Not really?"

"Well, she had this thing about that midget, Chad Lacewell. I told her, I said, now you look here, Hillary, don't make a ass of yourself chasing that runt. But it was nothing that radical, not rad enough to make her—make her—" She began weeping again.

"Baby, tell me about Glenn Schul and Al Hill."

Her tears dried up miraculously. "Woops," she said, smiling guiltily.

"Did you sneak out at night with Hillary to meet Glenn Schul and Al Hill?"

"God, you won't tell my mom, will you?"

"No."

"Promise?"

"Baby, you are not my problem. Hillary is my problem at

the moment. I'm trying to understand why she would kill herself. Now just what was her relationship with Glenn Schul?"

"He flipped out over her."

"And Hillary?"

"Oh, she liked Glenn."

"How well?"

"You're getting pretty personal."

"Baby, wouldn't you like to know why your best friend hung herself?"

She licked her large lips, blinked her eyes rapidly a few times. "Well, she worried a little after the first time."

"The first time for what?"

"You know."

"No," he said. "Are you saying that Hillary and Glenn engaged in sexual activity?"

Baby giggled. "Well, that's one way of putting it."

"More than once?"

"I told Glenn that if he didn't use a condom I'd cut off his balls. I didn't want Hillary getting knocked up."

"More than once?"

"Yes."

"How many times?"

"Oh, four, five."

"Did losing her virginity bother Hillary?"

"Naw. She told me that it was easy." Something occurred to her. She clapped her hand to her mouth and gasped. "Oh, God, she wasn't knocked up?"

"No," Munday said. "Could her conscience have been bothering her about having sex with Glenn?"

"It did at first, but then she couldn't get enough. One night my mom had to work and we had a party here. Hillary kept pulling Glenn back into the bedroom."

"In the last six weeks before the Christmas break Hillary's grades began to drop. Do you know why?"

"Gee, yes. I asked her about it. All of a sudden she got a little spacey, you know?"

"No."

"I mean she just lost it. Went around with her head on backward."

"No problems between her and Glenn Schul?"

"No. They couldn't wait to get together. She'd spend the night with me and I'd have to practically hold her in bed until my mom was sound asleep."

"So you think that the sex thing with the boy wasn't a serious concern with her?"

"Serious as hell," she said, giggling, "but good serious, not bad serious."

"And you don't know of any reason why she should have been unhappy."

"Nope. Hell, she even liked her parents. Said they were a little rad about church and stuff, but she didn't let that cramp her style."

Glenn Schul and Al Hill, minority members of the East Clarendon High School football team, being white, were out of town together visiting some of Schul's relatives in Jacksonville. Munday called it a day.

Father and daughter watched "Sherlock Holmes" on the A&E Network that night. Daughter made a huge pot of popcorn while father made hot chocolate. Daughter was up early the next morning in order to catch the school bus at her door at seven. Over the next few days Munday received answers to inquiries sent to law enforcement agencies along the lower North Carolina coast and the Grand Strand area of South Carolina. There had been no new reports of a missing white male, age fifteen to twenty.

Munday attended the graveside services for Hillary Aycock in the Summerton cemetery. When the minister had finished speaking and people were crowding around Tom and Fran Aycock to offer condolences, Munday was approached by a willowy blond in black. He didn't recognize Toni Aycock, Tom and Fran's older daughter, until she put out her hand and said, "Hello, Chief Munday."

"Jumpin' Jesus," Munday said.

Black was Toni Aycock's color. It emphasized the cornsilk softness of her hair, the green jewels of her eyes. She acknowledged Munday's reaction to her with a throaty laugh.

"Last time I saw you, you pulled me over and lectured me about driving too fast," she said.

"Well, you've come a long way, baby."

Her smile faded. "What happened to my little sister, Chief?"

He sighed and ran his hand through his hair. January had been kind for the funeral. The temperature was in the upper fifties, the sun winter-harsh and brilliant. "Toni, we just don't know. I've talked with her teachers and her friends. All we know is that her grades had gone to hell and she seemed preoccupied and maybe a little tense."

"I used to get a little tense when I sneaked around to smoke dope," she said.

"She had a blood test at school. Your mother had her to see the family doctor in mid-December. I don't think she was using."

"What then? Was she pregnant?"

He hesitated, then decided to answer. "There was not an official autopsy, Toni, but no, she was not pregnant."

"At least she didn't take another life with her."

"Yes, that's one way of looking at it, I suppose."

She let her green eyes bore into his. "Mom and Dad doted

69

on that little girl. If she'd been so inclined—as I was—to raise a little hell she could have gotten away with anything with those two. It's eating them away from the inside, Mr. Munday, like rust under a new paint job on a car. They need to know why. Until they know why they're going to blame themselves."

"Well, Toni, we may never know all the why of it," he said. "I don't think it's necessary to tell your parents, but she had become sexually active with an older boy."

"How do you know?"

"I got it from one of her friends."

"That little bitch Baby Lowman?"

He nodded. "According to Baby, Hillary was enjoying the sexual relationship." He sighed. "There are a few common reasons for teen suicide and I'm afraid I've ruled out most of them. She didn't seem to be on dope. She wasn't pregnant. She was not under pressure from her parents to excel, because high achievement seemed to come naturally to her. She was not an abused child. That leaves us with nothing but the fact that she neglected her studies, the change coming on rather suddenly, and for no known reason."

"I appreciate the support you've given the folks," Toni said.

"Your parents and I have been friends for a long time."

The funeral gathering was breaking up. Cars pulled away. The funeral home limo took Fran and Tom Aycock back toward town. Munday walked with Toni toward the few remaining vehicles, including Old Number One.

"I keep thinking of you as Toni Aycock," Munday said.

"Good thinking. That's my name."

"Modern usage, keeping your maiden name after marriage?"

70

"Old custom, going back to the maiden name after divorce."

"Sorry."

"No need to be."

She stopped beside a gleaming, silvery Porsche.

"You seem to be doing pretty well for yourself."

She laughed. "Good settlement and talent. I was the top salesman for our firm last year. This old high school drop-out listed and sold more properties than any other two of our staff put together."

"Good for you," Munday said. "I'm thinking of going into real estate when I retire."

"Well, for God's sake don't do it here in Clarendon County. You could sell half the houses in Summerton and on the beaches and still be broke."

"Well, the Yankees have discovered us. They're buying up the old houses along the river and restoring them."

"Good for them." She held out her hand. "No push, Chief, just asking for a favor. Find out why my sister did it and get that particular monkey off the backs of my mom and dad."

"I'll do my best."

January, having come in like a sonofabitch with snow and sleet, went out with cold rains. An instant northeaster slammed hurricane force winds against the cottage and made the structure sway alarmingly on its pilings. Jilly came into Munday's room in her gown and robe to say, "Hey, Dad."

He pulled her down onto the bed and put his arms around her, remembering how, when she was younger, she was afraid of thunder and lightning.

"I wasn't frightened," she said in a small voice.

"Course you weren't."

"I thought maybe you were."

"Thank you," Munday said humbly.

6

Clare Thomas had been out of high school for just twelve years when she carefully locked the C.S.D. black and white and left it in the staff parking lot at East Clarendon High School on an unseasonably mild morning in February. Two buses pulled in just behind her, snorting diesel fumes into the crisp, clean morning air. She felt more than a dozen years removed from the screaming and chattering hoard swarming out of the buses. A few eager ones ran. Older, more sophisticated students sauntered casually toward the front entrance. Two boys and a girl in a skin-tight, buttock-hugging hooker's skirt peeled off from the crowd to disappear around the corner of the building, cigarettes at the ready. Clare sighed. Students sneaking a cigarette on the school grounds was a problem to be listed under small stuff. She had not been assigned to East Clarendon High School to cause the tobacco farmers to go broke.

An armed sheriff's deputy stalked the hallways of East Clarendon because of an epidemic which had built to epic proportions in the last quarter of the Twentieth Century. Clair Thomas, with her 9 mm automatic in its shiny leather holster; her cuffs, walkie-talkie, and nightstick on her belt; her loins girded in police blue; her full breasts protruding under her nameplate and her badge, was pulling duty in a public school because a large and irate group of parents had decided something had to be done to stop the insidious growth of violence among their sons and daughters.

East Clarendon High School sprawled over a twenty-acre site scraped and bulldozed out of scrubby pine barrens seven miles from the nearest municipality. By far the largest portion of the acreage was devoted to athletics. There was a lighted stadium with wooden bleachers and an oval track, baseball and softball fields, a soccer pitch, tennis courts, and the towering basketball gym.

If educational priorities were to be measured by land use, the double-winged, one-story structure housing classrooms, labs, restrooms, multi-media room—the old-fashioned term library was out of fashion—cafeteria, teachers' lounge, and administration offices came in a poor third. On one parking lot a herd of yellow, top-heavy, garish buses shared asphalted space with the Fords and Hondas of the teachers and staff. Another, larger lot for students and visitors was packed with four-by-fours, big wheels, muscle cars, sports vehicles. One seventy-five-thousand-dollar Mercedes convertible stood out arrogantly amid a group of woebegone family-type gas-guzzlers, and a good representation of the South's most treasured mode of transportation, the pick-up truck.

Almost nine hundred juveniles of high school age converged on East Clarendon from that area of the county to the east of Catfish Creek. Those who lived in the rural areas near the creek, or on the western tip of Fortier Beach, waited for the buses in darkness in the morning and arrived back at their homes after four in the afternoon. Those who were over sixteen and, thus, allowed the great American privilege of driving, toted up half a hundred accidents per year on the highways leading to and from the school. For a pedestrian to be caught in the students' and visitors' parking lot when the dismissal bell rang at three o'clock in the afternoon was to live dangerously.

Not one of the student inmates of East Clarendon and only a few of the teachers and staff had been born when Brown v. Board of Education was decided by the Supreme Court on May 17, 1954 and the death song of the neighborhood school began to be heard throughout the land. It was not politically correct to advocate a return to the time when a relatively small number of rural students were bused to schools and townies walked a few blocks. To point out that in the field of education progression is often regression was to challenge not only the local but the state and national educational cliques who alternated between taking their lead from educational "experts" at Stanford University and some Ivy League tower on the opposite coast, "experts" who, in the majority of cases, had not set foot in an elementary, middle school, or high school classroom since their one-way passage through.

The situation in Clarendon County had deteriorated to the point where more than a few brave souls stood up at P.T.A. and School Board meetings to give their opinions on why Johnny couldn't read or make change for a dollar. Some said one reason why elementary school students might be doing poorly on the California Aptitude Test was they were just plain "wore out" from getting up before dawn and riding a school bus for over an hour each way every day of the school week. Some said if the educational establishment would go back to teaching reading, writing, and arithmetic most problems would be solved. Others questioned high-tech trends in the schools. When a member of the establishment from Raleigh spoke at the monthly School Board meetings advocating not only a computer in every classroom but a telephone and a modem as well so that "every teacher and every student would have the opportunity to interface with the scientific community" she received cold stares, only a smattering of applause, and one quietly voiced "bullshit" from the back of the room. The articulate lady went back to Raleigh to lie sidewise in the public trough while, presumably, dreaming up more advanced theories about the new wave of learning.

At School Board and P.T.A. meetings there were heretics who questioned, sometimes quite loudly, the wisdom of "new math," the abandonment of the teaching of phonics, and, most vigorously, the effort on the part of theorists on the leading edge of education to do away with books entirely. But by far, the greatest concern, if one judged by the attitude of parents who were involved in school affairs, was the issue of violence in the county schools.

Whatever the cause, education in Clarendon County was in trouble. The numbers of at-risk students grew with each school year. The dropout rate stood at sixty-nine-point-four percent. C.A.T. and P.S.A.T. test scores ranked the county near the bottom in student achievement.

Clare Thomas had been undergoing a crash course in the problems of education in Clarendon. On orders from Chief Deputy Lance Carver she had attended several confrontational meetings between parents on one side and school administrators and School Board members in opposition. With some outside help, the public servants and administrators had, at last, made a reluctant admission that, yes, something had to be done.

LeShane Dunn, East Clarendon's principal, usually acted as spokesman for the establishment. LeShane was a product of Clarendon County Schools. He had earned his high school diploma in the all-black high school in Summerton before construction of the consolidated county schools. He considered himself to be more tactful than some of his fellows, although he was not at all reluctant to let it be known he had paid his dues as one of the first blacks to teach in the new, integrated schools, and thus he was fully entitled to state his views as he saw them.

"What you parents seem to want," Dunn said, "is to start expelling students in a wholesale manner. I must remind you of this basic fact. For each student who drops out of school or is forced out of school there is an equal and corresponding increase in the potential for crime and, in most cases, in the welfare rolls."

In the opinion of the more vocal parents at the meetings there was dubious value in, for example, coddling three rather large boys who converged on a smaller victim with deliberate mayhem in mind and crunched his chest to the extent of breaking two ribs.

LeShane Dunn asked, "Would you have me apply draconian punishments to young people whose characters have been formed in abusive homes, whose main crime is poverty?"

Vocal parents demanded some form of punishment when, for example, a student came to school with a fully loaded .45 and told the science teacher she had better damned well give him a passing grade this time.

"I will be shamed, shamed," Dunn said, "to admit to this community that it is necessary to have an armed law enforcement officer in the halls of my school to keep order."

In the end, the decision was made at a high level. The word came down to the Clarendon County School Board to do something about the epidemic in the schools or have the state step in and take over the entire system. Suddenly, where there had been a shortage of available money to pay for the services of sheriff's deputies, there were ample funds. Those members of the School Board who were running for re-election immediately claimed credit for assuring the safety of "our sons and daughters" in the schools. And because of their courageous action Clare Thomas was spending the hours between seven in the morning and four in the afternoon going back to high school.

Clare discovered quickly the natives were most restless on Friday, and the later it got the more fretful they became. It was Friday. The second lunch shift had been summoned to the small school cafeteria by the clamorous bells. There was the usual amount of conversation, which, for teenagers, called for use of the voice at maximum amplitude. A bit of harmless pushing and shoving was going on in the food line. After three weeks of having an armed policeman in the halls most of the students had learned to ignore the threatening presence, to treat Clare as if she were a piece of the furnishings. She was leaning up against a wall watching the line move toward the entrance of the cafeteria when a group of athletes came jiving down the hall, one arm swinging out of rhythm, one leg bending slightly with each step. The tallest of the boys, the six-foot-nine-inch center of East's basketball team, seized a smaller boy by the shoulder and pulled him out of line. The smaller boy protested.

A knife appeared in the hand of one of the basketball center's satellites as if by magic. Clare saw the material of the small boy's shirt indent as the point of the knife was thrust against his back just above the left kidney.

"We're cutting in, mama's boy," the knife wielder said. "One way or the other."

The basketball star laughed. Clare moved swiftly, seized the knife man's hand, threw her weight behind her grip and had the boy dancing on his toes in a split second, his arm pulled up behind him painfully.

"Drop the knife," she said.

"I'll kill you, bitch," the boy said.

"Not with one arm broken, sonny," she said, yanking up. The boy cried out and the knife fell to the floor with a clatter. She released the arm. The boy whirled, went into a crouch. Clare was at least four inches shorter than he.

"Try it," she said.

"Come on," the tall center said.

The knife wielder bent. Before he could pick up his weapon Clare had her foot on it.

"Back off," she said.

"Want my knife."

"I said back off."

"Come on," the center said.

Clare was uncertain whether the tall boy was trying to call off the dogs or urge them on. She lifted her knee forcefully and sent the knife man flying backward to come to rest on his rump. She stepped forward.

"O.K.," she said. "That's it. You come with me." She picked up the knife, closed it with a snap of the switchblade.

"Better go with her," the tall one said.

She walked behind the boy to LeShane Dunn's office. Dunn listened gravely as Clare described the incident. When she finished he nodded.

"Thank you, Miss Thomas. I will direct this matter from here."

"You realize," Clare said, "that I could arrest this boy."

"Tell her to quit calling me boy," the knife owner said.

"I'm sure that the deputy means no disrespect in using that term, Leonus," Dunn said. "You realize this is a very serious matter, don't you Leonus?"

"I was just jiving that mama's boy," said Leonus.

"I'm afraid I'm going to have to give you a full week of In-School Suspension."

"Yes, sir," Leonus said.

"You may return to your lunch period," Dunn said.

"You're a hard man," Clare said, as the boy slammed the office door behind him.

Dunn raised his eyebrows.

Clare kept her voice calm with an effort. "Well, we certainly wouldn't want to apply draconian punishment simply because a kid threatened to give someone a kidney transplant, would we?"

Dunn seemed to be truly puzzled. I.S.S., In-School Suspension, meant for five days the boy who had pushed the sharp tip of a switchblade into another's back would have to spend his lunch hour and activity period in the multi-media room.

"What would you recommend?" Dunn asked.

"For a starter, how about suspending him from basketball?"

For years LeShane Dunn had been basketball coach at East Clarendon. He had never had a losing season. He had been in the bleachers for every home game during the past season, cheering for the Wildcats as they reached the semifinals of the state championships. Leonus was the finest high school point guard in eastern North Carolina. He would surely be offered a good college scholarship after his senior year. He and all the other starters were going to be back for the next season, which, Dunn figured, would result in a sure-fire state championship for East Clarendon. He didn't even bother to answer Clare Thomas' question.

The first period after the lunch break ended with clanging bells and a sudden din in the hallways. Clare stepped out into the hall, held out her arm to slow two boys who were running a race. During the first week of October last a boy had run into a female teacher at full speed, sending her to the hospital for a lengthy stay. The runners slowed to a walk, looked back, made half-audible comments about the big-titted fuzz. There was a crash of shattering glass from the front hallway near the main entrance. Clare broke the rules, running toward the sound. She saw a familiar form, the tall, lanky center of the basketball team. He was bending over a fallen form lying amid shards of glass from the athletic trophy showcase.

"I didn't mean to," the tall boy was saying over and over.

Blood poured from the fallen boy's upper arm. Clare lifted the sodden shirtsleeve, saw a gouged cut. A two-inch wide slab of flesh flapped outward, exposing bone. She applied pressure to stop the bleeding.

"Go to the office," she told the tall boy. "Tell Mr. Dunn to call the rescue squad."

"I'm here," LeShane Dunn said. "I have called the school nurse."

"Goddamnit, Mr. Dunn," Clare yelled, "this boy has a severed artery. Get your ass down to the office and call the rescue squad."

The rescue squad came close to setting a record in time of response. It was not the first time that they'd been called to the high school, and some of the volunteers had children at East Clarendon. A paramedic applied a tourniquet as the injured boy was being wheeled out the front doors.

"I didn't mean to do it," the tall boy said. "We were just jiving around."

"This is a very serious matter," LeShane Dunn said. "A very serious matter."

Clare went to the nearest girls' room to wash the blood off her hands. The stench of cigarette smoke was strong. She soaped twice, rinsed, examined her fingers and hands for any sign of an open wound. She decided she would bring a pair of surgical gloves with her on Monday. The door opened behind her. She looked up and smiled. She had not yet met all of the teachers personally, but she knew them by sight.

"I knew something like that was going to happen sooner or later," the newcomer said. "Too much glass too openly exposed."

"Well, it happened," Clare said.

"I'm Evie Baugh. I teach English."

"Clare Thomas."

"I have a break this period," Evie said. "Can I buy you a cup of coffee?"

"Soon as I wash away all the HIV," Clare said.

"That's all we need," Evie said.

"You *don't* have any AIDS patients in school here?"

"No, thank God."

Clare rubbed her hands together under the blower, which belched only cold air. A roll of toilet paper had been strung from stall to stall, up over a smoke detector, down to the floor. Clare's hands were still wet when she followed Evie to the teachers' lounge. The coffee was instant and decaffeinated, bitter and only lukewarm.

"Welcome to the battle zone," Evie said, lifting her Styrofoam cup.

"Peace," Clare said.

"I haven't had a chance to tell you that some of us appreciate your presence," Evie said.

"Just doing a job."

"Now if we could have a uniformed officer on each bus—"

"Before this past couple of weeks I'd have said, is it that bad?"

"It is."

"What kind of kids are we raising?" Clare asked.

"A good question." Evie rose. "Let's chat sometime. I'll be glad to tell you war stories."

"Sure."

Clare sipped the tepid coffee, made a face, got up to pour

the remainder down the sink, checked her watch. Quarter hour to the last classroom change of the day. She sat down, picked up a white and blue folder titled "NORTH CAROLINA 21st CENTURY. A Time For Action!"

"One of the most critical investments we can make for the future of North Carolina and its citizenry is education."

"Hummm," she said.

"NORTH CAROLINA 21st CENTURY is North Carolina's strategy for achieving the National Education Goals and a response to the challenge to ensure the United States will be a highly competitive nation during the 21st Century. Goal One: Readiness for School. Within one year, all children will start school ready to learn."

"Good trick," Clare said.

"Goal Two: During the first few years of the 21st Century the high school graduation rate will increase to at least 90 percent."

"That's a goal?" she asked.

A male voice came from behind her. "Do you answer yourself, too?"

She turned, smiling self-consciously. "Well, I'm never lonely."

"You're Deputy Thomas."

"I am."

"I'm Tom Williams. I'm responsible for the delicious lunch you had today—that is if you ate in the cafeteria."

"Did you toss the pizza yourself?"

"With these two hands," he said. He was not dressed like a cook. He wore Dockers, a Wildcat sweatshirt, and Michael Jordan sneakers. "You live on Fortier Beach, don't you?"

"Right."

"I wonder if I can ask a favor of you."

"You can ask."

"One of my employees hasn't shown up for work this week. She lives on the beach road. Her name is Ethel Eubanks. She works in the middle school lunchroom. I've tried calling her several times, but there's no answer. I wonder if, on your way home, you could just stop by and check on her."

Clare pulled out her pad, reached for her pen. "Eubanks?"

"Yes. She lives in that house sitting down in the fields to the left just where the road goes up the hill."

"O.K."

"I appreciate it."

"No sweat."

East Clarendon's juveniles managed to get through the rest of the school day without further mayhem or loss of blood. When the last of the buses pulled out of the parking lot trailing dirty exhaust fumes behind it Clare made a quick tour of the halls. Through an open door she saw Evie Baugh at her desk bending over a stack of papers.

"Hey," she said, "take the rest of the day off."

"Would that I could," Evie said. "Are you finished?"

"I'm off for a good, hot bath and a sit down," Clare said. "See you on Monday."

"Right."

The halls and the restrooms were empty. A gymnastics class was going on in the gym. The classrooms were open, and quiet. When she went out there was already a feeling of lateness to the afternoon, although it was only twenty past three. She started the engine of her black and white, called the dispatcher, gave her destination as 4333 Waterway Place, her home.

"No such luck, Thomas," the dispatcher said. "The Chief Deputy wants to see you."

She took her time driving to Summerton, parked in Sheriff

Jug Watson's marked place, knowing that Jug would not be back this late in the day for anything short of general insurrection.

"Hi, Clare," Lance Carver said, as she entered his office. "Have a seat."

Lance was the color of *café au lait*. His hair had silvered in a very attractive and distinctive way. He was as trim as he'd been as a rank rookie when old Jug Watson first added a black man to the Clarendon County Sheriff's Department back in the late 1960s.

"I had a call from an irate parent an hour ago," Lance said. "He said one of my white deputies insulted his son. Called him boy."

"Jesus Christ, Lance," Clare flared, her face getting red.

Lance held up one hand, grinned at her. "Said you almost broke his son's arm."

"Maybe I should have."

"Maybe you should," Lance said. "I had a call from LeShane Dunn, too. He said you cursed him."

"Oh, hell," she said.

"But even worse than that, *Deputy* Thomas, you asked him to kick his star point guard off the basketball team."

"The news traveled fast," Clare said. "Is there mental telepathy in the black community?"

Lance laughed. "Just a closeness, honkey." He winked at her. "Clare, you're doing a good job out there. You have to kick some ass, you kick it, whether it be white ass or black ass. I'll back you all the way, and so will Jug."

He squinted his eyes and stared at her. "Did you tell LeShane to get his black ass down to the office and call the rescue squad?"

"I didn't say black."

Lance laughed, waved his hand. "Go on home now and

get some rest. I just wanted to tell you that we're with you in case you begin to get static personally from LeShane or some of the parents."

"Thanks, Lance."

"But I'm glad you didn't break that boy's arm. I wanta see the good old Wildcats win that state championship next year."

"Jesus Christ," Clare muttered as she left the office.

She was under the shower when she remembered she'd promised Tom Williams to check on his truant employee. She said, "Oh, hell."

She had to get dressed again. From the top of the bridge she saw a conflagration in the sky. The old fireball was out of sight, leaving behind an afterglow of crimson and orange to creep upward into low, thin clouds. Lovely, lovely. And lonely. Beauty was for sharing. A sunset. A Barbara Mandell song. She slowed for a lingering look. Cars were piling up behind her. She shrugged. Being fuzz had its little perks. None of the impatient bastards were going to honk at *her*.

The Eubanks house was almost totally hidden from the road by softwoods growing along a sporadic creek, which flowed only in times of heavy rains. The approach road sloped steeply down from the highway, leveled off, skirted two big water oaks. A Duster was parked in the driveway. Lights glowed from the front windows. She left the motor running and the car lights on, walked up two steps to the porch, knocked on the door. The face of a boy of about twelve appeared as the door opened partially.

"Hi," Clare said, "I'm looking for Ethel Eubanks."

"She isn't at home."

"Is she your mother?"

"Yes." The boy's voice was soft and high, almost feminine. He had a sweetly regular face, large, brown eyes, long, black lashes. His hair was full, but neatly trimmed.

"What's your name?" Clare asked.

"I'm Larry."

"Where is your mother, Larry?"

"I don't know."

She noticed the smell then. Her back stiffened, and a shoot of adrenaline lanced into her stomach. Once experienced it is never forgotten, that smell.

"Larry, when was the last time you saw your mother?"

"About a week ago." He sounded eminently believable. He was a kid, a twelve-year-old boy, small, vulnerable, likeable.

"A week ago?"

"She's probably off with some man."

There was a wrongness about it. The smell. His sweetly spoken words. The offhand way in which he brushed off the absence of his mother for an entire week.

"Larry," she said, "do you mind if I come in? I'm Deputy Clare Thomas, of the Clarendon County Sheriff's Department."

He hesitated for long moments, shrugged, opened the door. He wore blue jeans and a Wildcat sweatshirt. His feet were bare. Worthing local news was on the television, a mutter of voices in the background. The smell was very strong. Larry Eubanks put his hands in his pockets and looked at her with youthful innocence. She walked toward a hallway. To the left was the kitchen-dining area. Straight ahead, door open, was a bathroom. Two doors opened off the hallway to the right. The smell was almost overwhelming in the hallway. She tried the door to the first bedroom. It was locked.

"Larry," she asked, "do you know how to unlock this door?"

He shook his head. "No."

"Why is it locked?"

"Well, it's my mother's bedroom. She keeps it locked so my friends and I won't go in and mess with her things."

"Do you mind if I try to open it?"

He looked around the room, said, after a long pause, "No."

She removed the ink cartridge from her ballpoint pen. The lockset on the bedroom door was a passage lock. On the hall side the knob had a small, round hole. When she inserted the cartridge the lock was sprung.

Ethel Eubanks lay on her side on the bed with her back toward the door. She was covered to her shoulders by a blanket and a sheet. She had been shot once in the back of the head. A window air conditioner roared out a blast of frigid air, but in spite of the cold in the room the stench was more than Clare could stand. She wadded her handkerchief and held it over her nose, stepped closer to the bed, looked over her shoulder with her hand on the butt of her weapon.

The hydrostatic forces of projectile entry had caused the dead woman's eyes to protrude. Fluids had run from her nose and mouth to dry to a sheeny hardness. For a head wound there'd been very little bleeding, but it was enough to have soaked the pillow. In the area of the wound those omnipresent companions of death, maggots, worked busily.

Clare backed out of the room. Behind her Larry Eubanks cleared his throat. She whirled, her hand on her pistol. He looked young and innocent as he said, "I knew someone would come sooner or later."

"Larry," she said, "I want you to come outside with me."

"All right."

She let him lead the way. She told him to stand in front of the black and white while she called in. She stood by the open door in order to hear the radio.

"Larry, what happened to your mother?" she asked.

"I don't know."

"I think you do know, Larry."

He nodded.

She unbuttoned a pocket on her shirt, pulled out a small card. "Larry, before you say anything else I'm going to read you your rights, O.K.?"

"Just like on television, huh?"

She, herself, always felt that she was on some slock tube drama when she read, "You have a right to remain silent—"

She finished. The standard stuff. You have the right to be represented by a lawyer. If you cannot afford an attorney the county will provide one, etc. etc. etc.

"Do you understand what I've just told you?" she asked.

"Yes."

"Do you have anything you'd like to tell me, Larry?"

He looked at her with his wide, childish eyes. "I waited and waited. And then it was getting late and I knew that I had to do it if I was going to have time to get dressed and go to the banquet."

"What banquet is that?"

"The celebration banquet for the basketball team."

"You had to kill your mother so that you could be on time at the banquet?"

"I just opened the door. She was sleeping. She was always sleeping. I shot her once."

She heard the far-off pulse of a siren. Less than ten minutes had passed when a black and white left the highway with a squeal of tires and bounced down the dirt lane toward the house.

Clare stayed outside with Larry while Lance Carver and a senior deputy entered the house. Lance came out gasping for air.

"How the hell you happen to be here?" he asked Clare.

She told him about the request from Tom Williams. Lance wrote down the name on a little pad. Larry Eubanks was still standing in front of the car. She leaned toward the chief deputy and whispered, "The boy did it."

"No. That little kid?"

"I'm afraid so. There's a .22 rifle leaning up against the wall beside the T.V. set. An axe and a shovel in the kitchen."

"You've got sharp eyes. Has he made an admission of guilt?"

"Yes. He said he had to kill her so that he could be in time for a banquet at the school. He'd been thinking about doing it all afternoon, ever since he got home from school about three-thirty."

Lance wiped his mouth with the back of his hand, blew his nose into his handkerchief. "Once you get that smell in your nose it stays with you," he said.

"Yes."

"Did you read him his rights?"

"Just like on T.V."

"Sonofabitch. The kid can't be more than twelve."

"He's fifteen," she said. "He didn't like it because his mother slept in the afternoons. She worked days at the middle school lunchroom and went to school at night at the community college. She was going to become a nurse."

"This one is going to be a mess," Carver said. "Look, I'll want a complete report from you first thing in the morning. If you want to you can go on. We'll have to take the boy to the Juvenile Detention Center in Worthing. I'll have someone else do that."

Two more deputies arrived, leading the ambulance up to the house. Clef Burns was riding with one of the deputies. He examined the body and directed the deputies as they rolled it up in the sheets and the blanket. They put pillow and all into a body bag and carried it to the ambulance. The entire bundle would be transported to the medical officer in Raleigh.

"Larry," Clare said, "I want you to go with Deputy Blackburn here."

"Where?" the boy asked.

"It's all right," she said.

He came around the car and looked up into Lance Carver's face. "Does this mean that I'll get the car and the house when I'm sixteen?"

7

February weather was so mild a few impatient crocuses were sending up green shoots to measure the warmth of the sun. Clare slept late. Saturday was supposed to be her day off, but the unexpected results of having done a favor for Tom Williams took care of that. She ventured out into a winter-brilliant morning. The thermometer on her front porch showed a reading of sixty-four. The woodlands between her house on the Waterway and the ocean, half a mile distant, blocked the southwest breeze.

Chief Deputy Lance Carver was waiting for her on the steps of the courthouse. He took the passenger side seat. The conversation during the drive to the Blue River County Juvenile Detention Center in Worthing was shoptalk. In cooperation with the State Bureau of Investigation the department was moving closer to the biggest drug bust ever in Clarendon County, where half a dozen inlets from the sea and miles of thinly populated shoreline on the Intracoastal Waterway made business profitable for entrepreneurs dealing in popular but socially unacceptable commodities. The drug trade was C.S.D.'s biggest problem. A full three-quarters of the cases put before the Grand Jury were drug-connected. The remaining quarter of Grand Jury presentations dealt with more interesting subjects such as incest, rape, manslaughter, and breaking and entering, the latter prevalent in the winter when vacation homes stood empty and unused on the beaches and the Waterway.

First-degree murder was a rarity in Clarendon. First-degree murder committed by a fifteen-year-old boy who looked twelve would be, Lance Carver concluded, when the conversation turned to the Larry Eubanks case, one for the books.

There was no doubt in Clare's mind that Larry's shooting of his mother had been premeditated. He spent the afternoon thinking about it, then decided that he had better do it or be late for the school banquet.

Lance accepted custody of the juvenile, Larry Eubanks, with a flourish of his pen. He gave the receipt to Clare.

"For your collection," he said.

Larry was still wearing the same blue jeans and Wildcat sweatshirt. He walked between them to the car, small, silent, a half-smile on his face. No one spoke until Clare cleared Worthing traffic and set the speedometer at fifty-five on the river road.

"I want my Aunt Carla here," Larry said.

"She's been notified," Carver said. "I spoke with her myself. She is driving up from Columbia this morning. Should be here early in the afternoon."

On the radio a deputy in the western sector of the county was chatting with the dispatcher. The deputy's voice broke up occasionally. It was a big county.

"Where are you taking me?" Larry asked.

"To the courthouse," Carver said. "We want to ask you a few questions, Larry. Is that all right?"

"Yes."

The chief deputy had asked the S.B.I. to send an agent to monitor the interrogation. He was appropriately named Gene Justice. He'd worked with C.S.D. before. He had not met the new deputy. Clare gave him her hand and accepted as a matter of course his obviously favorable appraisal of her as a woman.

Carver gave Larry a soft chair in front of the desk in the Chief Deputy's office. Clare and Gene Justice sat to the side. Carver turned on the tape recorder, spoke time and date into it, identified the suspect. He told Larry of his rights, adding, "Larry, since you're a juvenile, you also have the right to have a relative present. Do you understand all that?"

The good looking, almost pretty boy nodded.

"Would you answer so that you can be heard, please," Carver said.

"Yes."

"Do you understand your rights?"

"Yes."

"And you are willing to answer some questions now?"

"Why not?" Larry asked with a shrug.

"Larry, did you shoot your mother while she was asleep in her bed?"

"No, sir."

Carver looked at Clare, raised one eyebrow. "Larry, didn't you tell Deputy Thomas last night that you shot your mother?"

"No."

"Larry, didn't you tell Deputy Thomas that you thought about it all afternoon and decided you had to go ahead and do it because if you didn't you wouldn't have time to get dressed and get to the banquet?"

Larry answered without hesitation. "Maybe she misunderstood what I said. I hadn't seen mama for a week. I thought she was probably off with some man."

"How could you think that when her car was in the driveway?"

"Well, she was getting ready to buy another car. I thought she was driving the new car."

"What did you think when the smell began to get strong in the house?"

"We had a dead rat in the wall once. I thought maybe that had happened again."

Carver picked up a .22 rifle from his desk. "Is this your rifle, Larry?"

"No."

"It was found in your living room, leaning up against the wall behind the T.V. Do you deny that this rifle was in your house?"

"No."

"But it isn't yours?"

"No."

"Your mother's?"

"No."

Lance was keeping his voice soft, mild. "Whose, then?"

"It belongs to a friend of mine."

"What is his name?"

"His name's Hersh."

"Is Hersh his family name or his given name?"

"His name's Hersh Jenrette."

"Did he lend you the rifle?"

"Yes."

"Why did you want to borrow the rifle, Larry?"

The boy looked down at his sneakers. "Rabbits."

"You went hunting for rabbits?"

"They eat Mama's garden."

"In the winter?"

"Well, I've had the rifle a long time."

"Larry, you've been in trouble before, isn't that right?"

"Yes, sir."

"In November you took your mother's car without permission. You hit a parked car on Fortier Beach and left the

94

scene of the accident to drive to Columbia, South Carolina. You didn't make it all the way to Columbia because you were picked up by the South Carolina Highway Patrol west of Florence and held in custody for driving without a license."

"I wanted to see my Aunt Carla. Mama wouldn't let me have the car. She told the fuzz—the highway patrol—to keep me there in Florence until she got there. She wouldn't let them call Aunt Carla." The tone of his voice had changed for the first time. It had become freighted with juvenile protest. "Aunt Carla could have been there in about an hour. I had to stay in that place all night."

"Larry, you're just fifteen. Don't you know it's against the law to drive without a license?"

"Yes."

"Larry, last summer the man across the road from your home, Mr. Hershal Jenrette, caught you taking mail from his mailbox. Is Mr. Hershal Jenrette the father of your friend, Hersh Jenrette?"

"Grandfather. Hersh lives with his grandfather and grandmother."

"When one of my deputies questioned you, you admitted you'd been stealing the mail to get Mr. Jenrette's pension checks."

"I didn't cash them."

"You said, when you admitted taking the mail, that you wouldn't lie about it. Are you lying about shooting your mother?"

"No."

"Did the .22 rifle found in your living room belong to the boy, Hersh, or to his grandfather?"

"To his grandfather."

"Was Mr. Jenrette aware Hersh was lending you the rifle?"

"I don't know."

Clare leaned forward. "Larry, are you sure you want to go on playing this game with us?"

"I don't know what you mean."

"I think you do," Clare said. "Don't you?"

Larry shrugged. "I guess."

"Larry, why did you shoot your mother?" Clare asked.

The tone of his voice did not change. He still sounded detached, distant. "She wouldn't let me do anything. She hated all my friends. When she got off work in the afternoon she went to bed as soon as she got home. She was always sleeping when I got there and I had to get my own snacks and meals. She made me walk to work at the Food Lion. She made me clean up my room and all she ever did was sleep. And then I had to stay home by myself at night."

"While she was in school?" Clare asked.

"Or off with some man."

"Larry, was your mother in the habit of running the room air conditioner in the winter while the oil furnace was heating the rest of the house?"

"I don't know. What are you going to do to me?"

"That will be up to the court," Lance Carver said.

"You told me," Clare said, "you opened the door and stepped into the bedroom. You had the rifle in your hand. Why don't you tell us what happened then?"

"I shot her in the back of the head. She was asleep. She just twitched a little. I don't think it hurt her."

"What did you do then?"

"I closed the door."

"You didn't turn on the air conditioner in your mother's bedroom?"

"Not then."

"When?"

"She started to smell. Listen, what's going to happen to me?"

"We're going to charge you, Larry, with the murder of your mother. You'll stand trial."

"But I'm just fifteen."

"Under the laws of this state you can be tried either as a juvenile or as an adult," Carver said. "That will be a decision made by the County Prosecutor."

"Larry, let's get back to your statement," Clare said. "You said your mother's body started to smell and you went into the bedroom and turned on the air conditioner?"

"Yes."

"When was that?"

"I don't know. Maybe about Wednesday." He nodded. "Yes, it was Wednesday, because Hersh and some of the guys were coming over."

"Jesus Christ," Gene Justice said under his breath.

"You shot your mother on Friday, the day of the athletic banquet at the school. Did you go back into the room before you went in to turn on the air conditioner?"

"No. Listen, she made me pay rent, too. I had to give her some of the money I earned working at the Food Lion."

"Larry, there was a shovel and an axe in the kitchen. Why were they there?" Carver asked.

"I don't know."

"Were you planning to dispose of your mother's body?"

He nodded.

"Please answer aloud," Carver said.

"Yes."

"You were thinking about dismembering her?"

"I knew I couldn't move her. She was too fat. Too heavy."

"So you were going to dismember her and bury her?"

"She smelled so bad I couldn't stand it."

Lance wiped his mouth with the back of his hand, swiveled in his chair to look out the window. "Clare, any more questions?"

"No," she said.

"Mr. Justice?"

"I think you've covered the ground," Justice said.

"Clare, get someone to look after Larry for a while," Carver said.

Clare used the Chief Deputy's intercom to call a deputy. Larry was led off to a holding room.

"Not a story calculated to make young girls want to become mothers, is it?" Gene Justice asked.

Carver asked, "What do you think, Gene? Should we push to have him tried as an adult?"

"You have premeditation," Justice said. "He borrowed the rifle in advance. He admits sitting in the house thinking about it all afternoon before doing it. He's a poisonous little reptile, but he's cute, and that's your main problem. You won't have any trouble getting a True Bill from a Grand Jury, because the Grand Jurors won't be looking at the defendant, just at the cold facts. You'll probably be able to get whatever you ask at a Probable Cause Hearing, because you'll be dealing with just one person, a judge. The challenge will come if you try him for Murder One. You'll have twelve men and women in empathy with a cute little kid who looks as if he can't be a day over twelve. Any prosecutor would have a damned hard time getting a conviction because every woman on the jury will be thinking, what, that little darling do such an awful thing?"

"Well, I guess we'll have to rely on the judges and the County Prosecutor, won't we?" Carver asked. He turned to Clare. "Clare, I want every bit of evidence cast in concrete. It's your case. Start with the rifle. Find out what Larry was doing all week while Mama was putrefying in her bedroom. Get statements from that Jenrette kid and anybody else who had any contact with Larry during the week. I want us to be more than ready when the time comes, because it is my firm conviction that if young Larry walks away from this one he'll do it again. The next time someone licks the red off his candy he'll kill them, too."

Carver's intercom buzzed. He punched a button, said, "Carver."

"Chief, the Eubanks boy's relatives are here asking to see him."

"We'll be right there," Carver said.

"Lance, I'll leave it with you," Gene Justice said. "I'll send you a copy of my report on the interrogation for your records."

" 'Preciate it, Gene."

"No sweat."

Larry Eubanks' Aunt Carla was the archetypal Southern matron, broad of beam and proud of stance. She was obviously older than her dead sister. Her salt and pepper hair was cut short and permed for easy care. She wore little make-up, just lipstick and a tiny bit of eyeshadow. Her skirt was cut sensibly to hang just below the knee. An expensive leather jacket was draped over her arm. The man who was with her wore a black blazer, white shirt, red tie, and a pair of gray flannel slacks wrinkled in the seat and legs from the drive up from Columbia.

"I'm Carla Gaddy. This is my husband George." She turned. Two other women, one younger, one older, both cut in Carla Gaddy's image, stood just outside the door in the hall. "My sisters Grace and Evelyn."

Clare introduced herself and the Chief Deputy.

"We want to see my nephew now," Carla Gaddy said.

Larry was sitting in a hard chair in the holding room. Clare led the relatives into the room. Lance Carver came in last and stood against the wall. Clare stepped to one side. Larry's face twisted as if in pain. The three women and George Gaddy were bunched together.

"I shot Mama, Aunt Carla," Larry said in a low voice.

"God*damn,*" George Gaddy said. One of the sisters burst into tears.

"If we may be left alone with my nephew?" Carla Gaddy said in a husky voice.

Clare looked at Lance, who nodded. "We'll give you a few minutes," he said. "It can't be long because we have to return Larry to the Juvenile Detention Center in Worthing."

"They seem like good, solid people," Clare said, as she and Lance waited in the hall.

"Yep," Lance agreed. "Want a coke?"

"Sounds good." She put her hand into her pocket in search of change.

"My treat," Lance said.

"What is it, Christmas again?"

"I told old Jug Watson when he hired his first woman deputy," Lance said. "I said, Jug, first thing you know smart-mouthed females are gonna be taking over the place."

"Fat chance," Clare said.

Lance came back with two frosted cans. He drank his quickly. " 'Bout time," he said, nodding toward the closed door to the holding room.

Clare knocked, opened the door. Carla Gaddy was standing in the center of the room, her arms around Larry. His neatly trimmed head rested on her ample breasts. Two other sisters were near. One of them was patting Larry on the shoulder.

"Just tell us what we can do for you, honey," Carla said. "We'll do whatever we can. I promise you."

George Gaddy blew his nose loudly into his handkerchief. Carla Gaddy glared at Clare. "Do you have to take him now?"

"I'm afraid so."

Larry seemed relieved to escape the embrace. He followed Clare out the door. He spoke only one time on the way back to the Juvenile Detention Center.

"Do you know what they're going to do to me yet?" he asked.

On the way back to Summerton Lance Carver was humming a blues tune. Clare was driving seven-and-a-half miles over the speed limit. Her Saturday was shot.

"You said this is my case."

Lance nodded.

"You're putting someone else out at the school?"

"Um huh."

"O.K. I'll get on it first thing Monday morning."

"What's the matter, you religious or something?"

"You want me to work Sunday," she said with resignation.

"Ummmm."

"Meaning that it's not an official order, but I'd better by-God do it anyhow and forget about turning in overtime."

"Ummmmmm."

"Lance, did you catch that tender scene when I opened the door to the holding room?"

"I've been thinking about that and about what Gene Justice had to say about trying Larry on a First Degree charge. He turned three adult women and one man from cursing and shock over the murder of a sister or sister-in-law to concerned tears for him in just about five minutes flat."

"So what are you going to recommend to the prosecutor's office?"

"I'm going to ask for trial as an adult and for the maximum charge."

"Good," she said.

"There's just no other choice."

8

The parking lots at Fortier Beach's two churches were filling up when Clare drove eastward toward the beach road and the bridge. Rippled rows of high clouds foretold a weather change. A chill wind came from the southwest. The heater in the black and white cut in just as she turned north on the beach road. Traffic was light.

The Eubanks house, just barely visible from the highway, had an aura of neglect and decay about it. In contrast, the house across the highway was freshly painted. It was a frame structure of perhaps five rooms, a country-style front porch, a swing, and a rose trellis. Even in winter brown the yard showed the results of loving care. An old Buick station wagon sat in the driveway. Clare parked behind it.

Hershal Jenrette was attending church at the Crystal Cathedral via channel four. Massed voices at high volume overflowed onto the porch. Clare had to knock three times before she saw movement through a window.

The door opened to an assault of cigar smells both current and past. The man who peered at her through the screen door was of that indeterminate age between old and impossible. He had a thick mass of dirty-gray hair and a bushy moustache to match. Smoke curled up from a long cigar in his left hand.

"Mr. Jenrette?"

"The same."

"I'm Deputy Clare Thomas of the Clarendon Sheriff's Department. May I talk with you for a few minutes?"

"What's my grandson done now?"

"I'm not here about your grandson, Mr. Jenrette."

The old man puffed aromatic, nostril stinging clouds, stepped back from the door, motioned an invitation. The atmosphere of the room was breathtaking. Being a true-blue North Carolinian and the daughter of a tobacco farmer, Clare held the opinion that those who condemned smoking as the killer of hundreds of thousands did not take into account the effect on the human mechanism of the pukings of diesel trucks, automobiles, power and pulpwood plants, aerosol sprays, halitosis, home chimneys belching the smoke of fuel oil and wood, food preservatives, malfunctioning septic tanks, chemicals in the glue on the back of postage stamps and on the flaps of envelops, leaky condoms, and countless other sources of things bad for human lungs, stomachs, and assorted vital components. She, herself, had not smoked since she was a kid in high school. She usually didn't mind if others did, but the density of the air in the Jenrette living room strained her tolerance.

"If you're not here about my grandson," Jenrette said, "it must be about that young hellion across the road. I knew he was going to do something real bad sooner or later."

"Mr. Jenrette," Clare said, "Mrs. Eubanks was killed with a .22 caliber rifle, a Remington semi-automatic. Larry Eubanks told us he borrowed that rifle from your grandson."

"No such thing," Jenrette said. "Hersh knows better'n to loan out my gun. If Larry had my gun he stole it. He's good at stealing. Stole my old age check, you know. Took me two months to get it replaced."

"Is Hersh here, Mr. Jenrette?"

"The boy goes to church."

"Speaking of church, could we turn down the television just a little bit, Mr. Jenrette?" Someone had said something to make the choir burst into exuberant song again.

"All they do is beg for money anyhow," Jenrette said, as he switched the set off. He puffed a blinding, stinging cloud of smoke. "Little sonofabitch has stolen my axe and shovel, too," he said.

"When did you notice that your axe and shovel were missing?"

"Just this past week. I was going to clear out the drainage ditch on the back side of my property."

"Could you identify your tools?"

"Sure. Got my initials, H.J., burned into the handles."

"Sometime tomorrow I'd like for you to come to the courthouse and identify the shovel and the axe. If you'll set a time I can provide transportation for you."

"I'm not too old to drive yet," he said testily. "Morning all right?"

"Fine."

"Because I want to clear out that drainage ditch and I'll need my axe and shovel."

"I'm afraid we'll have to hold them for a while," Clare said.

"You gonna hold my rifle, too?"

"I'm afraid so. It's an important piece of evidence."

"Well, I guess it will be worth it if they put that little bastard where he belongs," Jenrette said.

"What time will your grandson be home?"

The old man shrugged.

"Where does he go to church?"

"Methodist church on the island."

Clare's eyes were watering, her lungs burning. She was breathing very, very shallowly and it made her feel breathless.

She had a compelling need to be out of the room with its suffocating residue of cigars living and dead.

"Thank you, Mr. Jenrette," she said, rising and moving toward the door.

"While that poor woman was lying dead that Larry boy was having parties and driving her car all over the place without a license," Jenrette said. "Seems to me you folks could stop kids driving without a license."

"Well, we can't catch them all, Mr. Jenrette," she said. She opened the door and took a long, deep breath of blessedly fresh air.

She arrived at the Fortier Beach Methodist Church just as Sunday School classes were ending. The minister pointed out Hersh Jenrette to her. "I do hope that Hersh is not in trouble," he said.

"No. I just want to ask him some questions."

"About the Eubanks boy?"

"Just routine questions," Clare said.

"Terrible thing," the minister said. "Can you imagine the mental agony that poor boy was going through, knowing his mother was lying dead in her bedroom?"

"Ummm," Clare said. During his interrogation Larry Eubanks had been more concerned with what was going to happen to him than with his mother's death. If he had felt even a slight twinge of remorse he had not shown it.

Hersh Jenrette was a sturdily built, thick-chested boy. Like many young people who had been slighted in the looks department he seemed to be intent on emphasizing his bad points through his choice of hair and clothing styles. He was about five-feet-six-inches tall, had sandy hair butchered punk style, sandy gray eyes, a rather large nose. His Sunday best was a denim jacket and jeans to match. A redneck hat, billed variety with a portion of the advertising slogan showing, protruded from his back pocket. Clare guessed he would wear it with the bill turned backward in the current Doofus style. He looked worriedly at the pastor, whose face was showing his own concern.

"Hersh, I'm sorry to have to pull you out of church," Clare said.

"I ain't done nothing,'" the boy protested.

"I just want to ask you a few questions, then you can come back in. Wanta come with me? We'll sit in my car."

He sat hunched over, his hands between his knees. He looked straight ahead.

"You and Larry Eubanks are friends?" Clare asked.

"Yeah, I guess so."

"When did Larry borrow your grandfather's .22 rifle from you?"

"Hey, I didn't loan Larry any rifle."

"You were not aware that Larry had your grandfather's rifle?"

"No. No way."

"Hersh, are you telling me the truth?"

He shifted uneasily. "Yeah, sure."

"Were you with Larry at any time during the past week?"

"Yeah, sure."

"When?"

"Oh, a couple of times."

"Your grandfather said Larry had a party at his house during the past week. What night was that?"

"Oh, yeah. That was Wednesday."

"And you went to the party?"

"Yeah."

"Who else was there?"

"Let me see." He gave her three names.

"What was the occasion for the party, Hersh?"

106

"Well, Larry seemed to be loaded. He spent a lot of money on snacks and beer. I guess he was lonely." He turned, looked at her for a moment, let his eyes shift away. "Look, we all just thought his mother was off with another one of her men."

"Is that what Larry told you?"

"Yeah, well, I don't remember exactly. We just knew Miz Eubanks wasn't going to come in and bust up the party."

"Did Larry seem all right to you?"

"Well, Larry's always a little flaky."

"Did he seem to be tense, upset about something?"

"Naw."

"And you had no idea Mrs. Eubanks was dead in her bedroom?"

"Well, there was this funny smell."

"Did you ask Larry about the smell?"

"Naw. Miz Eubanks was gone and the kitchen was a mess. I just figured the smell was there because the place was dirty, that's all."

Clare nodded. After living in the acid atmosphere created by his grandfather's cigars the boy's sense of smell was probably out-of-order.

Hersh looked at her again, and his sandy eyes did not shift as he said, "It gives me the creeps, knowing she was in there all the time. I tell you, if I'd a-knowed there was a dead person in there I'd a-been long gone."

"Do you know where Larry got the money to buy the stuff for the party?"

"Well, he was loaded. He had five cases of beer, lots of goodies." He added quickly, "We didn't drink all of the beer."

"Did you see Larry at other times during the week?"

"Once or twice I saw him driving his mother's car. He always looked so funny. He's a little kid, you know. When he's driving he has to sit way up on the edge of the seat so he can see. You see him coming and all that shows over the wheel is the top of his head and his eyes."

"And you didn't think anything about that?"

"Well, he was always sneaking the car."

"Did you attend the athletic banquet at the school a week ago last Friday?"

"Yeah."

"Did you see Larry there?"

"Yeah, sure. He was there."

"How did he act? Did you notice anything unusual about him?"

The boy was thoughtful for a moment. "No, not really. He was just Larry." He turned toward her again. "Some of us did wonder why he wasn't in school."

"He didn't come to school at all last week?"

"He'd come. I guess he drove his mother's car. I saw him in the hall a couple of times, but he wasn't in the classes we had together."

"O.K., Hersh, you can go back to church now."

He shrugged. "I don't think I want to go back in there."

The sound of a choir came from the church.

"Why?"

"They'll think I've done something, what with the fuzz pulling me right out of church."

"The best way to show them that you haven't done anything wrong is to go back."

He shrugged. "Yeah, I guess you're right."

Clare watched the boy until he disappeared into the church, cranked up, drove to a street-side telephone, looked up the number of Tom Williams. He lived in the unincorporated Charlestown area. She identified herself.

"Is it true what I hear?" he asked. "Did Ethel's own son kill her?"

"It's true," Clare said. "I'd like to talk with you about Ethel."

"I don't know much about her. She was a good worker."

"If you can give me a few minutes I'll drive on out."

"On Sunday?"

"I'm working on Sunday because you asked me to do you a favor," she said with a laugh. "Turnabout is fair play."

"I guess so."

She got directions to his house, was there twenty minutes later. Tom Williams shooed three children ranging in age from ten down to three out of the living room, introduced Clare to his wife, Anne, who showed no inclination to leave.

"Deputy Thomas is here about Ethel Eubanks," Williams said to his wife.

"I can't believe a son would do that to his mother," Anne Williams said. She was a pleasant faced woman. Her body showed the results of having given birth to three children.

"What do you want to know about Ethel?" Williams asked Clare.

"Larry has given the impression she often went away with men."

"If so she did it on weekends," Williams said. "She never missed a day of work. I could depend on her. I spend more time at the high school than at the middle school. Ethel practically ran the middle school cafeteria."

"Was she divorced?"

"Yes, at least from the first one. Eubanks was her second husband."

"Eubanks is Larry's father?"

"No, his father left for parts unknown a long time before Ethel married Eubanks. I know that because she asked me once how to go about finding her first husband so she could get child support for Larry. We don't pay much more than minimum wage at the cafeteria, you know, and it was rough for Ethel keeping up a house, a car, and a teenage boy on her salary while going to night school at the same time."

"Did the stepfather adopt Larry?"

"I don't think so. I think they just started using the name."

"So if Ethel Eubanks went off with men, as Larry said, leaving him alone, she could only have done it on weekends?" Clare asked.

"She never missed a day of work."

"What will they do to the boy?" Anne Williams asked.

"We're going to charge him with first-degree murder. After that it will be up to the county prosecutor, the courts, and, ultimately, a jury."

"What *do* you do with a fifteen-year-old boy who has killed his mother?" Tom Williams asked.

Clare's investigation into the life and times of Ethel Eubanks and her son, Larry, extended into the next week. Monday and Tuesday were wet and raw. She had her report ready for Lance Carver Wednesday afternoon. By that time the image of a woman slowly decaying in a room with the window air conditioner roaring while her son entertained friends in the living room had been front-paged in the *Summerton Weekly* and the *Worthing Morning News,* on dozens of local radio news breaks and the morning, evening, and night T.V. news. Sheriff Jug Watson, fortyish, tall, regally slim, the last of the Southern gentlemen, sat in on Clare's briefing.

"On Monday morning he used his mother's bank card to draw money from her account by using the outside teller machine. Monday night he took three friends to Myrtle Beach. He treated. Beer and pizza. They tried to sneak into a topless bar, but they didn't have I.D.s. On Tuesday he bought a CD player for the car. On Wednesday night he had a party at his home. I questioned all of the boys who were there. The consensus was Larry gave a great party, even if there was a funny smell in the house."

"Do you think any of the boys knew Larry's mother was in the bedroom?" Jug Watson asked.

"I know it's a fucked up—" She paused, grinned in embarrassment. "—a fouled up world, Sheriff, but I can't bring myself to believe any of those boys could have continued drinking beer and eating pizza and chips if they had known they were smelling the odors of decay coming from a dead body."

"I think I would tend to agree," Jug said.

Lance Carver was silent. He saw nothing to be gained by stating he had been disillusioned of his faith in the human animal, even the young of the species, early in his career as a law enforcement officer.

"I think we're on solid ground asking that he be tried as an adult," Clare said.

"He cannot, of course, be given the death penalty, since he is a juvenile," Jug said. "Do you agree with Deputy Thomas, Lance?"

"I'm all for asking for a first-degree murder indictment," Lance said.

"He'll get a lot of sympathy from the knee-jerkers," Jug said.

"What about some compassion for the dead woman?" Clare asked. "She was a hard-working single mother, rearing her son as best she could. She didn't get food stamps and she didn't apply for any other form of welfare. She worked a full shift in the school lunchroom and went to night school at the Community College from six in the evening until ten. She was studying to be a nurse and the homework load was pretty heavy. She was making good grades, A's and B's. Larry said several times she was always going off with men, but according to the neighbors, her teachers, and her boss, she was dependable. As far as I can determine the last time she dated a man was well over six months ago. She has been divorced twice, but in this day and time that's not a fatal character flaw. I think Larry's stated reasons for killing her are going to make him look like some kind of little monster."

"Summarize his statements regarding his rationalizations," Jug said.

"She made him walk to work at the Food Lion, a quarter of a mile. She wouldn't let him drive the car on his learner's permit without her in the vehicle. When he took the car, smashed it up, got picked up by the South Carolina Highway Patrol, she wouldn't call his Aunt Carla to go to Florence to get him, but had him detained overnight until she could get there the next day. She made him clean up his room, do his homework. Because of her work and class schedule she had to get some of her sleep in the afternoon, so she was in bed when Larry got home from school. He often had to prepare his own meals, which consisted mainly of heating a T.V. dinner. She made him give her some of the money he earned bagging groceries to help with the house payments. She didn't like his friends, some of whom were two years older than he. At least one of them was into dope."

"An obvious case of child abuse," Lance said with flat-voice sarcasm.

Jug looked out the window, giving Clare and Lance his distinguished, rather handsome profile for a moment. "Go for it," he said. "Nail this little creep's hide to the wall."

9

The white, hazy days of March brought a minor crisis to the Fortier Beach Police Department. An irate citizen appeared before the Board of Commissioners claiming one of Dan Munday's policemen, namely Officer Carl Young, had been harassing his seventeen-year-old daughter.

Munday attended the regular meetings of the town's governing body to be on hand in case a question arose regarding the police force. He usually sat in his office, which was separated from the conference room where the board met by a thin partition and an open door. The complaining citizen was a transplant from New Jersey, where, it seemed to Munday, the art of conducting both business and personal affairs in a confrontational, in-your-face manner was invented or, at best, perfected.

"Ask Chief Munday to step in," the mayor said.

Munday stepped in, stood just inside the door.

"Chief," asked the mayor, "did you hear what Mr. Bellizzi had to say?"

"Yes, sir," Munday said, neglecting to add that he could have heard Mr. Bellizzi if the door to his office had been closed.

"I'd like for you to look into this matter," the mayor said.

"Yes, sir, I will," Munday agreed.

"That's all?" Mr. Bellizzi asked. "Just, I'd like for you to look into this matter?"

"Sir," Munday said, "if one of my officers has been acting improperly I can tell you right now he'll be disciplined and your daughter will not be bothered again unless I see her driving sixty miles an hour in a forty-five-mile zone the way she was the first time Officer Young stopped her."

"My Sophia is a good girl," Bellizzi said, obviously looking for more confrontation.

"She certainly is," the mayor said soothingly. "And I assure you Chief Munday will look into this matter."

The Kid. Munday called him into the office on Monday morning. Carl Young looked like a policeman. He had been a linebacker in high school, missed playing college ball after being blind-sided in his freshman year by a two-hundred-forty pound tackle. He said his knees bent both backward and forward for a while. He kept in shape by surfing and scuba diving. He was blond. His hound-dog brown eyes made him look just a bit sad, but apparently the look endeared him to females of several ages, if not to seventeen-year-old Sophia Bellizzi, who drove a red Japanese convertible as if she aspired to be a female Richard Petty.

"Hi, Kid," Munday said. "Coffee?"

"Bad for the prostate, Chief," the Kid said.

Munday sighed. Carl Young was twenty-four. He drank lots of mineral water and orange juice and ate things like bean sprouts and yogurt.

"Papa Bellizzi came before the Board last night and accused you of being a mad rapist," Munday said.

The Kid flushed, grinned. "I'll admit I've been tempted, Chief."

"All right, tell me about it."

"Well, you know I stopped her going sixty on Atlantic Boulevard."

"I know."

"She's a beautiful girl," he said, as if that explained everything.

"I know. So?"

"Oh, now and then when I'd see her out in that nice little convertible, her black hair blowing in the wind—" A dreamy look came over the Kid's face.

"Never mind the romantic images," Munday said.

"Well, the next time I saw her I pulled up behind her and flashed the lights and when she stopped I walked up and she was expecting me to say, 'let me see your driver's license, miss.' She was already pulling it out of her purse. But I said, let me see your best smile, Miss Bellizzi.' "

"Jumpin' Jesus," Munday said, rolling his eyes toward the ceiling.

"Well, she smiled," the Kid said defensively.

"How many times have you pulled that stunt?" Munday asked wearily.

"Not many, Chief."

"Three, four?"

"Maybe six."

"Six times you've pulled Sophia Bellizzi over without cause?"

"Well, maybe it was just five."

"Carl, you know better, don't you?"

"Yes, sir. But she seemed to enjoy the attention. She never gave me a definite no when I asked her to go out with me."

"All right. I want you to go to the Bellizzi house and apologize to Mr. Bellizzi and to the girl. I want you to assure them it won't happen again."

"All right. You got it, Chief."

"And find some other way to meet girls," Munday said.

"Sure thing, Chief," the Kid said, grinning as he seated his hat on his blond, close-cut hair.

"As if you need it," Munday said to himself and to the Kid's departing back.

There was time before lunch for a leisurely patrol of the town. On back streets in the wooded sectors he kept his eyes open for fresh tracks in the driveway of summer cottages. They had been lucky. The winter was over and there had been very few break-ins. He ate the businessman's lunch—meat loaf and three vegetables at Sellers' restaurant with Hector McRae and a couple of his salespeople. He listened to their shop talk with interest. He was going to have to take his real estate license examination sometime soon if he intended to join Heck in the business of selling Fortier Beach. It didn't bother him that statistics showed the average income of a real estate salesperson in North Carolina was twenty-two-hundred dollars a year. In selling property as in most other endeavors twenty percent of the participants put out ninety percent of the effort and did eighty percent of the business. What bothered him most about his imminent day of retirement was the fact that he would have to learn to wear a white shirt and tie to work instead of police khaki open at the neck. He went back to the office with his stomach too full of John Sellers' "home" cooking.

It was budget planning time. He spent the early part of the afternoon working up his requests for the next fiscal year beginning July 1. Aside from cost of living pay increases for himself and the three men on the force he could follow the current year's figures, adding in a couple of hundred here and there to give the members of the Board something to cut in the name of economizing with the taxpayers' dollars. Old Number One was due to be replaced by a brand new used Ford with a Police Interceptor engine driven only one hundred thousand miles by the Highway Patrol. With a crooked grin he penciled in $30,000 and allowed himself the luxury of dreaming of having a gleaming, new vehicle with the latest radio equipment. He was erasing the five digit figure to write in $7,000 when the phone rang.

"Fortier Beach Police, Chief Munday."

"Dan, this is Vince Stamps."

"Yeah, Vince, what's happening?"

"You got time to drop by the store?"

"Sure." Stamps ran a convenience store located just off the bridge. It was the first stop on the beach. Stamps thought the location was convenient enough to justify charging five cents more per gallon of gas than anyone else and ten cents more on a pack of cigarettes. He did not get many repeat customers, but he got them first.

Munday wrote in "$7,000.00, Chief's car." He put the budget worksheet in the top drawer of his desk. The warm March day and cold Atlantic waters had procreated a fog creeping in from the strand.

"On little cat feet," Munday said, remembering the line from some long ago English class.

Traffic on the three lane main street was being held to a crawl by an overly cautious oldster who was following driving rules meticulously. Lights on, reduced speed, although the fog was not yet dense on the street half a mile from the ocean.

Vince Stamps was waiting on a customer buying a six pack of Coors and a *Hustler*. The young man looked at Munday guiltily and rolled the magazine up in his hands. Munday nodded, walked to the wall of coolers, took out a can of Dr Pepper. Stamps waved off Munday's dollar. Munday shrugged, put the bill back in his pocket.

"My daughter's gone," Stamps said. He was a tall man, his body going soft after years of twelve and fourteen hour days in the store, his hair dark and full. He wore the modern uniform, jeans and T-shirt.

"Lori."

"Yes."

Lori Stamps was Jilly's age. "All right, Vince, tell me about it." Stamps did not seem to be the frantic father. He was quite calm.

"She spent the weekend with a friend of hers. When she wasn't on the bus this afternoon my wife got a little worried and called her friend's mother. She didn't spend the weekend there at all."

"Did you check with her other friends?"

"Yeah. Mary, the wife, called around. No one had seen her since school Friday."

"And I assume she wasn't in school today."

Vince nodded. "That's right."

"Vince, any reason you know of why Lori should run away from home? I mean, any big family hassles lately? Have you punished her for anything in the past week?"

"No. We believe in giving Lori as much freedom as she can handle. If anything, I guess Mary leans over backward for the girl. I have to admit I don't spend too much time with her, what with the hours I work here in the store. I see her at breakfast in the morning and by the time I close up here she's in bed."

"Does Lori have a special boyfriend?" Munday asked.

"She dates Al Hill, quarterback on the football team. Mary called him. He said he and Lori hadn't had a date over the weekend because he had other things he had to do. He hasn't seen her since Friday."

"Do you have any relatives in the state?"

"You're sounding as if you think Lori just picked up and ran off."

Munday nodded. Because of its seclusion, Fortier Beach had been insulated from many of the evils of the times. It was not the kind of place where fifteen-year-old girls were victims of violence. "That's the most likely thing, Vince. Don't you agree?"

"Well, I guess so."

"Did Mary check Lori's things to see what was missing?"

"I don't know whether she did or not. She got pretty upset when Lori didn't show up after school."

"Is Mary at home now?"

Vince nodded.

"I'll run over there and ask her to check around. What about relatives or friends—people she might turn to if she did decide to run away?"

"Mary has people in West Virginia. My folks are all gone."

"Friends? Anyone closer than West Virginia?"

"Well, there was the Crowley girl. Lori and she used to be great friends until the Crowleys moved to Charlotte."

"What's Crowley's first name?"

"I don't know. I think Mary would know."

"O.K., Vince," Munday said. "I'll get on it."

Mary Stamps had been crying. Her red nose and puffy eyes made her look older than her thirty-five years. She was dressed in tan slacks and a floral blouse. "Have you found her, Dan?" she asked, as she opened the door to Munday's knock.

"Well, not just yet," Munday said.

She closed the door behind him.

"Mary, I'd like for you to check Lori's room to see if any of her clothing or personal items are missing."

She put a hand to her mouth quickly. "I hadn't thought of that."

Munday followed her down a hallway to a door with a sign

that read: THIS ROOM PROTECTED BY A RABID PIT BULL WITH AIDS. The room was as neat as the rest of the house, not at all like Jilly's room at home, which Munday often called the disaster area. Mary opened a closet, filed through clothing hung neatly on racks.

"Her Calvin Klein jeans are gone," Mary said. "And the sweatshirt she decorated in the art class. A couple of skirts and blouses, too." She went to the bathroom. "Her tooth-brush is missing and her skin medication."

"A bag? Something to carry her things?"

Mary went back to the closet, looked at the top shelf. There was a vacant spot there. "The leather suitcase is gone."

"All right," Munday said. "I think we can safely assume she left here of her own free will, Mary. So we can eliminate some of the real nasty possibilities. Now all we have to do is figure out where she might have gone."

"My God," Mary said. "She's only fifteen."

"Vince mentioned a friend of hers who moved to Char-lotte."

"Dana Crowley."

"Have they kept in touch since Dana moved?"

"They wrote regularly at first, but they gradually tapered off. You know how it is with teenage girls. There are so many demands on their time and attention."

"Do you have the Crowleys' telephone number?" Munday asked.

"No. Lori probably does. Somewhere."

"We can get the number from information if you know her father's name."

"John. John Crowley."

Munday nodded toward the telephone on Lori's bedside table. Mary Stamps was moving toward it when it rang. She glanced at Munday, hope in her eyes, picked up the instrument, said, "This is the Stamps residence, Mary Stamps speaking."

She listened, her eyes going wide, said, "No, Mrs. Adams' I haven't seen Julie at all since the middle of last week when she and Lori went to the movies together. No, she definitely did not spend the weekend with Lori."

She looked at Munday, her mouth open as she listened. Munday could hear the tiny, excited sound of a woman's voice escaping from the telephone.

"Chief Munday of the Fortier Beach Police Department is here with me now, Mrs. Adams. We've just discovered my Lori packed her favorite clothing and her personal care items."

She nodded, nodded again. "Yes, yes, I think that is the thing for you to do."

"That was the Mrs. Adams who lives out in Charlestown?" Munday asked.

"Her daughter, Julie, told her she was going to spend the weekend with Lori. She didn't know Julie was missing until just a few minutes ago, because Julie has music lessons on Monday after school and is late getting home. I told her she'd better call the Sheriff's Department."

"I take it Lori and Julie are friends?"

"Oh, yes. They're very close."

"My guess is that Lori has company, wherever she is," Munday said. "That's good." He didn't say two girls together offered a more difficult challenge for the human predators of the world. "Wanta make that call now, Mary?"

There had been a listing for John A. Crowley, but the telephone had been disconnected in November. After thirty minutes of struggle to overcome telephone company red tape, Munday was told Mr. Crowley's deposit had been returned to him by mail to an address in Huntsville, Alabama.

"Mary, I'm going back to the office and get out a bulletin on the police network," Munday said.

Mary Stamps was weeping quietly as he left.

The town clerk buzzed Munday's intercom as he walked in the back door to his office. "Chief, you're to call Lance Carver at C.S.D.," the clerk told him.

Munday dialed, asked for Carver.

"It looks as if we have a couple of hot teeny-bopper runaways," Carver said. "I've got a man out at the Adams house now. Did the Stamps girl pack for the trip?"

"Yes," Munday said.

"You figure they're together, Julie Adams and Lori Stamps?"

"They told their parents identical stories," Dan said. "Julie Adams said she was spending the weekend with Lori. Lori didn't give Julie's name, but used the name of another friend."

"Hold on, Dan, my man's on the radio," Lance said.

Dan heard Clare Thomas' voice, distorted by radio and telephone, but still recognizable. Lance was back on the phone quickly. "The Adams girl packed clothing and personal care items," he said. "Her mother is in shock. She has no idea where they might have gone."

"We had one idea out here," Munday said. "Didn't pan out."

"Well, give me a description of the Stamps girl and we'll get out a bulletin."

Munday called Mary Stamps and briefed her on what was happening. He repeated the information to Vince, but had to hold in the middle while Vince waited on a customer.

It was late. The night man checked in, sat for a while chatting with Munday over a cup of coffee aged into pure acid on the heating pad. When Munday got home Jilly had spaghetti ready. She cooked it by adding meat and peppers to a canned sauce. With lots of Italian bread heated and soaked in garlic butter, it was one of Munday's favorite meals.

"You're gonna make some lucky man a good wife someday," he said as he savored the first bite.

"Unless I decide to become a nun or a big city call girl," Jilly said.

"I would call that an example of divergent ambitions."

"Both are dedicated to a cause," she said, with a sly little smile.

"How well do you know Lori Stamps?" he asked.

"We ride the same bus when Mrs. Stamps doesn't drive her to school. She's younger than I."

"She's fifteen."

"She acts younger."

"What sort of girl is she?"

"She runs with the in-crowd. Her mother lets her car date."

"With Al Hill?"

"Him and others."

"I think I note disapproval in your voice."

She made a face. "Don't mind me, I'm just a prude."

"I like you the way you are," he said.

"It's your fault," she said. "You and your old-fashioned morality."

"I will accept credit for morality," he grinned. He was proud of her. For a while, as she reached puberty and the miraculous changes began in her body, her actions, and her attitudes, he was fearful his approach to rearing a daughter as a single parent was skewed. He was always quite frank with her. There was evil in the world and he wanted her to be aware of it. He told her about the thirteen-year-old runaway who went from man to man during a Fortier Beach summer, using any kind of drugs supplied to her, skimming the oil off mayonnaise and mainlining it when she had nothing else. He talked to her about sexually transmitted diseases ranging from herpes and the common cold to the new strain of antibiotic-resistant syphilis and AIDS. He told her it was only common sense to save the important things in life for a time when she was in life and not just teetering on the brink of it.

"Tell me about Lori, and about Julie Adams."

"What kind of trouble are they in?"

"It seems they've run away together."

She nodded. "Julie's spacey enough to do something dumb like that."

"Not Lori?"

"Lori's a sheep. I guess Julie could have talked her into it. You've sent out bulletins?"

"Yep."

"I hope they're all right," she said sincerely.

"This spaghetti is," he said. "Very much all right."

"Dad, if I served you fried dog-do you'd say, hey, this is real good fried dog-do."

"Want me to say this is terrible spaghetti?"

"Don't you dare," she said, giggling.

Munday had a call from C.S.D. shortly after nine the next morning. Two girls answering the description of Lori Stamps and Julie Adams had been picked up Monday afternoon in a Charlotte shopping mall with their handbags stuffed full of shoplifted lingerie and make-up. They were carrying forged I.D.s showing they were eighteen. They blew a reading on the Breathalyzer indicating they were drunker'n skunks, but they refused to say where they bought the beer so there was no opportunity for the Charlotte fuzz to warn errant bartenders about selling alcoholic beverages to fifteen-year-old girls using obviously faked driver's licenses.

"Charlotte P.D. said figured they had our two runaways, but the girls stuck with the phony names until early this morning," Carver said. "Charlotte's more than willing to give them to us, Dan, if we'll come and get 'em."

Munday wasn't surprised. Handling juveniles, in any jurisdiction, was a pain in the ass. "No charges on the shoplifting?"

"The department store was willing to waive them," Lance said. "I guess you'd better send a man, Dan, since the Stamps girl is yours."

"Well, I guess I could send the Kid up on the bus."

Lance laughed. "You people will insist on buying H.P. discards."

"This people doesn't," Munday said. "But you have to remember we don't have a multi-million dollar budget like the county."

"Tell you what," Carver said. "Why don't you have one of your men ride up with the deputy I'm sending."

"I appreciate that, Lance," Munday said.

"Have him contact Clare Thomas here as soon as he can."

"Tell her I'll just send him on over," Munday said. "Be there in about half an hour."

He told the Town Clerk his plans, asked her to call Vince and Mary Stamps to give them the news. She was on the phone with Mary when he walked out the door, drove home, took a quick shower, put on a clean uniform. He left a note on the refrigerator for Jilly telling her that he expected to be home no later than ten. The drive to Charlotte was almost five hours each way.

As he drove Old Number One into Summerton he felt foolish, like a young boy on the prowl, but it was not an all bad feeling. He was whistling as he bounced up the steps to the courthouse.

10

The morning mail brought a manila envelope to Clare's desk from the County Prosecutor's office. She opened it carefully, pulled out a sheaf of papers. The top sheet read:

Defense Attorney: James Cottle
STATE OF NORTH CAROLINA
In The General Court of Justice
Superior Court Division
STATE V. LARRY EUBANKS
Offense in violation of GS14-17

The jurors for the State upon their oath present that on or about the date of offense shown and in the county named above the defendant named above unlawfully, willingly, and feloniously did of malice and afore-thought kill and murder Ethel Eubanks against the form of the statute in such case made and provided and against the peace and dignity of the state.

She needed to read no further. The Grand Jury had agreed Larry Eubanks should be made accountable for his actions before a judge and jury. It was no more, nor was it less, than she had expected.

When Dan Munday came into her office her smile was

spontaneous. She said, "Well, hi, Dan."

To Munday, Clare looked neat and comfortable in her C.S.D. blues. Her shirt had no hint of a wrinkle. Her pants had a perfect crease.

"Are you the representative from F.B.P.D.?" she asked.

"Today's your lucky day," Munday said.

"Sure." She grinned. "I'm ready if you are."

He followed her out the door, down the steps to the parking lot. She paused beside the driver's side door. "Is it going to insult your manhood if I don't ask you to drive?"

"Hey, my manhood will be perfectly content to let you do the work." He took the passenger's seat, strapped on the seatbelt. The engine started smoothly, hummed powerfully. Munday sighed and gave Old Number One a sorrowful mental wave of good-bye.

"I haven't driven from here to Charlotte before," Clare said.

"I'd take the cut-off, hit highway 30 south of Shallotte and the four lane at Whiteville."

"Roger," she said.

He watched her closely as she cleared Summerton traffic and eased the car up to five miles over the speed limit. She seemed quite competent. He settled back into the seat.

"I thought you'd send one of your men," she said as she clicked in the cruise control while passing a slow moving pick-up truck.

"And miss the chance to spend five hours alone with the sexiest deputy in the C.S.D.?"

"P'shaw and gosh," she said.

"Maybe you've have liked it better if I'd sent the Kid?"

"He's a nice looking boy." She put emphasis on the last descriptive word.

His heart was pounding like a teen on a first date.

"Actually, I've been wanting a chance to get to know you better, Clare."

"Really?" She cast a look at him out of the corner of her eye. "With honorable intentions or otherwise?"

"I'm not quite ready to get down on the floorboard on my knees and propose marriage."

She laughed. "I think you'd have to lose a little weight to fit in between the seat and the dash."

"That's it, build my ego."

"Sorry."

A sixteen-wheeler blasted past them in the opposite lane. The Ford rocked on its suspension from the shock wave. "He was doing seventy, at least," Munday said.

"I thought about trying out for the Highway Patrol," she said.

"Tougher for a woman to get on with them than with C.S.D."

"I fancied myself whizzing up I-95 at eighty with the siren wailing, busting drug kings from Miami to confiscate their Lincolns and Mercedes for the glory of North Carolina."

"And instead you got good old Clarendon County."

"Well, you can't say it hasn't been exciting lately," she said.

"I've been meaning to ask, how did you get out of pulling guard duty at the high school?"

She looked at him. "You've been keeping up with me?"

He took the plunge. "I'm interested in you, Clare."

She looked at him oddly, her brow furrowed in thought, her full lips twisted. She was not a beautiful woman, but she had a nice face, expressive eyes, and he liked her hair very much the way it swept forward onto her cheeks.

"Are you hitting on me, Munday?"

"My daughter cooks great spaghetti," he said. "I thought

maybe you could come for dinner one evening this week."

"I'm not sure but what that doesn't scare me more than if you were just making a pass," she said.

"What about it?"

"All right."

"Thursday night."

"Fine."

"We live at—"

"I know where you live."

"You've been keeping up with me?"

She laughed. The sound was throaty, and shiveringly feminine. "I've been interested in you for a long time, Munday."

"Jumpin' Jesus," he said. "And I was afraid all this time that you'd think I'm too old."

"I have a father complex."

"I'm not that damned old."

"I like distinguished older men."

"I'll accept that."

"After we eat spaghetti I'll take you for a run on the beach," she said.

"Have mercy," he yelped.

She laughed again, and he felt the richness of it in his gut.

He pointed out the turn onto highway 30. Traffic was light. Once she got behind a farmer in a battered pick-up and had to wait a while to find a place to pass.

"You haven't told me how you convinced Lance to take you off school duty," he said, wanting to hear her voice.

"The man who runs the lunchrooms asked me to go by Ethel Eubanks' house to see why she had missed a week of work. Since I was the one who found the body and heard the boy's first confession I guess Lance decided to keep me on the case. I suppose he was pleased the way I handled it. The District Attorney got a true bill from the Grand Jury for first-degree murder, and the judge who will preside at the Probable Cause Hearing has already indicated that he will honor the prosecution's request that Larry Eubanks be tried as an adult."

"Good for you."

"I think Lance is prepping me to be an investigator," she said, smiling. "He's sent me out on a couple of squeals with the department's top investigator."

"Maybe Lance needs to promote a woman to fill his minority quotas," Munday said.

"You have an eerie sense of humor," she said testily.

"That's what it was meant to be," he said, concerned. "Honestly. I think you'll make a damned good investigator."

"It wouldn't take much to beat what we've got," she said, "except for Tom Bragg. Wrap the others all together and you wouldn't have a paper sack full."

"I'm not so sure of Tom. Sometimes he acts as if he's got his feet on wrong and his eyeballs in the wrong sockets," Munday said.

She laughed again. "Tom says that he can't get any sympathy because both of his knees are so bad he can't limp."

He wanted to make her laugh more.

"And he's ugly," he said. "You know about ugly, don't you?"

"When I was in middle school I had a boy tell me one day that I was as ugly as a bucket full of assholes," she said.

He affected an atrocious English accent. "I say, you're a rather earthy child, aren't you?"

"It's the company I keep. Deputies and aging police chiefs."

"I wish I'd been there," he said.

"Where?"

"When the boy told you that you were ugly."

"Why, to see if he was right?"

"To make him eat his words," Munday said.

"Ah, my knight on a white horse."

"The horse has a bad leg and I have blunted my lance against the armor of the world."

"Poor old fellow." She gave him a teasing smile. "You were telling me about ugly."

"Well, ugly strikes one out of three people."

"Ummmm?"

"You can prove it next time you're in a crowd. Look at the person on each side of you and if you don't see it, guess what."

"Now *you're* doing it," she wailed in mock despair.

"You're a stunning woman, Clare," he said.

"Yeah, they look at me and go into shock."

"Now you're fishing for compliments." He chuckled. "I don't mind. You've got a great mouth. I like your lips."

"The better to eat you with, my dear," she said, with an evil leer.

"Beautiful eyes. Nice line of throat." He paused. "Hummm. Good legs. Not that I've ever seen them. But they look good because even uniform pants can't hide the fact that you've got a fine bottom."

"You're getting personal," she said, but there was no real objection in her voice.

"Damned fine breasts."

"This where we turn?"

"That's it," he said.

On the four lane she pushed the cruise control on and the powerful engine revved with a smooth snarl to get the Ford up to sixty again.

"How come you never married, Clare?" he asked, after a period of silence.

"You're misinformed, Munday. I did. I was seventeen, and I had my high school diploma in my hot little hand. I couldn't wait another minute to get away from my dad's farm. I told dad that I'd cropped my last tobacco, fed my last chicken, milked my last cow." She was silent for a moment before she said, "Ha, ha, ha."

"You're still milking cows?" he prompted.

"No, I waited tables."

"Look, if you don't want to talk about it it's all right."

"I don't mind," she said. "I was just remembering how it was. I don't think of little Jimmy too often."

"Jimmy was your husband?"

"High school sweetheart. Neither one of us had enough self image to mix with the crowd. We sort of took refuge from the world in each other. I started going steady with him before my dad would let me go off on a date. Never even so much as dated another boy. He sneaked around and dated one or two other girls. We had a civil ceremony. My dad wouldn't come. Then we headed for the bright lights and the action in Atlanta."

"What happened?"

"An old friend of mine, fellow named Travis McGee once said—"

"Fellow lives on a houseboat in Lauderdale?"

She laughed. "Well, well, you can read."

"Hell, I miss John D. I keep hoping that the rumor that went around when he died is true, that he wrote one last Trav McGee book for publication after his death."

"I read that somewhere," she said. "Trav was supposed to die in it. I don't know if I'd like that. Much as I'd love to have one more good visit with old Trav and Meyer I don't think I could stand it if John D. had killed Trav off. I like to think of him as ageless, still mounting that spavined steed of his to go off smiting the dragons of our society."

132

"I would have mixed emotions about that, too."

The car's heater was working smoothly, not at all like the machine in Old Number One. There was a hint of Clare's perfume in the air. He watched the winter fields flow by. "Clare, you're not old enough to live in the past."

"Oh yeah? What about you? Have you read any books written since the 1960's?"

He shrugged. "I go to the used book store and search out books about serial murderers."

"Really?"

"Well, I've always felt the best writers were in the crime field."

"Do you pull out the MacDonald books now and then?"

"I confess," he said. "You were talking about something John D. wrote in one of them."

"Remember what Trav said about men and women?"

"Well, he said a lot. He was quite the philosopher, Trav was."

"He thought that one of the problems of our society is a shortage of men," Clare said. "He said there are a helluva lot more grown up women than grown up men. In my Jimmy's case he hit it right on the snoot. Jimmy had trouble holding a job. I pulled the breakfast shift in an I-Hop and made enough money to keep us in beer and cigarettes, but I had a little trouble paying for Jimmy's other pleasures. A little bit of pot I could put up with, but when he got into coke—"

Munday thought it best to remain silent. Clare stepped down on the accelerator to pass a sixteen-wheeler, let the cruise control take over again.

"I didn't know Jimmy had started dealing until the DeKalb County fuzz woke me up from my afternoon beauty sleep with a warrant to search the place. Lucky for me Jimmy had enough sense not to keep his stash in the apartment or I'd have a possession rap on my record and Lance wouldn't want me to become his ace investigator."

"Was that when you left him?"

"I was eighteen years old. I was away from home for the first time. I thought the worst thing that could ever happen to me was to have to crawl home and ask my dad and mother to take me in. No, I didn't leave him. He left me."

"He was a damned fool."

"I don't think he wanted to leave me," she said. "They killed him. He moved in on the wrong people. The Atlanta police found him in a dumpster with his entrails hanging out of a slit in his belly. They'd cut off his gonads and thrust them into his mouth."

"Jumpin' Jesus."

"I ran like a turkey. Ended up in Houston waiting tables. I was working there when my dad died. I came home and helped my mother sell the farm. We got a good price and my mother insisted I take some of the money and go back to school. I didn't know what in hell I should study, had no idea that I could be anything other than a waitress. I had a talk with my advisor and he suggested that a big, strong girl like me might do well in law enforcement, and there you are."

"He was a wise man, your advisor," Munday said.

"After I got the job with C.S.D. I went back to the school and told him thank you, although I wasn't quite sure at the time I was all that happy about it."

"How do you feel about it now?"

"Pretty good, actually," she said matter of factly. "It's sort of neat digging around looking for clues just like Sherlock Holmes, and, if you'll excuse me for sounding a bit pretentious, I'm finding the human animal to be an endlessly eerie and often fascinating creature. Tom and I went out on an incest complaint last week. The fourteen-year-old girl had told her teacher at school her father was doing things to her that made her feel funny. It took Tom about fifteen minutes to find out papa had been throwing the meat to daughter ever since she was twelve and there had never been any complaints from her until one day when she decided that she wanted a pair of fifty-dollar designer jeans and papa wouldn't buy them for her."

"Sympathy for papa?" He laughed. "You're damned sure not a dedicated feminist."

"Dan, maybe I'm wrong. I've been wrong before, but that little snit of a girl, fourteen going on thirty-five, knew exactly what she was doing. I had a long talk with her while Tom was questioning the father. She had all the instincts of a born whore. She used her juicy little body to blackmail her father. She had that man wrapped around her slightly soiled little finger. She got anything she wanted out of him, except when he was so broke that he couldn't afford to buy her those fifty-dollar jeans. She was also getting it on with an older cousin and her boyfriend." She shook her head. "I sometimes wonder what kind of kids we're raising. One thing for sure, the rules have changed. Remember that old song about getting too soon old and too late smart?"

"Before my time, old lady," Munday said.

"Bull, don't tell me you never watched the *Lawrence Welk* show. Hell, they're rerunning it now on public television. Anyhow, these kids are too soon old. They see heaving and panting sex on prime time television shows. They watch about humpteen acts of violence per night, ranging from rape to cannibalism. That little girl who was servicing her daddy and enjoying it until he licked the red off her candy had probably seen hundreds of pretty girls pretending to be whores, and she lived in a world where condoms are distributed in high schools and where everybody from presidents on down to the girl next door thinks if you have an itch it's perfectly all right to scratch it. Marriage? An old, bad joke. Married couples holler and scream at each other and occasionally kill each other and always cheat. Love is all below the waist. Movie stars and leading characters in what my mother calls shitcoms have babies without the benefit of marriage."

"Young people are unilaterally oriented, most of them," Munday said.

"My, what big words you have, grandpa." She chuckled. "That girl who finally turned her father in for something they were both enjoying hadn't considered what was going to happen to her when we hauled dear old dad off to jail. She was thinking only of herself, and how mean daddy was not to buy her those fifty-dollar jeans. Well, that old boy has had it. His ass is grass. The Grand Jury won't discuss the case more than three minutes before returning a True Bill, and the legal lawnmower will go to work. A judge will lay on a longer sentence than he would hand down if the man had committed Murder Two."

"There are some damned good kids out there," Munday said.

"I sure hope so. I guess in our profession we see more of the other kind."

They rode in comfortable silence for a few miles, hit town traffic in Rockingham, pulled into a Burger King for a hamburger and a shake, ate sitting in the car watching the flow of vehicles on the thoroughfare. After a quick visit to the conveniences inside the restaurant they were underway again.

"Well," Clare said, "I've told you my life story. Now how about the life and times of Dan Munday?"

"As dull a subject as you'd ever want to investigate."

"I know you were married. I've seen you with your

daughter in the restaurant and I've seen her at school. She seems to be a fine little girl."

"Not so little any more, but, yes, I think Jilly is a fine girl."

"Some of them act like bubble-heads," Clare said. "They wear skirts up to their buns and wiggle at anything that wears pants. Why is it, Dan, that the only place you ever see those mini-mini skirts are on whorish looking models on the tube and in the halls of the high school?"

"Watch out or you'll hit one of my hot buttons," Dan said. "One of the things I kept pounding into Jilly's head from the time she was four or five years old was that those people on T.V. are not like us, that they live in another world, and that world is like Oz and New York and Hollywood, not real."

"If she understands that, you're very lucky." She slammed on the brakes to keep from rear-ending a Toyota with a South Carolina tag that had decided to come to a near halt to sightsee. She didn't speak again until she had passed the offending vehicle and was back to speed. A road sign said Monroe, twelve miles. "What happened to your marriage, Dan?" she asked.

"I think it just wore out," Dan said. "Elaine moved on to greener pastures."

"And you got custody of Jilly?"

"No contest," Dan said.

"Your wife didn't want her?"

"We don't express it quite like that."

"I can understand why," she said emphatically.

"Elaine wanted to travel, and an eight-year-old child would have been excess baggage."

"You don't mind if I take an instant dislike to your ex-wife?"

"Feel free."

"As they say in Oz and New York, is there a significant other in your life now?"

Dan looked out the window, pondered how to answer, decided on the truth, because, although he hated the phrase she'd used, it had taken only four and a half hours in Clare's company to make her significant in his life. "There was one lady," he said. "We dried each other's tears for a while after Elaine left. The relationship cooled over the years, and I hadn't seen her at all until just after Christmas. I'd say that rather than being significant to each other we're more like old friends."

She looked at him, squinting one eye. "That has the ring of truth."

He grinned, made the sign, "Cross my heart."

As they approached Charlotte traffic thickened. Munday acted as navigator, took her into the city past the arena where the NBA team played, into the relative calmness of the decaying downtown. The two Clarendon county runaways were being held in the juvenile detention section of the County Jail. Munday let Clare be the spokesman to get them pointed toward the right people.

Charlotte Policewoman Ruth Winestein escorted them to the room where Lori Stamps and Julie Adams were watching an afternoon game show on T.V.

"All right, ladies," Winestein said, "get your things and let's go. These nice people are going to take you home to mommy and da-da."

"Hello, Julie," Munday said. "Remember me?"

"Yeah," the girl said in a dead voice. "Hi."

"Does my dad know I'm coming home, Chief Munday?" Lori Stamps asked.

"Yep. He knows."

"I'll bet he's mad as shit."

"Naughty, naughty," Ruth Winestein said. "Little girls should watch their fucking language around adults."

"Piss off," Lori said.

"They're yours and welcome to them," Winestein said. Clare had signed a receipt for the girls at the desk. Winestein escorted them all to the front sidewalk. "They'll do it again," she said to Clare. "Next time they might not be so lucky." She was speaking in a normal voice so that the two girls could hear her. "This isn't New York or Los Angeles," she said, "but if we hadn't found them when we did, someone else would have." She looked directly at Lori. "And instead of going home to mommy and da-da they'd be working on their backs in a hot sheet motel room for the benefit of some stud pimp."

"You're scaring me shitless," Lori Stamps said.

"Get them out of here," Winestein said.

Clare held the door for the two girls to get into the back seat.

"Hey, there are no door handles back here," Lori complained.

"You're very observant," Clare said.

"Shit," Julie said.

Munday had taken the passenger's seat in front. He turned and said mildly, "I'd rather you didn't use language like that."

"Yes, sir," Julie said meekly.

The evening rush hour was underway. Clare handled it skillfully, although a bead or two of perspiration showed on her forehead.

"When we get out of town if you'd like me to spell you I will," Munday offered.

"I might take you up on that," she said.

"I'm hungry," Lori Stamps said.

"Didn't they give you lunch in juvenile?" Clare asked.

"Such as it was," Lori said.

"We'll have a bite down in Rockingham," Munday said.

"I want pizza," Lori said.

"We'll see," Clare said.

"Did yawl see my mother?" Julie asked.

"I saw her," Clare said.

"What did she say?"

"She was worried, naturally," Clare said.

"Is there any particular reason why you girls decided to run away from home?" Munday asked, turning to look at the two teenagers. Julie's hair was still lank. Lori's blond hair was frizzed into tight, tiny curls. Runny mascara smudged the eyelids of both girls. They looked at each other quickly.

It was Lori who answered. "We had to, Chief Munday. They were going to kill us."

"We were on their hit list," Julie said.

"I see," Munday said. "Who are they?"

"The Gang," Lori said.

"And what gang is that?" Munday asked.

"They just call themselves The Gang, that's all."

"I see, and who is the leader of this gang?"

Julie said, "I don't know."

"But, if they were threatening to kill you, you must know some of them."

"No, we don't," Lori said.

"Kids," Clare said, "if that's the best story you can come up with I think you'd better try again."

"But it's true," Lori said, her voice getting husky. "We know what they do. They got the word to us that we'd have to do what they wanted."

"How did they get the word to you?" Munday asked. He, like Clare, was assuming the girls had concocted the story of their lives being in danger to appease the wrath of their parents.

"In notes," Julie said.

"Did you save the notes?"

"No, we were afraid to. They said to destroy them."

"You said you know what they do. What is that?" Clare asked.

"Well, they worship the devil," Lori said.

Clare looked at Munday, made a moue with her mouth, lifted her eyes.

"They hold black mass and all that shit," Julie said.

"And suck chicken blood," Lori said.

"That's awful," Clare said mockingly.

"You don't have to believe us," Lori said. "I don't care. If you could ask Hillary Aycock why she killed herself I'll bet you'd believe us."

Munday kept his face passive, but turned to look closely at Lori. "What's that about Hillary?"

"Maybe you ought to ask yourself why she was so scared that she hanged her own self," Julie said sullenly.

"Do you realize you're talking about a very serious matter?" Munday asked.

Clare rolled her eyes toward the heavens, reminded of LeShane Dunn and other very serious matters.

"Just exactly what do you know about the reasons for Hillary killing herself?" Munday asked.

"Well, we don't know for sure," Lori said.

"You have indicated that you know something," Munday said sternly. "Why did Hillary kill herself?"

"She was one of them," Julie said, "and she couldn't stand it."

"One of who?" Munday asked.

"You know," Julie said.

"No, I don't."

"The Satan freaks," Lori said.

"Hillary was a member of a satanist group?" Munday asked.

"Well, we don't know for sure," Julie said.

"But we think so," Lori said. "She never came right out and said so, but she hinted at it. She wanted us to join, and that's why they were after us. Because they're afraid Hillary told us too much before she killed herself."

"Exactly what did Hillary say to you?" Clare asked.

"It's hard to remember the exact words," Julie said. "Like, she talked about these fun people, only she didn't sound as if they were really fun."

"What did she say about these people?"

"Well, that they really knew where it was at," Lori said, "and all that."

"All what?" Munday asked.

"That they did real neat things," Julie said.

"Such as?" Clare asked.

"She hinted that it was real exciting," Lori said.

"How exciting?" Clare persisted. "Like sexy?"

"Well, yeah, I guess," Lori said.

"Did Hillary ever state in so many words that she belonged to a group of people—kids—who were worshiping the devil?" Munday asked.

There was a long pause. "Well, not really," Lori said.

"And you received notes threatening you if you didn't join the same group?" Clare asked.

"Yeah," Julie said.

"This frightened you enough to give you reason to run away from home," Munday said, "but what are you going to do about it now that you're going back? You don't seem scared anymore, except maybe about what your parents are going to do or say. Won't the gang still be after you? Won't you need some sort of protection?"

It was obvious that the girls hadn't thought of that. There was a long silence.

"You don't have to believe us," Lori repeated.

"Just as long as your parents do?" Clare asked.

"Yes, smart ass," Julie said. "And what are you going to do about it?"

Clare said, "Oh, that's charming." She looked at Munday and "tsked" out of the corner of her mouth. It was to say, "Well, that's the end of that story, eh?"

It was after nine o'clock when they got back to the Courthouse in Summerton. Clare would deliver Julie Adams to her parents. Lori Stamps would ride to Fortier Beach with Munday in Old Number One.

"I'll call you tomorrow," Munday whispered to Clare.

"Do it," she whispered back.

On the way to the beach Munday had one more go at Lori Stamps. "Lori, you were very lucky not to be charged with shoplifting in Charlotte, you know."

"Big deal," she said.

"Do your parents deserve to have the worry you've given them by running away?"

"I don't know," she said sullenly.

"Why did you do it, Lori?"

"I told you."

"Because a gang of devil worshipers was threatening to kill you?"

"Yes."

"Lori, did you happen to see the Geraldo show on T.V. about a month ago?"

"No," she said, too quickly.

"About teenage devil worship?"

"No. I was in school."

"I was feeling a bit under the weather that day," Munday said. "Had a touch of the flu or something so I stayed home from work. It was an interesting show. The devil worshipers drank chicken blood and held what they said was a black mass and called the devil Master and all that. Are you sure you didn't see it?"

"I don't remember."

"Lori, if I were you I'd tell my parents the truth and forget the fanciful stories."

"You're not me, and it is the truth," she said.

At the Stamps house, Mary Stamps burst out of the door and engulfed Lori in her arms when she was halfway up the walk.

"Oh, baby," Mary crooned, "I was so worried. We're so glad you're home."

"Where's Vince?" Munday asked.

"He's still at the store," Mary said. "Thank you for bringing my baby home to me."

"Mother, I am not your little baby," Lori said angrily.

Munday had left Old Number One running. He drove just a little too fast on the way home, felt a sense of warmth and cleanliness when he saw the lights on in the cottage. Jilly was on the couch, her legs crossed under her, doing her homework to the beat of a Jerry Lee Lewis record on the CD player.

"Hi, Dad," she said, putting aside her notebook to come and kiss him on the cheek. "There's soup on the stove. Nine bean. Your favorite. Shall I get it for you?"

"I'll do it, honey. You go on with your homework."

"Have a good trip?"

"I rode up with Clare Thomas. You remember her. She lives here on the beach. She was on duty at the high school for a while."

"Ah, ha," Jilly said with a knowing smile.

"Ah-ha me, no ah-has, wench," Munday said, grinning back.

"She seems nice."

"I think so. I've asked her to dinner this week. Can I prevail on you to do your famous pasta?"

Her smile faded. "Isn't it a little early to be bringing her home to meet the family?"

"I think you'll like her," he said, feeling a bit uneasy.

She smiled again. "It doesn't matter whether I like her or not, as long as you do. She's your girlfriend."

"Thursday night all right?"

"Fine," she said. She lowered her head to her homework. Her hair fell forward, hiding her face.

11

With one exception, Fortier Beach voted Republican, the one deviation from a straight ticket being in the biennial Seventh District Congressional race. The Honorable Representative was a spend-and-tax Democrat, but he had developed the most efficient and enthusiastically helpful home front organization anyone in North Carolina had ever seen. If one wanted to know anything about Washington or had a problem with some pesky, red-tape, regally-minded gaggle of petty bureaucrats one had only to pick up the telephone and call the Congressman's nearest office, which, for Fortier Beach, was in Worthing. If the Congressman's aides didn't have the answer on hand they would find someone who did. No one in the Seventh District worried about government waste when it came to the expanded services offered so freely to the informed electorate of the Seventh District, because, after all, it was for *them*. Economies were to be practiced in other congressional districts, especially in the urban areas of the North and in the land of fruits and nuts to the west.

Mainly, Fortier Beach voted Republican because: One, the population was top-heavy in educated retirees. Liberal cynics said the older folks were conservative because they had theirs and didn't want to share it with the more unfortunate. More informed observers explained it by saying the retirees had lived long enough to attain wisdom. Two, the minority population of the island could be counted, kids, dogs and all, on the fingers of two hands. Three, when a big Diamond T tug and barge knocked out the swing bridge, which was the only access to the island, a Democratic governor, a bit irked by the rather loud complaints of Fortier Beach citizens, stated in a snit that a bridge to Fortier Beach was not one of the necessities of life. The Governor's rather questionable comment was in response to a flood of screams of outrage from the well educated, independent retirees, many of whom were of the Northern persuasion and had not, apparently, learned honey attracts more flies than vinegar. Their confrontational approach to the problem mussed the Governor's sensitive Democratic hair and provoked an intemperate response that solidified Fortier Beach's Republicanism then and thereafter.

Perhaps it was because the beach precincts had gone Republican in the Nixon landslide, carrying along every county office except Clerk of Court, that the Democratic regime then in power in North Carolina did some skillful foot dragging when the barge destroyed the swing bridge, making life on Fortier Beach rather exciting for a number of days. The Governor finally had to act because the accident occurred while a good number of summer people, many of them Democrats from the Piedmont cities, were on the island. Deprived of freedom of movement, the visitors added their clamor to the slightly less than people-skilled voices of the citizens.

The Coast Guard sent a helicopter to provide transportation to the hospital in Summerton in the event of medical emergency. In spite of this, one visitor, a heart patient, protested quite vocally that his life was in danger. He was fifteen minutes from medical care by helicopter. When the Coast Guard lifted him off the island and it was arranged for him to return to his upstate home, it was discovered he lived in a rural area a full forty-five minutes from the nearest doctor.

Young mothers panicked, fearing their babies would be without milk, but there was a good stock of groceries and supplies in the island stores and the necessities were soon flowing across the waterway by boat.

In spite of some initial inconvenience many of the permanent residents looked back on those months without a bridge as golden days. There were no vacationers on the island to give the small town its usual summertime big city traffic problems.

Bubba Dean maintained Fortier Beach did not have a traffic problem, only a driver problem, a contention having some validity when one got behind a summer visitor driving fifteen miles per hour for the length of the beach, or when one of them ignored the left turn lane on Atlantic and crossed both lanes from the far right.

As soon as the Department of Transportation borrowed a ferry boat from the Outer Banks and gave the citizens an opportunity to move one car off the beach to be parked on the other side of the Waterway, things smoothed out and it was "riiiite niiice" until, finally, the Democrats in Raleigh brought in a contractor from the mountains of West Virginia to build a high rise bridge across a saline marsh.

It was, by design, quite a handsome bridge. From the beach side it soared upward in a slow, graceful flow to a height calculated to pass the masts of the largest vessel capable of navigating the Intracoastal Waterway. The West Virginia contractor, who had never built a bridge with its pilings anchored in almost bottomless marsh mud, went bankrupt, and there was some delay, but eventually there it was, long, sweeping, low-railed so that one could look out over the wide expanse of the saline marsh to see the variation in color of the grass from season to season.

When a young man named Frank Werty won a case of beer by jumping off the Fortier Beach Bridge into the Waterway he did not gain instant fame. Knowledge of the feat was confined largely to those who frequented Red Nell's Raw Bar and Lounge. Frank Werty's high moment of notoriety came during the week of Dan Munday's preparation for Clare's visit on Thursday night. Munday got a haircut, had his teeth cleaned, bought a new pair of civilian slacks and an Oleg Cassini pull-over shirt made in Sri Lanka. Frank Werty jumped off the Fortier Beach Bridge again on Wednesday night.

It wasn't exactly swimming weather. The water temperature was still cold enough to keep the blue crabs in hibernation, but it was a rather nice, unseasonably warm night. Red Nell's Raw Bar and Lounge closed at one a.m., leaving a few of her patrons at loose ends, too wound up on Coors and Lite to go to bed and with no other place to go on a pretty spring night. Three car loads of them parked in the emergency lanes on top of the bridge. From there you could see the lights of a ship lying at anchor off the Blue River shipping channel, waiting for daylight and the tide for passage up river to the port. A big tug and barge train had passed at a walking pace and was muttering its way into the distance to the west and south. There was a moon.

The bet was two cases of beer. Werty didn't take off his boots. The first time he had taken them off and when he hit the water it stung the bottom of his feet something fierce.

He stood on the low rail with two of his buddies helping him balance. Moonlight sparkled on tide ripples in the dark water a mile or two down there.

"Let's forget this and go home, Frank," said his best friend.

"Nothin' to it," Werty said, stepping out. He fell forever

and felt the impact of the water on the bottom of his feet even through his boots. He took a deep breath just before he hit and held it.

The dispatcher at C.S.D. contacted Fortier Number Two by radio. The Kid, Carl Young, had the patrol that night. He drove to the top of the bridge, parked in the emergency lane behind a chrome-decorated, big-wheeled pick-up truck.

Frank Werty had not surfaced. He struck the water with a mighty splash and disappeared. The mighty cheers of the spectators faded into a long silence. The Kid called the rescue squad and the Coast Guard. By that time there was no possibility of finding Frank Werty alive. The Coast Guard's small launch came roaring down the Waterway shortly after the rescue squad arrived with siren wailing. The Kid had positioned cars on each side of the Waterway on the old causeway that had once led to a swing bridge. The lights illuminated the general area but didn't reach down to the water, which stood at dead low tide. A spotlight on the Coast Guard vessel played back and forth. The muddy bed of the marsh, exposed by the low tide, was aromatic of oysters and decayed vegetation.

Munday arrived on the scene about an hour after Frank Werty did his Brodie. He had to explain that expression to Jilly when he used it in front of her the next day. He saw the lights from the time he turned onto the bridge approach. Lights in the darkness, stationary lights of the cars, the moving lights of the Coast Guard boat, blinking lights on the ambulance from Summerton and the small fire truck from the Fortier Beach Volunteer Fire Department.

He drove to the top of the bridge and began clearing the emergency lanes. There were some protests which he quelled by asking the young men and women, most of whom were not residents of Fortier Beach, if they would like to take a ride with him into the Sheriff's Department and blow their breath into a certain instrument. He saw the Kid's car on the old causeway on the south side, drove back to the beach end and went down onto the old road.

Just before dawn Munday called C.S.D. and asked for a deputy to keep traffic moving across the bridge. The morning shift would be going in toward the industrial plants in Clarendon and the adjoining county soon. With the sun there were four boats searching the Waterway, just in case Werty's body had floated, which, Munday thought, was not likely. It takes about three to four days, depending on the temperature of salt water, for a body to become a floater.

The Kid summoned the Fortier Beach Scuba Club, of which he was President. Jimmy Small was among the school age members of the club who were only too happy to miss a day of school and participate in something new and exciting. The divers went down in pairs. Werty had jumped, as best it could be determined from the various estimates of the time from the patrons of Red Nell's Raw Bar and Lounge, just before the tide went slack at low. His body would have moved toward the west when the tide turned and began to flow in strongly, so the Kid and his young friends were working west of the bridge for the first couple of hours.

It was midday before the Kid asked the Coast Guardsman who was running the diving boat to tie up to the pilings directly under the bridge. The tide had flooded and ebbed to low again since Werty won his bet. Jimmy Small was diving partners with the Kid. Each of them had a fresh tank and powerful underwater lights that barely penetrated the murky waters at channel depth.

The muddy bottom was littered with bottles and beer cans. It was almost as much fun for the barbarians to throw litter from the window of a speeding car and see it arch out into space and fall into the water as it was to play smash-the-road-sign by trying to hit it with an empty can or bottle at sixty miles an hour. Jimmy was leading, the Kid comfortingly close on his left flank. They kicked down to the bottom immediately and swam against the tidal current.

Even with the powerful lights, visibility was no more than four feet. Jimmy was playing his light back and forth on the bottom when he saw something like a thick tree stump. He moved his light upward as he kicked a couple of feet closer and the beam reflected off the white, staring, dead eyes of Frank Werty. Jimmy yelped and came to a halt so quickly the Kid ran into him. Jimmy had to clear his mouthpiece of water, because he had almost swallowed it when he looked into the dead man's blank eyes and somewhat surprised look.

The Kid went close and made a quick examination. The body was buried in mud to its waist. The first time Werty won his bet he jumped on high tide. The second time there was five feet less water under the bridge and he went down, down, down, driving himself into the mud like a piling. The black muck was disturbed around him. The Kid could see finger marks and grooves where Werty tried to dig himself out.

The Kid motioned Jimmy to go up and get a rope. Jimmy was only too eager to get the hell out of Dodge. He surfaced, removed his mouthpiece and yelled. "We've got 'im. Gimme a rope."

He swam back down with the rope and missed the spot by at least ten feet because the tide was really whistling in by then. He oriented himself by swimming to the westward group of pilings that prevented passing vessels from banging into the huge, cement pier of the bridge, swam to the middle of the Waterway, played his light over the bottom and moved against the current. He had just spotted the glow of the Kid's light when he had his second thrill of the day. It was half buried in the mud. It gleamed in white, regular rows. Something other than beer cans and bottles had been tossed over the low rail of the bridge. It was the rib cage of a human being, bones picked clean by crabs and small fish.

Jimmy was just about ready to go up and let someone else have the pleasure of helping the Kid recover the body of Frank Werty, but he saw the glow of light. He came up behind the Kid, touched him on the leg. The Kid reacted violently, whirling with a great burst of bubbles, his eyes wide through the glass of his mask. He made a pantomime of wiping perspiration from his forehead.

They looped the rope under Werty's arms, which tended to float and wave gently in the tidal current. The Kid motioned Jimmy to go up again.

Jimmy surfaced and said, "Give a pull, easy."

Down below the Kid stood beside the body and held the rope, trying to guide the vector of force vertically. The body popped out of the bottom mud and went swaying off out of the beam of the light like a hooked fish. The Kid kicked upward, surfacing with a splash, removing his mouthpiece to gasp in fresh air. The sunlight seemed especially beautiful to him.

"Oh, shit," the Kid said, when Jimmy told him about the bones.

Four of them went down. Jimmy, made more bold by the brightness of the day and the presence of dozens of people, led the way. He went first to the pilings and repeated the route he'd followed to find the bones the first time. One of the divers carried a recovery basket. The Kid dug away mud from the bones and exposed a full torso, the rib bones connected to the spine bones, the shoulder bones connected to the spine bone, the spine bone connected to a stub of neck bone, and like that.

The whole thing was weighted by bricks tied together with wire through the mortar holes and to the spine. The torso had been hollowed out before the weight was inserted.

Munday boarded the Coast Guard launch while the Kid and the divers were conducting their search. When the partial skeleton was lifted aboard he noted not all of the softer material had been devoured by hungry marine creatures. Tough ligaments around the joints were bleached white and stringy, but they had not decayed away. The torso which had been discarded as if it were nothing more than a bottle or a beer can had not been at the bottom of the Waterway forever.

The spine had been severed at the small of the victim's back with a severe, smashing blow, a blow powerful enough to crush one vertebra. One vertebra of the neck extended upward from the shoulder bones.

The Kid and his divers, reinforced by a team of two from the Sheriff's Department, scoured the bottom of the Waterway for an additional two hours without finding any more body parts.

Lance Carver and Jug Watson showed up just as Frank Werty's body was being loaded into the rescue squad ambulance. Technically, the recently deceased body and the partial remains had been recovered in Munday's territory. The City Limits of Fortier Beach stopped at the edge of the marsh, but the town's authority was expanded by an Extraterritorial Jurisdiction Zone extending one mile from the boundary, taking in the bridge and a couple of hundred yards of the land on the north side of the Waterway.

The matter of Frank Werty was simple. There were a dozen witnesses to the fact that he jumped of his own volition. Stupidity was not legally punishable. There was no law to mandate man as his brother's keeper.

The partial skeleton posed a problem.

"Dan, what the hell," Jug Watson asked, "are you starting a bone yard out here?"

Munday shrugged. Jug was referring to the finding of the foot-filled sneaker on the beach.

"I think it will be interesting to see if the medical officer can make a D.N.A. match between this and your foot," Lance Carver said.

"Ain't science wonderful?" Munday asked.

"If you need any help, Dan, don't hesitate," Jug Watson said.

"I've never turned down help yet," Munday said, "and if you can think of any you can give me, feel free."

"I know what you mean," Jug said. "It's pretty hard to identify a foot and a rib cage."

"How are you going to ship this thing to Raleigh without busting it all up?" Lance asked.

"I've got some Styrofoam popcorn out in the storage shed at City Hall," Munday said. "You knew, those little things that blow all over everywhere if you spill them. I guess I'll put it in a big box and pack it down with that stuff."

"Send it U.P.S.," Jug said, chuckling. "What are the contents of this package, sir? Oh, just a man's bones, that's all."

"Or a woman's bones," Munday said.

It was Thursday. Munday had a fresh haircut and clean teeth and all he needed was a few hours sleep to make up for getting up again in the middle of the night. The Kid helped him pack the bones. He drove it to the package center and sent it to the medical examiner in Raleigh by U.P.S., calling the contents Police Evidence.

"What's the value, sir?" he was asked.

"Depends on your point of view. I know one fellow who would have said, at one time, that it was quite valuable to him, but I guess the minimum will cover it."

He could not quite figure out how he could justify a value over one hundred dollars if the parcel got lost. Back when he was in school he read somewhere the basic raw materials in a human body were worth about a dollar-ninety-eight. Even with inflation the human bones brought up from the bottom of the Intracoastal Waterway would not have much value, at least not to the United Parcel Service's insurance company.

He washed his hands twice at the City Hall and once again, before getting into a hot, long, soaking shower, when he got home. He lay down on his bed to make up for the hours of sleep he'd missed. His eyes popped open and stayed that way. He got a beer from the fridge, dark, Mexican *Dos Equis*, and went out onto the porch overlooking the Atlantic. The last near miss from a hurricane had put a respectable surge onto the sands of Fortier Beach, taking the dune in front of his cottage. City Commissioner Hugh Zachary was walking his dog. Munday waved. Zachary's two Yorkies, Mop and Doll, dashed into a flock of resting gulls, sending them off on a flare.

A light, northwesterly wind was blocked by the cottage so it was slumberously warm on the porch. Munday leaned back in a plastic, outdoor recliner and dozed off before he finished his beer. He was awakened by the slam of the front door. He heard footsteps inside the cottage. The back door opened and Jilly said, "There you are."

"Here I are," he said. "How was school?"

"It was school," she said. "Dad, since you're having company tonight I asked Jeanne Dabney to spend the night with me, O.K.?"

It was not O.K. He had in mind that Jilly and Clare would have a chance to get to know each other. He opened his mouth to say so.

156

"Hey, Mr. Munday," Jeanne Dabney said, sticking her frizzled head around Jilly. She waved.

"Hey, Jeanne," Munday said.

"You don't mind?" Jeanne asked. "We've got ever so much to talk about, Jilly and I."

"No, it's all right," Munday said.

"Jeanne's going to help me cook. How about brownies after?"

"That'll be nice," Munday said. He took a sip of his beer. It was flat. He hated to waste it, because it was expensive, being imported, but he went to the rail and poured it into the white sand. The wind had shifted. A chill had crept into his bones while he slept. He went into the living room and laid a fire. He didn't light it until half an hour before Clare was due to arrive. By that time it was cool enough so that the fire felt good.

12

When Munday heard a car pull into the drive he had to force himself not to leap to his feet and run to the door. Jilly and her friend were in the kitchen putting the finishing touches on dinner. The cottage was filled with the mouth-watering aroma of baking cookies. It reminded Munday of a tip he had heard at McRae Realty one day. When showing an existing house for sale, put a sheet of cookies to bake before the prospects arrive. Nothing makes a house seem more like a home than baking aromas.

The doorbell rang.

"Want me to get it, Dad?" Jilly called out.

"I'll get it," he said.

The porch light made highlights in Clare's short, ash blond hair.

"Come in this house," Munday said.

"Am I too early?"

"You have come at positively and absolutely the exactly right moment," Munday said, stepping back to let her sweep past. She wore soft turquoise, a shirtwaist dress with a gored skirt to emphasize her waist and outflowing hips. A white sweater was draped over her shoulders.

"Take your sweater?" Munday asked.

She gave him her back, shrugged the sweater off into his hands. When she turned she was smiling. "It smells good in here."

"Cookies."

The sleeves of her dress were folded to mid-forearm. An abalone shell necklace and matching earrings picked up the color. When she walked, the dress moved with her and her good knees showed. Her stance was proud in heels that brought the top of her head to Munday's nose. He had never seen her in a dress. It emphasized her maturely plush figure. She was a big girl, solid but shapely. She exuded vitality. Around the orb of her deep, brown eyes there was a glow of healthy blue-white. She smelled of shampoo and an understated perfume.

She laughed, "Just what are you looking at?"

"By God," Munday said, "you're a girl."

"Disappointed?" she asked archly. "Or may I take that as a compliment, I hope."

Munday fell back on humor to cover his confusion. "I'm so broke all I can afford to pay is a compliment. That's why I asked you to dinner here at home instead of taking you out."

"Hi," Jilly said from the doorway leading to the kitchen, "you're out of uniform, aren't you?"

"Hello, Jilly," Clare said. "You're making delicious smells." Clare knew Jilly from having seen her having lunch or breakfast with her father at the Sellers restaurant. It was a small town. Although Clare had been there less than a year she knew most of the permanent residents by name or by sight.

Jilly shrugged. "Just brownie mix from the supermarket."

"Thank you for inviting me to dinner," Clare said with a smile.

"Well, Dad did that," Jilly said. She added, with a quick wink, "but he had my permission."

"I'm glad," Clare said.

"Something to drink?" Munday asked.

"I make a mean martini," Jilly said.

"Sounds great," Clare said.

They were still standing. When Jilly disappeared into the kitchen Clare said, "And you, sir, you look spiffy tonight."

"A good-looking man looks good in anything he throws on."

"Yes, Uncle Albert," Clare said, to show that she, too, remembered Walt Kelly's swamp critters.

"Don't do that," Munday said.

"What?"

"You're too young to know what I'm talking about *every* time."

"Poor old fellow," she said. "Hadn't you better sit down and rest?"

"Good idea," Munday said, indicating the best chair for her. She sat with her knees together, long legs on a diagonal to her crossed ankles, the line leading upward to a hint of hose-smoothed thigh just above the knee.

Jilly delivered two icy drinks in crystal stems. "I gave you three olives," she said to Clare. "That's the way Dad likes them."

"That's the way I like them, too," Clare said.

"Dinner in about ten minutes," Jilly said. "So drink up."

"Yes'um," Munday said, grinning at Clare.

"I think you're proud of that girl," she said.

"Indeed I am."

"You should be." She lifted her glass. "Health, wealth, and the time to enjoy them."

"I'll drink to that," Munday said. "My health and yours, although I've drunk to the other fellow's health so much I've ruined my own."

Clare acknowledged with a small smile. He decided he was overdoing trying to be witty.

A ripple of girlish laughter came from the kitchen. Clare looked at Munday questioningly.

"Jeanne Dabney," he said. "Jilly wanted some help with the meal."

She nodded, sipped her drink.

"You look very, very good," Munday said.

"Thank you." She had spent not a few minutes deciding what to wear. She was not the type to devalue an invitation by showing up for dinner in jeans and sweatshirt. "It's nice to know that my efforts are appreciated."

"More than you know," Munday said.

"Nice cottage."

"Jilly keeps it straight, mostly," he said. "I try to help and she says I don't know anything about cleaning house. She does let me do the windows."

"Do you like living on the beachfront?"

"Mostly," he said. "There are times when you get a little tired of constant wind, and the sand is a pain in the hootchy. It can be cold in the wintertime. I've added some insulation but most beach cottages weren't built for winter comfort. I like it here especially in September and October."

She had moved to the beach in October. Lovely days of low humidity; a sun just warm enough; flat, calm seas; gliding pelicans; white-flaring gulls. "A great time of the year," she said.

"You have a nice place on the Waterway."

"Well, I'm just renting."

He laughed. "Aren't we all? The only difference between renting and owning is that your landlord is responsible for upkeep and the so-called owner has to keep up the mortgage company's property. If I don't pay my payments they can kick me out faster than they can evict a renter for non-payment."

"Well, you have a little more freedom of action. You wouldn't have to ask the mortgage company's permission if you wanted to paint your bedroom black and silver."

"You painted your bedroom black and silver?"

"No, because I didn't want to have to ask permission."

"You hear about the blond terrorist who was ordered to go out and blow up a car?"

"I think you're going to tell me."

"She burned her lips and got lipstick all over the tail pipe."

"Didn't that used to be a Pollock?"

"You can't tell ethnic jokes anymore."

"Just feminist jokes, huh?"

He flushed. "Hey, no offense."

"None taken," she smiled. "Know what you get when you turn a blond upside down?"

"Tell me."

"A brunette with bad breath."

"*That* is gross," Jilly said, from the doorway. "But I like it." She winked at Clare. "Lady and gentleman, loosely speaking in the latter case, your delicious repast is serve-ed."

With giggling, exaggerated servility, Jilly and Jeanne piled Clare and Munday's plates with pasta. "You may indicate when you've had enough," Jilly said, ladling sauce onto Clare's plate, "by either saying when or nodding your head."

"When," Clare said.

"Are you sure?"

"Well, just a little more."

The salad was crisp, the sauce meaty, the garlic bread crisp outside, soft and hot inside. Clare ate with obvious gusto. "Jilly, if you ever decide you'd had enough of this old bear, you're welcome to come live with me if you'll cook spaghetti once a week."

"You hear that, don't you, old bear?" Jilly asked. "You better be sweet to me."

"I am always the soul of sweetness," Munday protested.

"He has morning breath," Jilly confided.

"Gross," Jeanne said.

"You're Donald Dabney's daughter, aren't you?" Clare asked in an effort to include Jeanne in the conversation.

"Yes," Jeanne said, slaying Clare's opening gambit with one word.

"Jeanne," Jilly said, "Clare is the one who found Larry's mother's body."

"Ugg, gross," said Jeanne.

"What are they doing to Larry?" Jilly asked.

"He's being held in the juvenile detention center in Worthing for psychiatric studies."

"Why haven't they let him go home with his aunt?" Jeanne asked.

"He's charged with first-degree murder, and the state is trying to determine whether or not he is mentally responsible enough to stand trial," Clare said.

"He's just a kid," Jilly said.

"She wouldn't let him do anything," Jeanne said in a teenishly belligerent tone of voice. "She charged him rent and everything. She was real mean to him."

"The possibility of parental abuse was investigated," Clare said. "If anything his mother was too lax in disciplining him. As far as we can find out he was never punished physically."

"I'll bet you're one of those who would like to allow spanking in schools again," Jeanne said.

Clare finished chewing a bite of salad. "I don't set school policy," she said, "but it's my opinion, and I think it was borne out by what I observed during the time I walked the halls at the high school, students there are crying out for guidance."

"Oh, yeah," Jeanne said sarcastically.

"What do you think of the parents who are trying to take over the job of the school administration to force a new system of punishment on us?" Jilly's voice was pleasantly soft, her accent only slightly colored by her Southern background.

"If you're talking about the Comprehensive Management Concept, it's not just a system of punishment," Clare said. "It's primarily designed to help teachers do what they should be doing, that is to teach, while giving the students a series of guidelines that protect the rights of those who are in school to learn and not disrupt."

Munday saw the steel curtain clang down over the blue eyes of Jeanne Dabney. Closing the gate was, he thought, a teenage talent. Clare could talk for the next hour and Jeanne wouldn't allow one word of it to penetrate.

"Don't you think there's too much disruption of class time?" Clare asked, looking at Jilly.

"If it's algebra I don't mind," Jilly said with a smile.

"Just wait until you have to stay after school," Jeanne said to Jilly. "Just wait until they try to make you go to school on Saturday."

"The purpose of the proposed extra period at the end of the school day is to allow students to re-learn and re-test," Clare said. "In schools where the system has been installed it has reduced the number of at-risk students dramatically."

"Some of the boys say the parents had better not hold another meeting at the school," Jeanne said angrily, "or they'll have to buy four new tires to get home."

Clare put down her fork. She was looking intently at Jeanne. "We've heard about those threats, Jeanne. If you have any friends who might become involved in such illegal and destructive activity, you'd be doing them a favor to tell them there will be law enforcement officers watching the parking lot."

"Gestapo," Jeanne said.

"Now I don't think you've got the background to make that judgment, Jeanne," Munday said.

"Yawl forget we're people too," Jeanne said, "that we've got rights. Just like with Larry. It's easy for you to say, well, he's a criminal, but you don't have any idea what he went through, do you? Any time something happens involving a teen the teen is automatically in the wrong. It doesn't matter what's been done to us."

Munday looked at Jilly. Her eyes were flashing back and forth between Jeanne and Clare as she ate her salad.

"As a matter of fact," Clare said, "I had a long talk with Larry. I made a list of his reasons for having killed his mother. Would you like to hear them?"

"No," Jeanne said.

"I would," Jilly said.

"He was angry because she wouldn't let him go around in cars with older boys, some of whom were known to be using illegal substances—"

"A little bit of pot," Jeanne said.

"She wouldn't let him drive the car alone, although by law he was supposed to have a licensed adult with him at all times," Clare continued. "She made him clean up his room."

"She never cooked him a meal," Jilly said.

Munday jerked his eyes away from Clare's face to look at his daughter.

"She worked long hours at the lunchroom," Clare said, "and then was up until very late with classes and homework."

"She made him give her money from what little bit he made bagging groceries," Jeanne said.

"She was working for just over minimum wage," Clare said. "She was having a tough time keeping up house and car payments and meeting all the other expenses."

"Well, that wasn't his fault," Jeanne said. "He didn't ask to be born."

"Hold it a minute," Munday said, raising one hand. "Jeanne, this isn't just a matter of whether some kid deserved or did not deserve to be grounded, or paddled, or something like that. This isn't you against us—"

"Isn't it?" Jilly asked, with a little smile.

"No, it isn't," Munday said. "Whether you think Larry's mother was doing the best she could and Larry was in the wrong in his relationship with her, or whether you go with what Jeanne apparently thinks, that Larry's situation was so bad he was the victim, the fact remains the boy violated the most basic of all human rules. Whatever his mother did or did not do was not justification for her death. Whatever real or imagined teenage right she deprived him of did not balance out the fact he violated once and forever her most basic right, the right to life. He killed her, kiddies. He picked up a .22 rifle and opened the door to her bedroom and very calmly and skillfully shot her in the back of the head. She is dead, dee-eee-a-dee, dead."

Jeanne was poutingly silent. Jilly put down her fork and let her hands rest on the table on either side of her plate.

"It hasn't been so long since I was your age that I can't remember how it was," Clare said. "When you're fifteen death is something that happens to someone else, someone you usually don't know, or to the very old."

"I know about death," Jeanne said. "My grandmother died."

"Did your folks leave her to rot in a closed room for a week?" Munday asked.

Jeanne tossed her frizzed hair and disdained to answer.

"I think if you could have seen Mrs. Eubanks you might have a different slant on the matter," Clare said. "It was not a pleasant sight. The smell—" She paused.

"Was it really awful?" Jilly asked, wide-eyed.

Clare shook her head. "I don't think we want to talk about that while you're still eating your salad."

"That's all right, the boys tell grosser than gross jokes at lunch in school," Jeanne said, brightening with anticipation.

"Does it smell like a dead dog or something?" Jilly asked.

Clare looked at Munday. He nodded almost imperceptibly.

"It's a very penetrating smell," Clare said. "It's thick, and it clings to the membranes inside the nose like oil. When you're in it, it's the whole world. There's nothing else but the smell, and when you leave, it stays with you in your nose, and you can taste it in your mouth."

"Gross," Jeanne said.

"It finally sinks in you're smelling decaying human flesh, and you know one day you're going to smell like that and there's an abhorrence in you that is more personal, and more frightening, than any horror picture you've ever seen. It's the smell of the grave, and of hate, and of finality. You want to vomit it away, but even if your stomach does come up it's still there."

Jilly stood. "Dessert time," she said. She moved rapidly into the kitchen, came back with a plate of brownies. She stood beside Clare's chair. "These about the color of dried blood, aren't they?" she asked innocently.

Munday was startled, but Clare just smiled and said, "Dried blood isn't quite so brown. It's more blackish."

The brownies were rich and sticky. Munday ate two chocolaty squares. He was still mulling over Jeanne's attitude toward Larry Eubanks' solution to his self-defined problems. It seemed incredible even a bubble-head like Jeanne could excuse murder because a kid was made to clean up his room and heat his own frozen dinners. Even more astounding were the comments made by Jilly that seemed to indicate she at least partially shared Jeanne's viewpoint.

The two young girls left the adults to finish their coffee. They cleared the table and disappeared into the kitchen. Munday offered brandy.

"I promised you a run on the beach," Clare said.

Munday groaned loudly and patted his stomach.

"Do you think I'll need my sweater?"

"I think you'll need more than that, including a bulldozer to get me moving."

"Get your coat, old man."

He groaned again, but obeyed. He pulled on a fur-collared leather jacket, held out another for Clare. She pushed her arms through the sleeves and turned. She was standing quite close. He could smell her perfume. Her breath carried memories of garlic bread and brownies.

The night was still. The temperature had dropped into the upper fifties. The heavy leather jackets felt snug and good. They walked toward the east into the glow of a half moon making glittery, silver tracks on the smooth water past the dark sands.

"Do you walk the beach a lot?" she asked.

"I'm ashamed to admit that I don't," he said. "Elaine and I—" He halted guiltily.

"It's all right if you mention her," Clare said. "She was a part of your life for a long time."

"We used to walk a lot at night before Jilly was born."

"I come over to walk at night sometimes, usually later than this." She laughed. "Last summer I had this crazy friend who came to visit, wanted to go skinny dipping."

"Ah-ha," Munday said.

"A *female* friend," she said, punching him on the shoulder. "We'd been having a few and talking about old times and it was one o'clock in the morning. Well, you know how many accesses there are to the beach."

He did. There were access areas at the end of each street, and the entire island was cut into a grid.

"I thought it would be no problem at all to find a street end all to ourselves, but I drove down half a dozen streets and there were either cars already parked there or cars coming in behind us. We finally decided everyone on the beach was also looking for a place to go skinny dipping and went home and had another big orange—or something."

"I don't go skinny dipping, not in the ocean," Munday said.

"Coward."

"It's not the same with you females," he said. "Listen, I've flown up and down the beach in an airplane and I've seen the big hammerhead sharks lying off just off the breakers and it happens I have a piece of equipment that dangles like a fishing lure. I feel vulnerable when I'm naked in the bathtub, much less an ocean habitat for things with very large teeth."

"You're terrible," she said, laughing.

He put his hand on her arm and pulled her to a halt, turned her to face him. "Clare, if you really think I'm terrible, or just an old fool, now's the time to tell me."

"The girl is not saying a word," she whispered.

"Last chance," he said, moving his face toward hers. Her lips met his. She kissed in the old-fashioned way. No open-mouthed face eating, no wild snortings and pantings, just soft, wide, moist lips and a sweetness engendering a tremble in him he hadn't experienced in decades. There was just a hint of tongue, the shared taste of food and drink, bodies separated by the thickness of the two leather jackets.

"I think I've been kissed," she whispered, not trying to pull away.

"I think you need to be kissed again."

"Since you are older and, presumably, wiser, who am I to argue?"

They walked back toward the cottage side by side, hips brushing now and then, hands clasped.

"Dan, there's just one thing that bothers me," she said.

"What's that?"

"Jilly?"

"Jilly?"

"She doesn't like me at all."

He considered the matter. "I think you're wrong. She seemed to like you very well."

"Well, we'll see," she said.

"Listen, lady, you've kindled fires in me I thought had been banked permanently years ago. Don't you try to escape now."

"What are your plans, sir?"

"Ravishment, rape, and rapine," he said, putting his arm around her.

"Before or after you put Jilly and her little friend to bed?"

"Neither," he said. "No push, no shove. When you're ready. Not before."

"Fair enough," she said.

The girls had finished cleaning the kitchen and were watching television. Clare and Munday had brandy at the kitchen table. There was little talk, much probing of brown eyes, some hand holding, and a shiver of anticipation when Clare said, "I think by the time you can sneak over to my place after the girls are asleep I'm going to be ready."

Munday took her by the hand, pulled her to her feet, led her into the living room and got her sweater. "Clare has to go, kids."

" 'Night, Clare," Jilly said.

"Yeah, goodnight," Jeanne said in a tight little voice.

"I'm gonna walk her to the car," Munday said, "and while I'm out I'll take a little run up the beach and check out the business district."

"O.K., Dad," Jilly said.

"School tomorrow," Munday said. "You two had better hit the sack after this program."

"We will," Jilly said.

"Wasn't that pretty obvious?" Clare asked once they were outside.

"Normal procedure," Munday said.

What happened in Clare's rental place by the Waterway had not been normal procedure for a long time for either of them. The totality of it was so unique they were forced to experiment, to see if there had been some mistake the first time. There had not been.

13

Bubba Dean, he who had celebrated a myriad of birthdays, was never to be seen without a book in his hand or his pocket or in front of him on his desk at Dean's Realty or on the seat of his Lincoln Town Car next to him. His books were mostly paperbacks made limp by repeated thumbings and readings, and they were of a kind. Bubba was a student of success theory. To the core of his three-hundred-pound being he believed you can if you think you can. He lived by rules stated in simple but ringing language by a long and distinguished line of positive thinkers ranging from ancient Greek and Egyptian philosophers to Norman Vincent Peale, Robert Schuler, and Zig Ziggler. He was a walking encyclopedia of adages. He remembered Lee Iacocca's tagline to the old Chrysler ads on T.V.: "Lead, follow, or get out of the way." He knew whatever the mind of man can believe it can achieve. When the going gets tough the tough get going.

Bubba had learned long ago that it is easy to find the key to success, the hard part being finding which door to open; and that the only thing you ever get on a silver platter is tarnish. He agreed with Ann Landers that there is no known successful surgical procedure that will replace macaroni in the spine with a rigid backbone, for that operation is a do-it-yourself project.

Bubba was fond of passing along his knowledge about success to his salespeople. "You can always make time to do the thing you want to do," he would say, quoting Al Koran, "if you want it enough." And he liked to make up his own success adages. One of his favorites was: "The size of your dream determines your success. If your dream bucket holds only a gallon, you'll never get five gallons."

"Dan," Bubba said, on a sweet morning in early spring, "did you ever wonder why people who should have inferiority complexes never do?"

Munday and Bubba were alone at the redneck table next to the kitchen door at the Sellers Harbor restaurant. It was North Carolina's primary Tuesday. Bubba had already been over to the City Hall to cast his vote, and it was the list of candidates on the Democratic slate to which he was referring. Munday was in no hurry to vote. He had some definite opinions about the candidates who would face off for county offices such as the Commission and the School Board, and in those races he would vote for the man and not the party in the general election, but as a registered member of the G.O.P. his primary choices were limited. Although the beaches usually voted Republican for statewide and national offices it was necessary to be a registered Democrat if you were to have a say in who was going to fill local and county offices, for it was almost always the Democratic primary that decided local races.

"What all those clowns forget," Bubba said, "is the eighty-twenty rule. From the beginning of written history—and probably before that—eighty-percent of the wealth has been in the hands of twenty-percent of the people. If the tax-and-spend Democrats could wave a magic wand and divide the wealth equally world-wide it wouldn't take more than ninety days before eighty-percent of the wealth would be back in the hands of twenty-percent of the people."

"Being among the eighty-percenters I can believe that," Munday said.

"Eighty-percent of the world rides on the back of the twenty-percent," Bubba said. "It's a historical problem. The twenty-percenters have always had to get together and decide how much of their productivity they were going to distribute to the non-producers to keep them from burning down the world. In the past thirty years or so we've spent a couple of trillion dollars to keep 'em happy and it didn't work. The Romans had the right idea. The government threw big circuses for the mob and gave them free bread and beer and lots of blood in the sands of the arena. In ancient Israel they just kept the worst of them, he that pisseth against the wall, outside the city. That bottom-side element, the pissers, is different from the poor. The poor are mentioned a couple of hundred times, mostly with compassion, in the Old Testament, the pissers only five times. Being poor has never been anything to be ashamed of. The infamy comes from not being willing to do anything about it."

"Are you running for something?" Munday asked.

"I'm running hard to keep what I've worked for," Bubba said. "To paraphrase what old Satchel said, I'm afraid to look back because I *know* something is gaining on me. But when they catch up with this old boy they're going to find out that the fat boy has a partner named Smith and Wesson. Meantime, I just keep on keepin' on, because in real estate twenty-percent of the salesmen do eighty-percent of the business and are rewarded accordingly. You'll want to remember that when you go to work for McRae."

"I appreciate the advice, Bubba."

If Munday sounded a bit distracted it was because he was like a teenager in the throes of first love. Since the night he

174

had invited Clare Thomas to dinner the main thrust of his existence had been to be with her.

"Who throws the trash on the shoulders of the highway?" Bubba asked. "The eighty-percenters. We're developing a third-world sub-population, Dan. I'm not talking color or race. I'm talking apathy, ignorance, and doubt. I'm talking a kid who push-a-waits from high school with just one ambition, to take a surf board and a six-pack to the beach and catch a wave. You know some of 'em. You ask 'em what they're going to do with their lives and they say, 'Oh, I'll get me a job,' and what they mean is that they'll hire on with some construction crew because it doesn't take much skill or preparation to hammer a nail or carry bricks. They live with momma and papa and they're thirty years old. They'll work now and then, just enough to keep themselves in beer and cigarettes."

"I know some like that," Munday said.

"Responsibility is the greatest right in citizenship, and service is the greatest of freedom's privileges," Bubba intoned. "Know who said that?"

"Nope," Munday said, remembering the taste of Clare's lips, the firm bulge of her breast in his hand.

"Robert Kennedy. Not John. Robert."

"Ummm," Munday said.

"That's why I signed on to pick up the trash on the beach road from the city limits to the shopping center," Bubba said. "But in this instance the eighty-twenty rule is shot to hell because one-tenth-of-one-percent of the population is picking up the hamburger wrappers and cigarette packs of the other ninety-nine-and-nine-tenths-percent."

"Well, Bubba, there are those of us who appreciate what you do."

In exchange for policing up the roadside for two-point-nine-tenths miles, Bubba was given a sign at each end of the stretch of road, a metal rectangle attached to a Department of Transportation advisory sign, that read: Adopt a Highway, Dean Realty.

"You got the wrong people out picking up trash," Bubba said. "We oughta put the road gangs back to work, but, hell no, those criminals in the county jail and over in the prison camps have rights. It's beneath their dignity to pick up trash, so we of the one-tenth-of-one-percent do it."

Munday chuckled at the impossible image of Bubba bending over to pick up roadside debris. Bubba wore slip-on shoes without socks because he couldn't reach his feet. "Well, Bubba," he said, "at least you give some employment to a small portion of that third-world type labor pool."

"Yeah," Bubba said, "and speaking of that—" He drained his cup. "I'd better go see how my boys are doing."

Bubba's "boys" ranged in age from eighteen to sixty-six. There were four of them, two on each side of the road. They had put out signs reading: Shoulder clean-up ahead. They had started their work shortly after eight o'clock and by the time Bubba drove his Town Car slowly up the long incline to the crest of the bridge they had cleared away the paper tracks of the hordes all the way past the entrance to the small airport, which Bubba called Clarendon International.

All four of the workers were on the east side of the road about two hundred yards to the north. Bubba turned on his emergency blinkers and parked on a narrow shoulder alongside the drainage ditch.

"You fellows having a convention?" he asked, as he grunted his way up and out of the car to waddle ponderously toward the gathering.

"Look here, Bubba," said the senior citizen in Bubba's work crew.

A very sorry specimen of dog was crouched in the grassy bottom of the drainage ditch. The animal's ribs stuck out piteously. It had a long bone clamped in its jaws and it was growling warningly. One end of the bone looked bent.

"Bubba," asked the oldster, "is that what we think it is?"

Bubba saw that the bend was a joint. Just beyond the joint the bone had been shattered in twain. Rusty, dried, stringy things connected the shorter piece with the longer. Bubba was no student of anatomy, but it damned sure looked like what they thought it was to him, and what he thought it was was a human thigh bone with the knee joint still attached.

With an agility that surprised his workers, Bubba jumped down into the ditch and launched a kick at the starving dog. It wasn't a kick meant to hurt the animal, just to surprise him. The dog yelped and dropped the bone. Bubba kicked again and the animal decided that retreat was more satisfying than chewing on a bone that didn't have any meat left on it anyhow.

Bubba puffed his way out of the ditch and said to the youngest member of his crew, "Bring that thing up here, Mike. I'm gonna call Dan Munday."

"I ain't touching that thing," the boy said.

"Oh, for heaven's sake," Bubba said. "Wrap a piece of paper around it or something."

"You can get AIDS from something like that," Mike said.

"I'll get it, Bubba," said the old man.

Bubba grunted loudly as he sat down and swung his legs into the car. He dialed the restaurant on his cellular telephone.

Munday was just going out the door when the cashier called him back. "All right, Bubba," he said, "I'll be there in a minute. You on your car phone?"

"That's right," Bubba said.

177

"How 'bout giving the Sheriff's Department a call while I'm on my way? You're in the county over there."

"I'll do it," Bubba said, suiting action to words as soon as he'd broken off the call to Munday.

It took Munday just eight minutes to drive from the restaurant to the scene of the discovery. The old man had picked up the bone with a sheet of newspaper that had been left in the ditch by an obliging member of the barbarian sector, and it was lying in state on the grass beside the road.

"It might be from a horse," the old man said.

Munday stood looking down at the bone with his hands hanging loosely at his side.

"Or a goat?" said the boy, Mike.

"I don't think so," Munday said. "Why don't you boys take a look on up the road and see if there's anything else?"

The grade of the road seemed to be flat until one looked closely, then there was a very gentle rise to a crest about five-hundred yards to the north, the difference in elevation being the reason why the Department of Transportation had dug the deep drainage ditches. Bubba's work crew split up and began to scout around on either side of the asphalt. A C.S.D. car arrived ten minutes after Munday. Munday knew the deputy slightly, greeted him, let him examine the evidence in silence.

"It's human," the deputy said.

The search of the roadside ditches turned up nothing but more signs of daily barbarian passage. The deputy cupped the newspaper around the bone and lifted it gingerly into the trunk of his car. He left slowly, as if driving a hearse.

"Dan," Bubba said, "now it's bad enough to have my boys picking up beer cans and bottles and fast food wrappers and plastic cups and the occasional used rubber. I don't think it's reasonable to ask them to police up human remains."

"Bubba, you're absolutely right," Munday said.

Munday drove into Summerton. There was a gathering in Lance Carver's office. Jug Watson was there, along with the Chief Deputy, the deputy who had brought in the bone, and Deputy Clare Thomas, the department's newest investigator.

"Dan," Lance said, when Munday walked in, "I wish to hell you'd keep this stuff on your side of the bridge."

"Mornin'," Munday said. He winked at Clare.

"Chief," Jug asked, "have you heard from the medical officer regarding a possible match between the body parts recovered from your strand and the Waterway?"

"Not yet," Munday said. "They said it was going to take a while." In truth, he knew that tests on the body parts had been put aside in favor of more urgent investigations. You didn't have to be a member of Mensa to know that the likelihood of assigning a name to the partial remains was infinitesimal and, therefore, that the complicated D.N.A. comparisons were low on the list of priorities.

"I think, if you'll pay for the call, Jug, that it might be a good idea to check with them," Munday said.

Jug nodded. "Use the phone in my office."

It took a few minutes for Munday to wade through three different extensions and three different and irritatingly indifferent state employees before he had someone on the telephone who knew what he was talking about.

"As a matter of fact, Chief Munday," he was told by the lab technician, "I have my report on tape ready to be transcribed and sent to you. I'll see if I can't get it out tomorrow."

"Well, in view of the fact that we've got another little tidbit for you, I wonder if you could check that report and tell me now whether the foot and the ribcage came from the same body."

"I don't have to check," the technician said. "They definitely did not come from the same body. The torso bones were those of a young woman, somewhere between the ages of fourteen and eighteen."

"I appreciate it," Munday said. "Look, it's getting pretty complicated down here. I wonder if you could put a rush on this bone that we'll be sending up to you today to see if it goes with either of the others."

"I think that's a reasonable request, Chief. Yes, we'll get right on it."

Jug decided that the situation was getting interesting enough to send the leg bone to Raleigh by car. The deputy who had answered the call was assigned to the task and was soon underway, the bone still wrapped in the original faded newspaper.

Jug ordered coffee to be brought to his office. The female deputy who worked in records didn't seem to think that she was being put down by male chauvinists when she was asked to bring in four cups and a fresh pot.

"All right," Jug said, "what the hell have we got here?"

"What I'm afraid is going to become one royal pain in the neck," Lance Carver said. "I'm betting that when they run the tests on this latest find it's going to belong to a different individual."

Jug looked out the window and sighed. "If you're right, Lance, we're going to be famous. You know the media's fascination with multiple murderers." He turned to face them. "We need that kind of publicity like we need a major hurricane."

"I don't see that we have any more choice than we have in a storm," Munday said. "What is there to do except just ride it out?"

"Damned if I know," Jug said, "but, damn, I hate this."

"One thing we can do," Lance said. "We can alert all of our people to be on the lookout. There are more pieces missing than have been found."

"With the warm weather, the Adopt-A-Highway folks are going to be out working," Clare said. "We can alert them, too, in case more pieces have been discarded along the roads."

"Good idea," Jug said. "Dan? Any comment?"

"If you lose an hour in the morning, you have to hunt for it all day," Munday said.

"What?" Jug asked.

"Old Chinese proverb," Munday said, grinning. "I heard it from Bubba Dean."

Jug looked puzzled. "Meaning?"

"That it's getting close to lunch time," Munday said.

Jug rolled his eyes.

"Lance, you said that if I decided I needed to tie in with C.S.D. to yell," Munday said. "I'm yelling. I think it might be a good idea if you'd assign a man to work with me. I asked Raleigh to hurry up with a comparison on the new piece, so we'll be hearing from them in a day or so. If, as you suspect, it turns out to be from a third individual we're going to have to start kicking ass and taking names or we'll be eaten alive by our little friends from the newspapers and T.V. If we can announce that we've formed some sort of joint task force that'll hold them off for a while."

"I agree," Jug said. "Lance?"

"You and Thomas have worked together," Lance said. "Either of you have any objection if I put her on it?"

"None from me," Dan said, as his heart jumped in anticipation of spending precious daytime hours with Clare.

"It will be my pleasure to work with Chief Munday," Clare said.

"Pleasure is for your off duty hours," Lance said, looking first at Munday, then at Clare.

Munday was impressed. To that date he and Clare had not appeared in public together. There'd been a lot of beach walking and popcorn eating while watching old movies on the VCR and telephone calls and long, hand-holding talks that extended well past midnight.

"Not much gets past you, does it, Lance?" Munday asked.

"Very damned little," Lance said.

"I want to know what Raleigh says about this latest thing," Jug said.

What Raleigh said was that the femur shaft submitted to the medical officer for examination had been truncated slightly below the lesser trochanter by an edged instrument and that a similar blow had smashed the head of the fibula and the tubercle of tibia just below the medial condyle, that the medial condyle of tibia was loosely attached to the lateral condyle of the femur by atrophied ligaments, and that the main shaft of the femur showed evidence of having been gnawed by a fanged animal. Translated, that meant that the bone taken from a starving stray dog was the thigh bone of a human being that had been chopped off, probably with an ax, at points just below the thigh joint and the knee. Further, testing indicated that the femur was that of a male between the ages of fifteen and twenty, and that there was no D.N.A. match to either of the two previously submitted pieces of evidence.

14

Clare had slipped off one shoe. She touched Munday's ankle under the table. The feel of her hosed toes through his sock was electric.

"Let's stick to business here, Deputy," he said, grinning with almost foolish pleasure.

The joint C.S.D./F.B.P.D. task force for assigning an owner's name to certain errant bones and body parts was meeting in a back booth at the Blue River Restaurant on Summerton's waterfront. A window wall gave a view of the wide river. A container ship was passing. The channel came in close to River Street, so close you could see the Japanese name of the vessel and small, yellow men walking her deck. Neither Munday nor Clare had eyes for the beauty of the water or the spring day that poured sparkling sunlight on small wind ripples in the river.

"All right, business," she said. "Shall we discuss it at your place or mine?"

Well, after all, he was only human, and he was in love. They adjourned the meeting of the joint task force to the cottage on the Waterway and got down to a business that absorbed all of their attention for thirty-five minutes.

Munday got up first. When he came out of the bathroom Clare was lying on her side, knees curled up. She had a beautiful rump; and the curve from waist to hip, emphasized by her position, was a thing of beauty and a joy forever.

"Get up, wench," he said, slapping her playfully on the rump. It felt good, so good, just to touch her.

"You're not fooling anyone but yourself," she teased, as he caressed her large, firm breasts, let his hand explore the flat hardness of her stomach, the bushy vee below.

"You already know me too well."

"Not as well as I intend to."

"Go for it," he said.

"I'm getting up," she said. "Just another minute or two."

"Want me to put on a pot of coffee?"

"Ummm," she said.

She came into coffee smells dressed only in a pair of sensible white panties.

"Woman, woman," Munday moaned, "what are you trying to do to me?"

"Gimme coffee," she said sleepily.

He poured. She was an individual who wanted a full measure of life, meaning, in the case of coffee, a cup filled to the brim with both half-and-half and real sugar.

"O.K.?" he asked.

"Just right."

She sat down at the dinette table. Munday sat opposite her.

"So where do we start?" Clare asked.

Munday moaned. "You start by putting on some clothes."

She raised one eyebrow. "First complaint I ever had."

"I can't concentrate with two pairs of eyes looking at me," he said, reaching across to trace the brown circles around her nipples with his forefingers.

She laughed. "It's my femi-Nazi tendencies," she said. She faked a comic accent. "Like zis, I haf' you in my power."

"Clothes," Munday said.

She took her cup with her. She called out to him from the bedroom. "Where do we start?"

He didn't answer until she came back into the kitchen in uniform.

"You're the investigator," he said, "you tell me."

"Well, we could go to the beach and sit in the sun and see if the tide washes up anything."

"Meaning," he said, "that you're at as much of a loss as I am."

"You got it."

"How about you make us a list of missing persons within, say, a couple of hundred miles of Clarendon County."

"You've just defined a career for me. That would take in half of South Carolina and most of North Carolina. Myrtle Beach, Charleston, Florence, Charlotte, Raleigh-Durham, the Piedmont."

"And the service towns," Munday said. "Fayetteville and Jacksonville. Don't forget them."

"Well, I guess I could ask Lance to get me some help with it."

"You can confine the list to young people."

"Can we make that assumption?"

"Well, we've got three individuals, all in their teens."

"While I'm at it I might as well include older people. I'll keep them on a separate list."

"You're such a smart girl," Munday said.

"True, true," she said. "Dan?"

"Speak."

"I know it's wild, but have you given any more thought to what those two girls said while we were bringing them back from Charlotte?"

"About being afraid they were going to be killed?"

"By devil worshipers."

"They'd been watching too much television. They probably saw the Geraldo program. They were just looking for a way to ease the wrath of their parents."

"I think I'd like to talk with them again."

"Well, as a man said in a book I read once, it's something to do. Want me to call their parents and arrange it for this afternoon after school?"

"Ah, ha, you haven't read that one," he said.

"You're still way behind," she said. "Want me to call the parents?"

"Suits me."

There was no telephone in the kitchen. She went into the living room. He could hear her voice, but could not catch all the words. She was back in five minutes.

"Wow," she said.

"What?"

"I just stepped into a buzz-saw. It seems that both parents have swallowed their little darlings' story hook, line, and sinker. They not only said it was all right for us to come out, they wanted to know why in the hell we weren't doing something about the dire threat to their daughters. It was apparent that they'd been talking together, comparing notes, because I got the same thing from both mamas. They think East Clarendon High is a nest of evil, that satanism is rampant. They're afraid to send the kids to school, afraid they won't come home again."

"Jumpin' Jesus," Munday said.

"Dan?"

"Ummm?"

"We have a couple of hours before school is out."

"Get thee behind me, woman."

"Silly, it doesn't work as well that way."

"Go to work. Start those lists. I have a job, too, you know."

"Hell, nothing ever happens in Fortier Beach in the day-time."

"Don't tell the Commissioners that. I've had 'em fooled for years into thinking that it's my sterling presence that prevents things from happening. What do you want to do, fix it so that I'll have to work nights?"

"Nights, sir, belong to me."

He rose, went to the door. "Look, I'll meet you at the courthouse at three."

She came to him, lifted her face for a kiss. "Mrs. Stamps and Lori are going to be at the Adams house, so that'll work out fine. You behave."

"You, too."

"I've never had anyone to give me an incentive to behave before. It's a nice feeling."

He nodded. As he cranked Old Number One and drove up the island toward City Hall he thought a little prayer of thanks for having Clare in his life.

Nothing much was happening in Fortier Beach. With schools still in session around the state the beachfront cottages were largely empty, but the business community was looking forward to a prime season. They used the Easter weekend as a prediction factor, and the beach had buzzed with activity during that indicator period. Munday passed the time of day with the Town Clerk, looked over the time sheets of his men, noted that the Kid was going to be tied up in traffic court for at least two days during the coming week, causing a need for adjustment of the duty roster. What with sickness, the occasional accident suffered in the line of duty, court time, vacations, and time off for required police training it was difficult to give the town decent police coverage with a total of four men counting himself.

Thoughts of Clare kept flashing into his mind. He picked up the telephone and dialed C.S.D. She was on the telephone quickly.

"I guess I'm going to have to marry you," he said.

"Do it," she said.

"All right."

"All right."

"See you at three."

He was still grinning fatuously when the Clerk called out, "Telephone, Chief."

"Munday," he said.

"Hi, Dad, what are you going to do for lunch?" Jilly asked.

"I thought I'd have something to eat."

"Good plan. It's pizza day in the lunchroom, and Mrs. Baugh wants you to talk with her class first period this afternoon."

He hadn't thought about Evie Baugh in days.

"Pretty short notice, honey."

"No big deal," she said. "We're having career days at school. You know, people come in and tell about what they do for a living, and Mrs. Baugh's speaker for the afternoon cancelled out."

"So I'm second choice."

"Not with me," she said with a delightful giggle.

"All right, honey. Just for you."

He found a parking place in the visitor and students lot at the school. Jilly was waiting for him just inside the entrance door. The halls were noisy as they walked to the lunchroom, the dining area itself only slightly less so.

"You furnish ear plugs with this?" Munday asked Tom Williams, who was standing behind the counter watching his help dish out the pizza.

Williams laughed. "You get used to it, Chief."

Jilly led Munday to a table. Jeanne Dabney joined them, saying, "Hey, Mr. Munday."

"Hey, Jeanne," Munday said. "How's it going?"

"Same old same old," Jeanne said. "Who did you come to arrest this time?"

"Dad's going to fill in for Mrs. Baugh's speaker who couldn't come," Jilly said.

"If you're looking for police recruits I don't think you're going to find them here," Jeanne said.

"Why not?" Munday asked.

"They don't want to be the Gestapo in the halls," Jeanne said.

"You're a little shit, Jeanne," Jilly said.

"Language, girl," Munday said, but he was pleased that she wanted to defend him.

"Or do you think someone here in the school is spreading those body parts all over the county?" Jeanne asked.

"Why, do you?" Munday asked.

"Well, we get blamed for everything else," Jeanne said.

"Jeanne, are you being obnoxious again?" Evie Baugh asked, having come up behind Munday without his notice.

"Only her usual lovable self," Jilly said.

"May I join you?" Evie asked.

Munday pulled out the fourth chair for Evie.

"It's so nice of you to come on such short notice, Chief Munday," Evie said.

"My pleasure. How long do you want me to talk?"

"About a half hour. That will leave some time for questions."

"Yeah, like how many black men have you beaten up lately, Chief?" Jeanne asked.

"Jeanne, just shut up," Jilly said.

"I only beat up smart-mouthed teenage girls," Munday said. "Shut up, Jeanne."

"Shut up, Jeanne," Evie said, smiling to try to make the moment of tension into a joke.

"All right, all right," Jeanne said. "Let's not make a federal case out of it."

Pizza gave Munday indigestion. Good, though. He looked around at the young people at the other tables while he ate and listened to the comments of Jilly and Evie. The second shift in the lunchroom was for juniors and seniors. Some of the boys had attained most of their growth, were, physically if not mentally, on the brink of manhood. The girls? Ready for the fruit pickers, plush, lush, and sweetly ripe. More mature in mind and body than the boys. Some of them dressed like street walkers in short hobble-skirts and tees without bras, others in the uniform—jeans and sweat shirt.

As the saying went, the lunchroom was desegregated but not integrated. Black sat with black, white with white. But, black or white, none of the pride of Clarendon County, its youth, looked like devil worshipers.

Jilly and Jeanne finished eating first. "I have to go to my locker, Dad," Jilly said.

"I have to go to the bathroom, too," Jeanne said.

Left alone at the table among a chattering, laughing, yelling host of future members of the informed electorate, there were moments of strained silence between Munday and Evie.

"Are the telephones lines down between the beach and town again?" Evie asked.

Munday felt a quick flash of resentment. "Things have been pretty hectic," he said.

"Sure." She sighed. "I've been reading, of course, about the mutilated bodies."

"Just pieces of bodies, actually."

"It's frightening."

He laughed. "You and I don't have to worry. They only do youngsters."

"And teenagers don't count unless you know them personally?" she asked, with a certain measure of belligerency.

"Hey, what have I done to deserve that?"

"Nothing. Sorry."

"Can we go somewhere where we can hear ourselves talk?"

She led him to the teachers' lounge. It was empty. She looked at him with interest as she sat down facing him.

"I don't know whether or not you've heard, Evie, but Lori Stamps and Julie Adams said that they ran away from home because they'd been threatened by some satanic cult."

Evie was unable to hide her disappointment in Munday's choice of subject. There was a long pause before she said, "Nonsense."

"No devil worshipers at East Clarendon High?"

"No. Of course not. Devil worship is not exciting enough for today's teen."

Munday looked doubtful.

"Have you seen any of the cut and slash movies kids watch nowadays?"

"I watched one of those things about Freddy with Jilly once."

"Freddy Krueger. Now tell me, after seeing Freddy drench the world in blood, how excited could a kid get over saying prayers to the devil while standing over a naked girl?"

"If I were standing over a naked girl I wouldn't have time to say prayers to anyone. Is that as good as it gets?"

"Modern kids would find it all boring and silly. Actually, satanism was an invention of the clergy, based on resentment of the church's power by the people. In dreaming up reasons for punishing heretics for their alleged crimes against God, the priests drew on pagan religious practices, such as a fertility ritual performed on the naked belly of a barren woman. Confessions were obtained by torture, and some of them were moderately inventive. One priest who had angered his superiors tried to ease his pain by saying that he had made the sign of the cross backward and replaced the final benediction with the words, 'Go, in the name of the devil.' Isn't that truly evil and exciting?"

"I see what you mean," Munday said.

"One famous historical case is the Chambre Ardente Affair during the reign of Louis the Fourteenth in France. It began with a couple of marriage triangle poisonings and was fed by so-called confessions obtained by torture. One of the methods used to get unfortunate people to confess to vile things was called The Boot. It was a metal contraption which could be tightened on the victim's leg by driving in wedges, tightened so severely that the leg and foot bones were crushed. In the course of such treatment people would say anything to get relief. They confessed to saying black mass over the bellies of young girls, while, of course, debauching the altar."

"Such big words, teacher. Debauching how, exactly?"

"The priest might take time out from his black mass to kiss the young girl's *parties honteuses,* her shameful parts."

"Oh," Munday said, "he was giving her head."

"You have such a delicate way of putting things."

"How about human sacrifice?" he asked.

"Some of the black masses centered around slashing the throat of a new born baby," she said.

"How about older kids, teenagers? Were they ever used in sacrifices?"

She shook her head. "Mostly new born babies, and if the

placenta was available it had special significance." She cocked her head. "You can't seriously believe that what's going on is the work of school children?"

"Not really," he said. "I just wondered if there might be some fire under the smoke that Julie Adams and Lori Stamps are blowing at their parents. The parents believe them."

"I know," Evie said. "The mamas have been giving poor LeShane Dunn hell, demanding that he ferret out the witches and warlocks and, I suppose, exorcise all the demons from good old East Clarendon."

"Tell me some more about black masses and stuff."

"It's all very unimaginative, and, as I said, a lot of it is fiction. And in popular fiction witchcraft, satanism, and Voodoo are all mixed in together. Actually, you have to go back a couple of hundred years to find accounts of true satanism, even in fiction. For example, the Marquis de Sade, in Justine, had some evil monks dress up a young girl to represent the Virgin Mary." She laughed. "I remember the phrasing. Each of the monks, de Sade said, whipped up his filthy desires to commit the vagaries of his lusts with the girl while she was dressed as the Holy Virgin. To cap the ceremony they thrust the host—" She paused, looked at him questioningly.

"The wafer representing the body of Christ," he said.

"—into a certain lower body orifice and then the ministering priest crushed it with repeated lunges of his monstrous dard, emitting foul surges of the torrent of his lubricity over the very body of the Saviour."

"Well, that could get pretty exciting," Munday said.

"Sometimes the black masses were held inside a circle of black candles. The use of menstrual blood was common, and sometimes the girl who was being used as an altar copulated with a goat."

"That would make for a big Saturday night, wouldn't it?" Munday asked with a chuckle.

"Almost as much fun as drag-racing on the river road." She looked at him for a long moment. "When the writers mix Voodoo with satanism, the blood sacrifice is an animal, or a chicken." She looked at him with a little smile on her full lips. "Aren't you going to ask me why I know so much about the subject?"

"O.K. How do you happen to know—"

"Lori and Julie have been telling their story all over school. I went to the library—excuse me, the multi-media room, and read a book. I happen to have a good memory."

A bell rang. Evie rose, said, "You're on, Chief."

There were twenty-four students in Evie's first afternoon period English class. Jilly sat half-way back. She slumped down in her seat self-consciously as Evie introduced her father. Munday spent most of his thirty minutes telling tales of amusing mishaps and comic malfunctions. At first there was indifference in the eyes of the students, then some interest, then laughter. When he finished and asked for questions, the first one was, "You ever blow away anyone with that gun?"

"No," Munday said, "and I'd hate to have the first one be a smart-mouthed kid."

One boy asked about the pay scale for policemen. Another wanted to know what it took to be an F.B.I. agent. One bright looking girl demanded to know why there were no women on the Fortier Beach Police Force.

"Because, when we were hiring last time, no woman applied," Munday said. "Want me to get an application for you when you graduate?"

When another bell emptied the room Evie said, "That went rather well, Dan. Thank you."

"No sweat," he said.

She stepped close, lowered her voice so that she wouldn't be overheard by the students who were beginning to filter into the room for the next class. "If you've forgotten my number, I'm in the book."

"I haven't forgotten it," Munday said.

She raised her eyebrows in question.

He wondered whether he should tell her not to expect a call from him, decided, rather quickly, to take the coward's way out and avoid the issue.

"Duty calls," he said "Thanks for asking me, Evie. I know it's good policy to make the police more visible, but I'm never sure whether or not I've made a good impression on the kids."

She didn't answer. She turned her attention to a girl who was standing patiently, waiting for a chance to pose a question for teacher. Munday sneaked away, feeling just a bit guilty. That feeling faded, however, when he met Clare at the courthouse and they drove to the Adams house in her black and white.

Lori Stamps and Julie Adams sat side by side on the couch. Their mothers hovered anxiously. Neither father was present.

"Dan," Mary Stamps said. "I'm worried sick. Something has got to be done about this situation."

"Well, we're checking into it, Mary," Dan said.

"We'd like to ask Lori and Julie a few questions," Clare said.

"We told you all we know," Julie said sullenly.

"You said, as I remember, that you received a note, or notes, threatening your life," Clare said.

"From them," Julie said.

"We're going to make this real simple," Clare said. "All you have to do is tell us who them is."

"I don't know," Julie said.

"Now we're getting somewhere," Munday said, rolling his eyes.

"What exactly did the note say?" Clare asked.

"I don't remember," Julie said.

"Lori?"

"It said about giving yourself to Lucifer, and how the devil is brave and real swift and smart, and how since God hasn't done his job it's time for us to do something else," Lori said in a low voice.

"That was the first note," Julie said.

"Were they trying to get you to join some sort of group?"

"Yeah," Lori said.

"They said we should because the devil knows everything. He can tell you all about the Bible and he knows all about humans and the stars and all that," Julie said.

"If you didn't know who sent the note," Munday asked, "how were you supposed to get your answer back to them?"

"We were supposed to leave a note in a certain place," Lori said.

"Where?" Clare asked.

"Under a certain table in the library," Lori said.

"The multi-media room?" Munday asked.

"Yes."

"Did you leave a note?" Clare asked.

"No. We decided that what we'd better do is ignore them," Julie said.

"Did you by any chance try to see who looked for the note you didn't leave?" Munday asked.

"No," Lori said.

"Not even a little bit curious?"

"We were scared."

"Lori," Clare said gently, "did either of you ever consider that maybe it was all just a bad joke?"

"They said that if we told anything they'll cut us open like a fresh mullet," Julie said.

"That was in the second note?" Clare asked.

"Yes."

"And you have no idea who wrote either note?"

"No."

"I remember when I was in high school," Clare said. "It was pretty hard to keep a secret. Isn't there some rumor or hint about the identity of these kids who are supposed to be invoking the devil?"

"They're real tight," Julie said. "No one has a clue."

"Any rumors about what they do?" Munday asked.

"They torture people and kill them," Julie said. "If it's a girl they debauch her."

Munday raised an eyebrow at the use of the uncommon word. "Can either of you add anything to what you told us about Hillary Aycock's death?"

"Just what we said," Lori said.

Munday looked at Clare and nodded.

"Look, girls," Clare said, "if you think of anything that might help us find out who sent you the notes, will you call me at the Sheriff's office?"

Lori stared blankly. Julie nodded reluctantly.

In the car Munday said, "Not home, James. Take me to the aforementioned multi-media room at East Clarendon High."

"Going to check out a book?"

"How often do you hear a Clarendon County high school girl use a word like debauch?"

"Come to think of it, not often."

"Second time I've heard it today," Munday said.

The librarian, who disdained being called custodian of multi-media, knew exactly which book to show Munday. It had been checked out twice in the past few weeks, once by Evie Baugh and once by Lori Stamps. It was Rossell Hope Robbins' *The Encyclopedia of Witchcraft and Demonology*. Someone had underlined the names of the hierarchy of devils. Lucifer was listed first. Also underlined was a quote from a 16th century witch judge, Jean Bodin: "Satan possesses great courage, incredible cunning, superhuman wisdom, the most acute penetration, consummate prudence."

"She said the devil was brave and real smart," Clare said. "She read this to bolster their story."

"Well, you see, it's not all bad," Munday said. "You have no idea how difficult it is to get a teenager to read."

"Whatever it takes?"

"Right," he said.

"O.K., now what?"

He shrugged. "First, we don't waste any more time looking for a Satan cult. I guess we just wait. There are enough body parts left over to insure that something will turn up sooner or later."

15

As it is with many men who find themselves face to face with the world after a safe and relatively carefree period of childhood, adolescence, and young manhood, the times in which he lived and chance events determined the course of Dan Munday's life and had a direct bearing on the substance of Jillian Jane Munday's 16th birthday present. When Munday graduated from high school in the Wake County system he was a strapping lad, hardened by sports, big of arm and thigh, strong of back, but not quite agile enough or fleet enough to be recruited by one of the state's Atlantic Coast Conference football powers. He accepted a scholarship to what was then a small, little known college in the eastern part of the state.

Those who played their sports for Duke, Carolina, State, or Wake Forest referred to the little coastal school sneeringly as Eee-Cee-Tee-Cee, for East Carolina Teacher's College. The coach at East Carolina switched Munday from running back to linebacker, assuring that Munday's college career would be brief. He played exactly thirty-five seconds of football in his freshman year.

At fall practice before his second year he told the coach he wasn't interested in playing linebacker, to put him in the offense or take his scholarship and do uncomfortable things with it. With the coach's explicitly expressed negatives ringing in his ears he joined the Army where faceless and nameless people whom he would never know made a life-career decision for him. Because he was strong and rather large those anonymous people felt he would make a good Military Policeman.

He served his time, was an acceptable M.P., took his discharge, went back to East Carolina and took one look at the campus and decided that he had had enough college. So it was that the course of his life and the kind of car he would be able to afford for his only daughter's sixteenth birthday had been determined by a football coach who didn't need a straight-ahead, bull-like runner in his backfield and by whoever it was who decided Munday should mark his time in service as an M.P. His Military Police experience and his one year of college helped him get signed on as a rookie cop in Greensboro where he found police work can be endless boredom interspersed with moments of shameful panic. He earned his promotions and merit raises, won a commendation for being instrumental in setting up one of the city's largest drug busts, and met Elaine McWhorter, who wanted to live anywhere other than in Greensboro, preferably where sand met salt water.

It wasn't that Munday was incapable of making his own decisions, it was just that circumstances and Elaine's love of the sun guided him into filing an application to fill an opening on the Fortier Beach Police Force. The City Commission jumped out of their cushioned seats in their rush to hire the most qualified man who had ever been willing to accept a salary considerably below the national average for a law enforcement officer, a wage sweetened only slightly by health care and retirement benefits. When Munday was made Chief just before Jilly was born, he was earning less than schoolteachers, truck drivers, dental assistants, Fortier Beach waitresses who knew how to jolly visiting upstate drunks and fishermen into leaving large tips, and only a fraction of the salary of the longshoremen who handled cargo at the port in Worthing.

The one decision that could have been called his own was to stay in Fortier Beach when Elaine began to be bored with soaking up rays in the summertime and watching daytime television in the winter. He was working toward retirement at an age when he would still be young enough to start a second career. The timing was right. He would be a civilian and be established as a real estate salesman by the time Jilly was ready to go off to college. With his retirement pay as a secure base and armed with Bubba Dean's secret of positive thinking, he would make up to Jilly all of the lean years when she had only one pair of designer jeans and had to go to school wearing generic garments from KMart.

There had been times when he regretted his decision to be a small town policeman. He knew men who had gone off to join some big city force to get regular promotions and retire on more money that he made working full time, but then they sometimes had to dodge bricks and bullets, so it wasn't all bad. He didn't question his decision to opt for the quiet, relatively safe life in Fortier Beach too often, but the consequences of his decision hit him full in the face when he drove Old Number One to Worthing and made a round of the car dealers. He had envisioned Jilly driving slowly up Atlantic Boulevard in a tasty little convertible, top down, hair streaming in the breeze. His own hair stood on end when he looked at the price stickers.

He moved his search to the used car side of the lots and began to feel as low as a piece of wet toilet tissue on a tile floor until he found the little Le Baron convertible, five years old, just sixty-thousand-miles on the odometer, upholstery neat and clean, paint like new. With the help of his friendly personal banker he managed to attain something he hadn't had since Elaine sought tropical sun and the rich life in Florida, a car payment. In lieu of a raise, he had an unwritten agreement with Fortier Beach allowing personal use of the Chief's car.

Jilly's birthday gift was dark silver. The color blended well with her hair and her eyes. The upholstery was wine red. When, at a quiet little pre-birthday party on the evening before the great date, he handed her the keys and said, "Maybe you'd better take a look outside," she let out a very unladylike whoop and was down the stairs before Munday and Clare, who had driven the convertible over from its hiding place in her garage, could get out onto the deck.

The top was down. Jilly was behind the wheel. Her face was abeam. She looked so much like her mother had looked at twenty-one that Munday had to shake off the image.

"Come on," Jilly yelled, "I'll give you a ride."

"The first one's all yours," Munday said.

She backed the car sedately out onto the road and accelerated carefully, turning once to wave.

"You've made one young lady very happy," Clare said.

Munday was feeling just a bit of resentment against the world. Other men's daughters got new cars on their sixteenth birthdays. His daughter had to settle for someone's five-year-old discard. For one moment he was vulnerable. If, as Jilly braked for the corner with a glow of red, someone had offered really big money for him to turn his head long enough for a fast boat to bring a profitable cargo into one of the coves along the Waterway, he might have been tempted.

Clare's arm around his waist dispelled his malaise. He grinned down at her. "You'd look good in a convertible, too."

"Convertibles are for young kids. The wind gives me an earache."

"Poor old crone."

Jilly was gone for a half hour, just about long enough, Munday figured, to make the grand round of the beach and drive past Jeanne Dabney's house and, of course, the service station where Chad Lacewell worked. Chad had turned sixteen in March, and was driving his own car, waiting, Munday thought wryly, for the fruit to ripen at the Munday house.

"How was it?" Munday asked when Jilly came back.

"I love you," she said, leaping out to kiss him on the cheek.

"Have you driven it?"

"I checked it out in Worthing and drove it home."

"Wanta go for a ride, Clare?" Jilly asked.

"I'd love to," Clare said.

"I thought the wind gave you an earache," Munday said.

"Only when I'm driving," she said, getting in on the passenger side.

"Well, let me in the back," Munday said.

"Sorry," Jilly said, hitting the gas to spin wheels in the gravel drive, "ladies only this time."

It pleased Clare to think that Jilly wanted to be alone with her. Munday's proposal of marriage had not come as a surprise. She had been expecting and dreading it, dreading it because it would force her to make a decision. She loved Dan, there was no doubt about that, but the last thing she wanted was to become a subject for an advice column.

"Dear Ann, I am in love with a man who has a teenage daughter who adores her father and is adored in return. Will I be the fifth wheel?"

"You drive well," Clare said, as Jilly took a corner and accelerated to the forty-five miles speed limit.

"I've been wanting to talk to you," Jilly said.

Jilly's hair was streaming in the breeze. Her skin was flawless. For a moment Clare was stricken with sentiment, wondering how it would feel to have given birth to a beautiful little girl like Jilly.

"Well, now's your chance," Clare said.

"I've thought a lot about this," Jilly said. "I finally decided that there's no nice way to say it."

Clare felt a chill. She turned to stare at Jilly's pleasing profile.

"What's the problem?" Clare asked.

"You."

"Would you like to explain that?"

"Get your claws out of my father," Jilly said coldly.

At first Clare felt more shock than hurt. She was busy for a moment wondering how she had so miscalculated her relationship with Jilly. She had thought that they were getting along well, that, in fact, there was a foundation for a good, solid friendship. When the shock faded she felt an almost physical pain, as if she'd been hit in the face. She said, with forced calm, "You're right. There's no nice way to put that."

"You're a nice enough person, Clare," Jilly said, "and I don't mind you and dad getting it on—"

"Hold it," Clare said sharply.

"Don't pretend you don't," Jilly said. "Do you think I'm stupid?"

Clare had regained control of herself. "Stupid? No. Judgmental in affairs that do not concern you, yes."

"I guess even men as old as my dad need to have their ashes hauled," Jilly said. "So—"

"He'd be so proud to hear you talk like that," Clare said bitterly.

"Oh, come on. Look, what I mean is this. To put it very clearly, there's not room in the Munday cottage for two women."

"Yes, that's quite clear," Clare said, "but is it your decision to make? Don't you think it might be advisable to have a talk with your father about it before you start laying down the rules?"

"This is between you and me," Jilly said. "If you come in, I go. That much, at least, is my decision. I'll walk out the door headed for Florida as you walk in."

"I'm puzzled, Jilly," Clare said, still fighting for control of her hurt and anger. "Why do you dislike me so?"

"I don't. I said you're a nice person. But I've seen my dad shattered by one woman. I won't have it happen again."

Clare was shocked into silence for long moments. "But you can't judge me by your mother, or by what has happened in the past."

"Dad's too easy. I see how you wrap him around your little finger. He'd do anything you asked. He was that way with my mother. He babied her. He let her get away with stuff that should have caused him to give her a good swift kick. Even when she'd go off and leave me alone in the house he wouldn't get down and dirty with her. He's not that kind. He let her take advantage of him and he'd let you do the same and I don't intend to have it."

"I love him," Clare said. "I would never do anything to hurt him."

"Bull shit."

"Jilly, deep down, aren't you talking from a selfish desire to have your dad all to yourself, the way it's been for the past few years? Are you afraid that there's not enough love in him to share with me?"

"I've said what I have to say," Jilly said.

The car was approaching the cottage.

"And what happens if I tell Dan that you've given me an ultimatum, that you've said that you'd run away if he marries me?"

Jilly stopped in the drive, turned to glare at Clare, hard-eyed, lips set. "If you're ready to force him to make a choice between you and me, go for it."

Clare was silent. She mounted the stairs ahead of Jilly. Munday had turned on *ABC News*. "How was the ride?" he asked.

"O.K.," Jilly said quickly.

"Interesting," Clare said.

"I'll see to dinner," Jilly said. "Soup and salad all right, Dad?"

"Fine, honey," Munday said.

Clare was still standing.

"You're tall enough," Munday said. "Have a seat."

"I thought I'd go on home," Clare said.

"I've got enough for all of us," Jilly called out from the kitchen. "Please stay, Clare."

"I guess I'm having a sinking spell," Clare said with a wry smile. "I need an early night, Dan."

He rose and took her hands in his, concern on his face.

"It's nothing, really," she said. "Just tired, I guess. You don't mind?"

"I'll come over later," he whispered.

"No, I really do want to get to bed early, and this is Jilly's time."

"O.K. I'll check with you tomorrow." He kissed her lightly and walked her to the door. She picked up her purse from a lamp table, remembered that she had bought a gift for Jilly.

"I forgot something," she said, taking the small, gold-wrapped package from her purse. Jilly turned to face her when she entered the kitchen. "I was about to forget to give you your gift," she said.

Jilly flushed, perhaps, Clare thought, with guilt, or shame. "That wasn't necessary."

"I wanted to get it for you," Clare said. "I hope you enjoy it."

Jilly took the gift. Her face became expressionless. "If this is your way of sucking up to me—"

"Good night, Jilly," Clare said.

At home, Clare showered, washed and dried her hair, put on a comfy old robe, turned on *Jeopardy!* and curled up in her chair. It was college student time on the program. A very pretty little girl with a band holding back a healthy mass of dark hair reminded Clare of Jilly. The girl on T.V. affected an eastern finishing school drawl.

Kids, Clare was thinking. A world of their own. Alien creatures. Jilly so endearingly congenial and mature in her actions until something threatened the world as she knew it, then so poisonously selfish and cruel.

She tried to put the scene in the convertible out of her mind, found it difficult to do so. She had been more than ready to marry Dan, to move into his house, to be not mother but friend and sister to Jilly.

She wept silently as the pretty girl on *Jeopardy!*, looking so sophisticated, over-used the affected drawl, thus showing her youth and inexperience. She was so much like Jilly, girl going on adulthood, child-woman.

Jilly would be going off to school in what? She was in the tenth grade. Two more years of high school after this one.

The question was, for Clare, was she willing to wait? Her tears came more wetly when she decided that she had little choice.

16

Upon arriving at work Clare Thomas was informed the County Prosecutor wanted to see her in his office at ten-thirty. She welcomed the distraction. She had spent a restless night, not sleeping soundly until well after two in the morning. The shock of Jilly's surprise attack and the ramifications of it were still with her when she climbed the stairs to the second floor of the courthouse and said "Hey, Iris," to the prosecutor's secretary.

"They're waiting for you," the secretary said.

"They" were Adcock Burns, the choice of Clarendon's informed electorate to prosecute the county's criminal element, and James Cottle, a Summerton attorney.

Adcock Burns was a Lincolnesque man without the crags, warts, and sad look. He had a shock of coarse, silvering hair, dark, bushy eyebrows, keen brown eyes and a practiced smile that could disarm the suspicions of the most skeptical juror. He rose from his chair and bowed with old south charm when Clare entered.

"Thank you for coming," he said. "You know Jim Cottle, I believe."

"Yes. How are you, Mr. Cottle?"

"Fair to middlin'," Cottle said. He was in his late sixties, a straight, small man with a bantam rooster chest, a crest of red hair, and a face sharp enough to cut a path through the world.

"Clare," Burns said, "Jim, here, has been appointed by the court to defend Larry Eubanks. I asked you to come here this morning because Jim has brought up a few points about which I felt you should be aware, since you were the arresting officer."

Clare brushed her uniform skirt into smoothness behind her knees and sat down.

"Deputy Thomas," Cottle said, his green eyes squinted and staring directly at the bridge of Clare's nose, "I want you to understand it is the duty of every attorney who practices criminal law to accept court appointments when the defendant is unable to secure adequate representation through his own resources."

"I do understand," Clare said.

"Further, let me state I did not ask for the assignment. Indeed, I told the judge it would be a hardship at this time for me to accept it."

Clare nodded.

"But I am not the sort of attorney who is willing, once he has accepted an assignment, to lie down and play dead for the prosecution just to get the trial over with."

"Hell, Jim, you're like a bulldog," Adcock Burns said. "You get your teeth into something and you don't turn loose until it thunders."

"That's a snapping turtle," Cottle said.

"What?" Burns asked.

"That won't turn loose until it thunders."

"Whatever," Burns said.

"Deputy Thomas," Cottle said, "I came to Adcock, here, to tell him I'm going to file a motion to dismiss based on gross illegalities in the gathering of evidence in this case."

"I think you're going to have to explain that," Clare said.

Cottle nodded and held up one well-manicured finger. "First of all, Deputy Thomas, you and other members of the

Sheriff's Department conducted an illegal search of my client's home. Therefore, the evidence you would expect the prosecution to present, including but not confined to the body and the .22 rifle taken illegally from—"

"Now wait a damned minute," Clare flared, "I had the suspect's permission to enter—"

"The suspect?" Cottle interrupted. "The suspect? Have you never heard of a principle of justice known as just cause? It happens to be one of the foundation stones of protection for the innocent. When you went to the Eubanks home you had no reason to believe a crime had been committed. When Larry Eubanks opened the door to his home he was not, by any definition, a suspect."

"Mr. Cottle—"

"Hold on a minute," Cottle said, raising one hand, palm out. "The defense is going to maintain that sheriff's deputies conducted an illegal search without warrant."

"He gave me permission."

"The defense will maintain the client's right to counsel was violated."

"We read him his rights," Clare said.

"Did you tell him he had a right to deny entrance to you without a warrant?"

"No. I smelled—"

"Ah," Cottle said with a smile, "you smelled what, Deputy Thomas?"

"I smelled the dead woman."

"And how many dead and decaying bodies have you smelled, Deputy Thomas?"

"Enough to know that once you have experienced it—"

"More than one?" Cottle persisted.

"Yes, more than one."

"More than five?"

"Look," Clare said, "this kid killed his mother after obvious premeditation."

"More than five?"

"No, damn it."

"Less than four?"

"Just once prior to going to the Eubanks house."

"And that makes you an expert on the odor of dead bodies," Cottle said with rich sarcasm. "Deputy Thomas, I will tear you a new one if I get you on the stand."

Clare looked at the prosecutor. Burns had tented his fingers in front of his face and was looking at her with hooded eyes.

"I will present to the court the statement upon which you people expect Adcock to base his case was not voluntarily given," Cottle said.

"Well, we have an outside expert to say it was freely given after questioning," Clare said. "Gene Justice of the State Bureau of Investigation."

"Was anyone else present at the interrogation that produced my client's alleged statement?"

"Lance Carver, myself, and Mr. Justice."

"What?" Cotter displayed exaggerated shock. "There was no attorney present to protect the rights of the accused?"

"Not at that time," Clare admitted.

"Were you not aware, Deputy Thomas, that as a juvenile Larry Eubanks had the right not only to have his attorney present during any questioning but also a member of his family?"

Clare's face was flushed, but she remained silent.

"So what do we have?" Cottle asked. "We have a defense request to the judge to disallow all evidence collected in the illegal search of my client's home." He waved his hands. "No body, Clare. No rifle. No bloody pillow or sheets. We have illegal search without a warrant. We have total disregard for the constitutional rights of my client during his questioning without either an attorney or one of his relatives present. And to cap it off, my client was not properly informed of his rights under Miranda v. Arizona."

"Oh, no," Clare said. "I read him his rights while we were standing on the front lawn, while he was wondering if, now that he'd killed his mother, he was to get the car and the house."

"Clare," Cottle said, in a soft voice. "I can understand why you are rather emotional about this. The fact is you and the others goofed. Did you really expect a kid like Larry Eubanks to understand his rights just from having the Miranda statement rattled off to him at speed?"

"I asked him if he understood, and he said yes. Mr. Cottle, he's heard the rights read a million times in movies and television. He understood."

Cottle shook his head.

"Mr. Burns?" Clare said in appeal.

"Jim wants to have the charge reduced to Second Degree Murder," Burns said. "I'm seriously considering it."

Clare shook her head.

"I want you to take a look at this," Burns said, handing an eight-by-ten photograph across the desk.

Larry Eubanks, in a neat white shirt and pressed trousers, smiled out at her. He looked unbelievably young.

"Cleans up real good, doesn't he?" Burns asked. "That's the face a jury is going to see. They're going to see this sweet looking little kid, *a kid,* maybe twelve years old. They're going to hear my words, but those words are going to pass through their compassionate little hearts like a wind in the night and all they're going to see is this." He tapped the picture with his forefinger. "This sweet little kid." He spoke in falsetto. "Why, goodness me, that sweet little kid couldn't have done a horrible thing like that. That sweet little kid must have been driven to desperation by *something*." He returned his voice to normal. "Now I think I can beat down Jim's claims that the evidence was obtained illegally, although there might be some doubt about the kid really understanding he didn't have to answer any questions without his aunt and a lawyer being present. If we had some grieving relatives to sit up front in the courtroom and wipe tears and sniffle every time I mention the dead woman, there might be a minuscule chance I could get a conviction."

Clare remembered the swift conversion of Larry's relatives from grief and shock over the death to smarmy concern for poor little Larry. "What are you telling me, Mr. Burns?"

"That there will be relatives in the courtroom and they'll be rooting for sweet little Larry."

Cottle said, "Larry's aunt and uncle have filed a statement with the court saying they knew of serious mistreatment of the boy by his mother. They are willing to take Larry into their care."

"There is this to consider, as well," the prosecutor said. "The county has already paid out thousands of dollars in fees to psychiatrists. It has cost money to keep the boy in custody. The county will be paying Jim, here, his fee. A long trial would cost—"

"We're talking about a dead woman, a woman who was murdered with premeditation," Clare said. "We're not talking about money."

Burns spread his hands. "Welcome to the real world, Clare. We *are* talking about money. It's my job to bring as much justice as possible to this county at the most economical cost."

"I will not accept that," Clare said forcefully.

"Another thing," Burns said. "Should I get a conviction on murder one, should I by some miracle convince a jury this sad-faced, sweet, little twelve-year-old boy actually shot his mother in the back of the head for selfish and criminal reasons, what do we do with him? You can try a juvenile as an adult but if he is convicted you can't send him to an adult correctional facility. He would have to be held as a juvenile until he reached sixteen, and the county, not having such facilities, would have to pay someone else to do the detaining. At sixteen, he could be sent to a young offenders' camp. He wouldn't see the inside of a prison until he was eighteen."

"It sounds to me, Mr. Prosecutor, as if you have some serious problems with the juvenile justice system in this county," Clare said.

"Agreed," Burns said. He paged through papers in a folder, lifted a sheet, handed it to Clare:

STATE OF NORTH CAROLINA
CLARENDON COUNTY
STATE VERSUS
Larry Donald Eubanks
The defendant, having offered a plea of guilty to Second Degree Murder and being first duly sworn, makes the following answers to the questions set out below:
1. Are you able to hear and understand me? Yes
2. Do you understand that you have the right to remain silent and that any statement you make may be used against you? Yes
3. Are you now under the influence of alcohol, drugs, narcotics, medicines, pills, or any other intoxicants? No
4. Have you discussed your case fully with your lawyer

and are you satisfied with his legal services? Yes

5. Do you understand that you are pleading guilt to the felony of Second Degree Murder? Yes

6. Do you understand that upon your plea you could be imprisoned for a maximum sentence of 30 years? Yes

7. Do you understand that you have the right to plead not guilty and be tried by a jury and at such trial to be confronted with and to cross-examine the witnesses against you, and by this plea you give up these and your other constitutional rights relating to trial by jury? Yes

There were more questions, and in the blanks following each one the defendant's answers were inked in printed block letters. The document was sworn and witnessed. The signature of the defendant was in its proper place. The only blank, at the bottom of the page, was for the signature of the Presiding Judge.

"It looks as if you have made up your mind," Clare said in resignation. She still felt Eubanks should face the maximum charge, but at least a guilty plea to second degree murder would take him off the streets and the time Lance Carver predicted, when he would kill again, would be postponed.

"I'm afraid so," Burns said. "I think it's the best course of action."

"There'll be no trial," Clare said.

"He'll appear before a judge," Burns said. "The judge will hear testimony from the court appointed psychiatrist regarding his mental competence, and the judge will pass sentence."

"You *are* going to ask for the maximum," Clare said.

Burns shrugged. "I imagine he'll get the mandatory minimum. The judge is human, too."

Clare was feeling the onset of a severe case of the can't-help-its as she left the prosecutor's office. It was not the first time she had experienced cynical disappointment over the disposition of a case she had considered to be wrapped up tightly, but never before had she felt such emotional involvement. She had been the first to see the dead woman, the first to smell the putrefaction of what had been living flesh. At odd moments the memory of wriggling, bloated, white larvae working in the entry wound in Ethel Eubanks' skull would flash into her mind. She felt as if she were the only one in the world who was crying out not for vengeance, but for justice, but her voice was too small, too late, too devoid of power. The process of justice was underway. The twists of the process could have different names. Lawyers and judges might call them practicality and common sense. Clare called them expediency, convenience, and compromise.

17

The time of spring flowers had come and gone. Roadside woodlands white with dogwood blossoms for a brief and glorious time were taking on the summer look of rank greenness as dense as an Amazon rainforest. A howling northeaster eroded the eastward facing beaches north of the cape and littered Summerton and Fortier Beach lawns with broken limbs and pine cones. At East Clarendon High School the inmates, instructors and instructees alike, were counting the days before summer freedom. Aside from one staggering, wild-swinging, non-damaging, drunken melee outside the Midnight Sun the Fortier Beach Police Department enjoyed a quiet time. The period was not so uneventful for the Sheriff's department.

On a day in May when the temperature climbed to the eighty-degree mark Investigator Clare Thomas was called to the ferry landing at Danton's Creek. Two C.S.D. black and whites were already on the scene. The captain of the ferry had spotted a body on the west bank, just over the creek from the ferry slip. Two deputies had crossed in a small boat and were standing on a damp, muddy oyster bed holding handkerchiefs over their noses. Clare yelled to attract their attention. One man came for her in the boat.

"Nice of you to join us, *Investigator* Thomas," the deputy said.

Clare nodded. It wasn't the first time she had been the target of resentment from a man who had been on the force longer than she. She didn't bother to speak as the boat was rowed across the mouth of the creek to the oyster bar and then she was experiencing the smell again. Aside from an appalling assault on her senses it was a simple matter.

The body was lying on its face so the results of having been in salt water for four days were evident only to the nostrils and in the bloated bulk pushing outward against wet, stretched clothing. She held her breath and tried to remove a sodden wallet from the dead man's pocket. The edema of decay pushed against the pocket so she had to slit the cloth with a knife borrowed from one of the deputies. She opened the wallet carefully. The plastic driver's license was in perfect condition, showing the dead man's face, name, and address. He had gone into the river just below Worthing and had been the object of a search by rescue squads and the Coast Guard. Coroner Clef Burns had a look, helped the Summerton Rescue Squad slip a body bag over the remains, and then it was over. The body was quietly taken away by ambulance to be held for pick-up by a vehicle from Worthing.

Clare's feet were wet. The sick-sweet, oily residue of death lingered in her nostrils. She drove to the beach, soaked for a water-wasting time in the shower and put on fresh clothing from the skin out. By the time she met Munday for lunch at the steak house on the beach road she had cleared her nose and her memory.

She had decided not to mention the painful confrontation with Jilly in the birthday convertible. That her position in relationship to Dan had changed was obvious, but after due deliberation, often extending into lonely post-midnight hours she concluded Munday in her arms was, to paraphrase an old adage, worth a faceless, nameless Prince Charming in the bush of an uncertain future. Having decided to continue to live in sin with Munday she felt shamefully self-indulgent when they were together.

Clare's morality was a whimsical mixture of residual shards from childhood in a Baptist home and the easy rationalisms of the pre-AIDS sexual revolution. When she first entered into intimacy with Dan Munday a small, inner sanctuary of her conscience tacitly agreed her actions were permissible because she was a consenting adult and because both she and Dan were single. Moreover, it was not only possible but quite feasible that the illicit but delicious activity would be whitewashed by marriage some day. With Jilly's ultimatum, that rationale was taken from her, at least for the immediate future. To fight Jilly for Dan's affections would be, she knew, a lose-lose situation. She refused to console herself by thinking that when Jilly went away to college things would be different, for it was an uncertain world. Too many things could happen in two-plus years. To her surprise, admitting she was indulging her libidinous nature without the comfort of semi-moral justification added a burn of excitement to Dan's visits to her rented home on the Waterway.

Munday, being male and, therefore, just a bit less swift to detect subtle changes, gobbled up the goodies without questioning his luck. He used Clare's love as a nirvana to obviate the trauma of seeing his new sixteen-year-old dash off on weekend dates with a fruit picker.

"Poor baby," Clare cooed, when she first recognized Munday's sufferings brought on by Jilly's sixteenth birthday and the consequent freedom associated with it, the freedom to go off in Chad Lacewell's Camaro with the sinister, darkened windows, and do—well, we won't say what—until eleven o'clock at night.

"You don't have to worry about Jilly," Clare said, more than once. "She's got her head on straight."

"It's not her I worry about," Dan said. "It's the fruit picker."

"Takes one to know one, huh?" She laughed. "You're remembering yourself when you were sixteen and dating girls, aren't you?"

"Don't rub it in," Munday said.

There were, however, some advantages to having a sixteen-year-old daughter with a driver's license and her own convertible. No longer did Munday have to provide transportation to birthday parties, after-hours school activities, or just to Rose's for a box of sanitary pads. If a loaf of bread was needed for dinner, Jilly went for it, for she seized any excuse to get behind the wheel. And, on Friday and Saturday nights, Munday needed to make no excuses about spending the whole evening, until just before eleven, with Clare.

Jilly drove to school, of course. That was one of the very important perks of being sixteen. No more school buses. Although Munday trusted Jilly implicitly, he was, after all, a career cop and, therefore, a student of perverse human nature. He knew the most stable personality often fragments behind the wheel of an automobile. He asked his acquaintances in the Highway Patrol and the Sheriff's Department to keep an eye out for the silver Le Baron convertible with wine red upholstery. Not to his surprise, but definitely to his pleasure, he was told Jilly observed the speed limit to the mile. She had never been seen passing on the three lane beach road. The general opinion was she seemed to be a "pretty good little driver."

Well, what the hell. It was all in the genes. He expected no less of his daughter. Solid minded Jilly. Dependable Jilly.

Trustworthy Jilly. He had a great daughter and he had a woman with whom he was in love. What more could a man ask, especially if the woman he loved indulged one of his little idiosyncrasies?

For some reason Munday had a thing about female navels. Some men were fanny men, some bust men. Munday liked to draw circles around Clare's belly button with his tongue.

"You're always *doing* that," she said one Saturday night shortly after ten o'clock. It was cool-off time, the main event over. Cuddle close time. Touch me softly and hold me time.

"Ummm," he said.

"It tickles."

"Tickles good?"

"Well, not bad," she admitted, "but what's with you?"

"Belly buttons are like opinions. Everyone has one."

"I think you've got that backward."

Munday traced a circle with the wet tip of his tongue, plunged it into the indentation. "I guess I just like belly buttons."

"You're a pervert."

He smoothed dry lips over the flat plane of her stomach and downward. She shivered. "Dan, it's getting close to your curfew time." He was always home before eleven to be there when Jilly came back from her date.

The telephone interrupted things just as they were getting interesting again. Munday rolled onto his back and listened as Clare said, "Yes," and "Ummm," and "O.K."

"Duty calls," she said, swinging her long, full legs off the bed.

"You're not on call."

"There's been a wreck over on the river road, so the duty man's tied up there."

"What's the squeal?"

221

"Drug-maddened teenagers," she said. "Complaint from Indian Tree Trace." She was dressing hurriedly.

Munday had to get down on his knees to retrieve one of his shoes from under the bed. She was ready before he was. It was ten-fifteen. She expected him to get into Old Number One and go home. Instead, he got into the black and white with her.

"You'll be late," she said.

"Maybe not."

Clare used the blinker as she hit fifty on Atlantic, slowed at the tee intersection, sped up the incline on the south end of the bridge. She turned right just past the bridge onto a paved road running eastward parallel to the Waterway. There were a few houses along the road, which ended at the abandoned site of a factory that once had processed menhaden into fertilizer and animal food. Ahead of them were deep woods, tall pine trees, a site that hadn't been timbered since the 1930s and, thus resembled, Munday believed, what the entire Blue River country had been before the coming of the first Europeans. The road became a sandy track. The lights of the black and white showed it was not the first automobile to leave tire marks in the sand since the last rain.

The saline marshes bordering Black Drum Creek began at the end of the wooded peninsula lying between the Waterway and a westward bend of the winding estuary. Just across the marsh lay a new yuppie development called Indian Tree Trace. The complaint had come from the owner of a new, two-hundred-thousand-dollar waterfront home on the creek. It was not the first time a C.S.D. car had answered a call to the tip of the menhaden plant peninsula, but it was the first time Clare was driving.

The sandy road made a long circle at the end of the wooded strip. Teenagers who often gathered there among the tall pines always mounted a lookout. Clare steered her car into the big circle. Those who had been gathered around a blazing fire poured into their own cars and roared down the other side of the circle back to the main road.

One car, a low-slung American sports coupe, was just a trifle late in leaving. The beams of Clare's headlights caught it as sand jetted out from spinning wheels. Both Clare and Dan noted the license number.

"Think I should give pursuit?" Clare asked.

"Too dangerous," Munday said, and she knew he meant for the teenagers in the car, not for the black and white.

Clare stopped, reached for her notebook, jotted down the license number. Munday didn't have to write it down. He had recognized the car. It belonged to Chad Lacewell, Jilly's steady boyfriend.

"I guess we'd better put out the fire," Clare said.

Dan got out of the car, bent to pick up a beer can. It was still damp with condensation, cool to the touch. A hastily discarded cigarette was burning.

The clearing near the Black Drum marshes was a popular place, too well known and too well frequented to have the privacy needed in a lover's lane. Dan was not too upset by knowing Jilly had been among those gathered around the fire. Jilly would not sneak around to drink beer. Jilly would not allow her date to drink and drive. He worried less about what Jilly did with a group of teenagers than what could happen when she and Chad were alone in Chad's car. How does a teenager turn on the light after sex? She opens the car door.

The fire was burning on a mound of ashes built up by dozens of previous fires. Before the construction of Indian Tree Trace and the houses on the east side of the creek, young people gathered in the clearing to drink; smoke cigarettes and, too often, another combustible drug-producing product of vegetation; and to rap about the state of that alternate universe, the teenage world. Munday considered it a relatively harmless way of blowing off steam, just so long as no one got drunk and started speeding on the beach road afterward.

"Hey, Dan," Clare said.

He looked up from his examination of the discards of a party in the woods. She was standing near the fire.

"What in the hell is this?" she asked.

Something bulky was burning wetly, snapping and cracking in the flames. The stench of burning flesh caused Munday's throat to tighten.

Later, he was to realize the unthinkable, the unbelievable, had been imbedded in his subconscious mind for a long time, from the time two young girls claimed to be on the hit list of other youngsters, from the time of his casual conversation with Evie Baugh concerning the devil worship stories told by Lori Stamps and Julie Adams. The suspicions that leaped into mind as he stood over a blazing fire in the darkness of the piney woods and smelled charring flesh had, previously, been too bizarre to credit, but now the shape and heft of the object in the fire caused him to cringe mentally. He looked around, saw a pile of gathered deadwood, selected a strong limb, began trying to roll the heavy, meaty mass out of the fire.

"What is it?" Clare asked.

It was not what he had at first feared. It had the bulk and the shape of the torso of a child, but it had four legs. He turned it with the stick. The stomach cavity had been emptied.

"Some kind of animal."

"What the hell?"

"I don't know," Munday lied, hearing Evie's words in his skull. *They sometimes use animals in their sacrificial ceremonies.*

"I guess they were having a cookout," Clare said. "But what kind of animal is it? It's not a pig."

"I don't know," Munday repeated. "Do you have a bag in the car?"

"Yes, but—" She looked at him by the light of the flickering flames. "What are you thinking, Dan?"

"I don't know."

"You're a silver-tongued bastard," she said teasingly.

He was staring into the flames.

"I'll get the bag," she said.

She held the bag and he lifted the charred animal carcass into it with sticks. He used the entrenching tool carried in the C.S.D. vehicle to heap sand onto the fire and put it out.

She reached for the radio. "I'll call in and get I.D. on that tag number," she said, as she steered the car back down the sandy road.

"I know who it belongs to," he said.

"Ho *ho.*"

"It's Chad Lacewell's."

"Well," she said.

"Yes, Jilly was probably with him."

"I'll hold off on it, then. Give you a chance to talk with her."

"I appreciate it," he said.

"Look, it's nothing, really. Probably nothing more than one of those teenage gross-out deals. Like, who's got the guts to eat roasted dog?"

"I don't think it's a dog."

She was silent a long time. The car came out of the dark tunnel of the woodland onto the asphalt.

"All right if I bring the subject we're flirting with out into the open?" she asked.

"All right," he said.

"I think it's a bunch of crap," she said. "I still think those two little slits we brought back from Charlotte dreamed up the whole bit about the satanic rites. And I know damned well Jilly wouldn't be involved in anything that stupid."

"No," he said. "She wouldn't."

It was five minutes of eleven. Chad's low-slung muscle car was parked under the Munday cottage next to Jilly's convertible. "Pull in behind him," Munday told Clare.

As soon as the headlights hit the car the passenger door opened and Jilly emerged, straightening her blouse, pushing back her hair. Munday opened the door of the black and white.

"That you, Dad?" Jilly asked. Her eyes were squinted in the glare of the headlights. Her lipstick was gone.

Munday got out. Chad stood beside his car. "Mr. Munday, you wanta have them move that car? It's time for me to get home."

"In a minute, Chad," Munday said. "I want you and Jilly to come upstairs."

"My mom will be expecting me," Chad said weakly.

"You can call her," Munday said.

Clare turned off the lights and the night was black in contrast. The porch light was on to light the stairs. Munday unlocked the door, turned on lights. Chad's hair was mussed. Jilly's lips were swollen and her chin was red. Whisker burn. Munday told himself, well, teenagers *will* do a bit of smooching.

"I really should be getting home, Mr. Munday," Chad said.

"Sit down, both of you," Munday said.

Jilly was looking at him oddly. "Down," he said. She obeyed, sat on the edge of the sofa, jean clad knees together, her hands in her lap.

"What were you doing in the fish factory woods?" Munday asked.

"What?" Chad asked. "The woods? No. We—"

"We were just getting together with some of our friends," Jilly said. She looked at Chad. "I told you they had time to get the license number."

"We weren't doing anything wrong, Mr. Munday," Chad said in a frightened voice.

"Should I smell your breath or give you a Breathalyzer test?" Munday asked, looking not at Chad but at Jilly.

"Whichever you prefer," Jilly said.

"Oh, we weren't drinking," Chad said. "Maybe one or two of the guys had a beer, but not me and Jilly."

"What was the purpose of the gathering?" Munday asked, again addressing Jilly.

"Jimmy Small's cousin was roasting a beaver," Jilly said.

"A what?" Clare asked.

"Skip's father is an official state trapper up in the Green Swamp," Jilly said. She looked at Munday with a smile. "You know, we were reading in the paper not long ago how the beavers were clogging up drainage ditches and flooding farmlands, and how the state allowed trappers to thin them out."

"A beaver?" Clare asked. "You were cooking a beaver over an open fire?"

"Jimmy and Skip said it tastes like rabbit," Chad said. "We were all going to try some."

Munday ran his hand through his hair, looked at Clare. She was grinning widely. "I think you'd better let Chad get home to his mom," she said.

"Yeah," Munday said. "Goodnight, Chad."

Chad swallowed hard, showing relief. "Nite, Mr. Munday. Nite, Jilly. See you in school."

"All right," Jilly said. She sat perfectly still until Chad closed the front door behind him. She looked up at Munday, her face serious. "Are you going to smell my breath?"

"No," he said.

"What did you think we were doing, Dad?"

"You were going to eat roast beaver?" Clare asked, trying to lighten things, to ease the tension between Dan and Jilly.

"What?" Jilly asked. "Just what am I suspected of?"

"Nothing," Munday said. "I was with Clare—"

"Naturally," Jilly said.

"—when she got a call saying someone over in the development was complaining about the noise coming from the woods."

"A few of the guys were singing," Jilly said. "What did you think we were doing, having an orgy?"

"We had a compliant," Munday said. "It was Clare's job to investigate."

"And you caught the criminals red-handed," Jilly said, "drinking, doping, fucking."

"That's enough," Munday said angrily. "Go to bed. Now."

Jilly's face flushed. Her jaw muscles worked as if she were fighting to hold back harsh words. She rose and ran out of the room.

Munday, face stricken, looked at Clare helplessly.

"I think we have just witnessed the resentment of an innocent young lady who had been wrongly accused," she said. "Hadn't you better go talk with her?"

Munday hesitated. He wanted nothing more than to go to Jilly, take her into his arms, and tell her he was sorry for doubting her, but there was an obstacle forged from twin ingredients, pride and resentment. He had been a law enforcement officer answering a complaint. It had not been a good feeling to discover—whether or not the complaint was a legitimate one, whether or not there had been anything more out of place than a bit of beer drinking and cigarette smoking—his daughter, solid minded Jilly, was involved.

"I guess you'd better take me over to your place so I can pick up the car," Munday said.

Jilly's door was closed, her light out, when he returned. He let her sleep late on Sunday morning, had his breakfast in the restaurant seated at the redneck table with the Kid, who was coming off night duty, a couple of the city commissioners who were up early for church, and Bubba Dean, who had a hangover. The Kid had made a difficult arrest just after the beer joints closed and was sporting a fresh shiner.

After breakfast Munday cruised the ocean front. Although schools were still in session and the summer season had not officially begun, most of the first row cottages were occupied. The tide was low, making the beach wide and flat. Children splashed in tidal pools, ran from incoming waves, dug in the sand. A young girl in a tiny bikini was playing Frisbee with a husky lad. Young mothers with oiled and gleaming limbs basked in the morning sun while keeping one eye on their offspring. It was a day that the Lord had made and things were normal in Dan Munday's town, but something deep down was nagging at him. He circled a block and drove eastward to the end of Atlantic before he zeroed in on what was bothering him.

Jilly said Jimmy Small and his cousin were barbecuing the beaver, but there'd been no spit, no way of suspending the animal over the fire.

He drove slowly to the top of the bridge. On low tide the creeks and channels lacing the marsh were largely expanses of black mud. The tired suspension of Old Number One squeaked and bumped on the sandy track leading to the end of the road in the woods. He killed the engine, stood for a while beside the car. A wisp of smoke was streaming upward from the sand-covered remnants of the fire. He got his shovel out of the trunk and began to scrape sand away. At one side, only partially burned, was a freshly cut forked limb that could very well have been part of a support for a spit. He nodded in relief.

Under the sand was a bed of embers. It hadn't rained in almost two weeks. Fire danger was high. He spread the embers and began to shovel dirt onto them, digging in the gray-black ashes of other fires built on the same spot. The second shovel full contained blackened shards like burned chalk. He thought nothing of it until his shovel struck something solid and the blade turned up a larger piece of burned, chalky material instantly recognizable as the curve of forehead and the empty eye socket of a human skull.

He felt a shiver of atavistic revulsion, looked around the clearing, turning his head quickly. A wind off the ocean was making wavy motions in the tree tops, a sighing, lonely sound accompanying the dance of the pines. From somewhere on the Waterway came the sound of an outboard motor. He picked up the fragment of skull and put it to one side, cleared away the glowing embers, began to sift through the old, hardened ashes carefully. Apparently all of the broken and burned chalky fragments were bone, and there was no doubt about the mandible, complete with fire-blackened teeth.

He stopped digging after uncovering the jawbone. He stood for a long time looking at the grisly relics of human life before he walked to Old Number One and called the Sunday duty man at C.S.D. He asked specifically for Investigator Clare Thomas.

18

While the investigative unit led by Clare Thomas sifted ashes in a clearing in the piney woods just north of the Intracoastal Waterway in eastern Clarendon County, Chief of Police Dan Munday was doing his best not to prove but to debunk a growing body of circumstantial evidence that troubled him seriously. As he drove back across the high bridge he could see the ocean out beyond the green of Fortier Beach's residential areas looking as if it were uphill, so that at any given moment the entire Atlantic might begin to seek a lower level and sweep all before it. A sense of urgency was in him. While he and Clare stood alone in the clearing before the investigative team from C.S.D. arrived, she said, while holding the charred mandible in her hand, "I think it's time to ask Jug to call in the S.B.I."

With parts of at least four bodies scattered over a relatively small portion of Clarendon County, Munday could do nothing but agree, not even if it meant his own daughter might come under questioning from the suit-and-tie types from Raleigh.

He parked in the driveway of the Small house and had to wait for a few minutes until Jimmy Small's father came to the door pulling on a shirt. Sam Small allowed that it just might be Jimmy and the cousin were on the beach.

The favorite gathering place for surfers was near the

fishing pier. Munday parked at the end of South Piper Street
and walked out to the end of the planked beach accessway.
He saw Jimmy standing on the strand. The boy wore a legless
wetsuit. The temperature was climbing toward the eighties,
but the water was still cold. A light southeast wind was
making a feeble surf. A slim lad Munday remembered as
Jimmy's cousin managed to stand up on his board for a full
five or six seconds before a small wave faded under him.

Munday got sand in his left shoe as he stepped off the
walkway. Jimmy saw him coming and licked his lips nervously
as he approached.

"Hey, Chief," Jimmy said. "What's happening?"

"That's your cousin out there?" Munday said.

"That's him."

"Living with you now, is he?"

"Well, he has been for this whole school year," Jimmy
said. "I thought you knew."

"I guess I didn't notice," Munday said. "I see him mostly
on weekends, I guess."

"You're here about Saturday night, aren't you?" Jimmy
asked.

"Pretty unusual barbecue, wasn't it?"

Jimmy nodded. "I guess I'll never know what roasted
beaver tastes like," he said.

"Why did you all run like turkeys?"

"Well, some of the guys had a few beers."

"Is that all?"

"We're not into dope, Chief, you know that."

"All right," Munday said. "What happened to the fixings,
if you were going to barbecue that animal? You took off in
pretty much of a hurry, but you didn't leave anything behind."

"I brought the sauce and the knives and all from home,"

Jimmy said. "I knew if I lost my old man's carving knives he'd skin me alive. I grabbed 'em. Ole Cuz, he tried to take the beaver. Wrapped his tee shirt around it, but it was too hot and he dropped it into the fire."

"Jimmy, who all was there?"

Jimmy looked uncomfortable. Munday was asking him to betray the foundation plank of the teenager's code. Never rat on your friends.

"I know Jilly and Chad Lacewell were there," Munday said.

"Maybe you'd better ask them, Chief," Jimmy said.

"Where did you boys get the animal?"

"From my uncle. He's an official state trapper. Cuz was telling me how his dad cooked beaver once and I thought it would be a fun gross-out, so my uncle saved a young one for us. He said it would be real tender."

"How can I get in touch with your uncle?"

"He lives over in Brunswick County. He's listed in the Shallotte telephone book. That's F. P. Small. You'll see a lot of Smalls listed, but he's F.P." He pushed back a mass of damp hair from his eyes. "We weren't doing anything really wrong, Chief."

"Just the beer," Munday said.

"Just the beer."

At the Munday cottage, Jilly's breakfast dishes were still on the table. She had made French toast with lots of sugar and cinnamon. The smell of it was still in the air, reminding Munday he had not eaten. Jilly was not in the house. He walked out onto the porch overlooking the beach. They called it "laying out," the young ones who, if they considered it at all, felt they were immune to skin cancer and exposure wrinkles. Such distasteful things happened only to the old and they choose not to participate in that unimaginable fate.

Jilly was alone, lying on her face on a large towel spread over the soft, white sand just below the dune line. She was wearing the strap bikini she'd brought home from Florida, naked buttocks gleaming with oil. Munday felt a flare of quick anger, controlled it. He remembered what Clare had said, that Jilly was reacting like what, in his heart, he believed her to be, an innocent wrongly accused. He went down the steps, stood for a moment on the walkway looking down at his daughter. She was so delicately formed, so slim, and yet she possessed all the attributes of womanhood, small waist, a lovely outflow of hips, long, shapely legs, a swell of compressed breast just visible at her side.

She was wearing earphones. He cleared his throat as he approached, but she didn't hear. When he bent and touched her on the shoulder she jerked her head up, eyes wide in alarm. He squatted on his heels, reached out and removed the phones from her ears. "I've asked you not to use those things at high volume."

"It's not too loud," she said sullenly.

Munday had fired too many guns, sporting guns, business guns, military guns. An ear specialist had told him the little cicada singing merrily in his left ear most of the time was the result of tiny, hair-like formations having been stunned or killed by the high decibel reports. The doctor said an entire generation was doing the same thing and worse to their ears with rock and roll music.

"You're exposing quite a bit of Jilly," he said.

"I wanted to catch some rays before all the summer people got here and the beach gets crowded. If it bothers you all that much—" She pulled a corner of the towel up over her lower body.

"Look, about last night—"

She made a face, "Hey, Dad, I was out of line. I shouldn't

have sounded off the way I did. I'm sorry. Chad and I hadn't been there over ten minutes when you came. Chad doesn't drink when he's with me. We settled that early on. I told him if he wanted to drink beer with the boys he could go out with the boys and I'd stay home."

"Good for you," Munday said.

"Friends?" she asked. Her beaming smile reminded him of a young Elaine.

"Jilly, there's a very good possibility you and your friends are going to be questioned about what you did there in the woods."

She looked puzzled. "I don't understand. Why is it a federal case just because a bunch of kids get together and maybe a couple of the boys have a beer?"

"The sheriff is calling in the State Bureau of Investigation because someone tried to incinerate parts of at least one human body exactly where you kids had your fire burning."

She paled, licked her lips. "Wow." She swallowed. "You mean—"

He nodded. "We found parts of a skull, a jawbone, and several bone fragments so badly damaged it will be difficult to tell what part of the body they came from."

"And all the time we were—" She turned her lips inside out, said, "Yuk."

"So the best thing you and all the others can do is to tell the truth. As they say in court, the truth, the whole truth, and nothing but the truth."

"Surely they don't think *we* did it?"

"They—we—have no idea who did it. All we know is we've now found parts of at least four bodies."

"I'm getting just a little bit scared," Jilly said. A shiver caused bumps to rise up on the oiled, sheeny skin of her shoulders.

235

"You don't have anything to worry about. It may not even be necessary to question you and your friends any more. I talked with Jimmy and his cousin this morning and I'm going into the house in a minute to confirm with the cousin's father the source of the animal left in the fire." He grinned. "Crazy idea, Jilly."

She giggled. "It was so gross. Just like Jimmy and Cuz."

"I'd appreciate it if you'd go into the house and change into something that shows just a little bit less of my only daughter."

"All right, you old prude," she said. She gathered the towel around her as she stood, telling him by her actions that she, too, considered the suit to be just a bit too revealing.

The phone started ringing as Munday and Jilly reached the porch. She ran ahead of him to answer it, stood in the living room holding the instrument out toward him when he entered.

Clare said, "Since it's Sunday we had a hell of a time reaching anyone at the state lab, but we finally got someone to agree to receive the remains if we get them up there. I checked with Jug and he told me to call Gene Justice, since Gene is the one who works most closely with C.S.D. I caught Gene on the way out of the house for church. He'll be here tomorrow morning. He said he'll see to it there's a rush-rush priority assigned to our latest find. Since we have a full set of lower teeth, with some obvious fillings, Gene says that will give the Bureau something to work with. A dental chart made from the jawbone will be sent out to all North Carolina dentists, and Gene says he'll also try to involve the F.B.I."

"You're going to have someone drive the stuff up to Raleigh?"

"Someone named me," she said. "Wanta go for a long ride?"

Munday hesitated before saying, "I'd like to, Clare, but

236

Sunday is sort of family togetherness day at the Munday house."

Jilly, who had been listening, lifted one hand and whispered something Munday didn't catch. "Hold on a minute," he said.

"If you want to go somewhere, go ahead," Jilly said. "Chad wants me to go to the mall in Worthing with him. He has to buy something to wear to Tammy's wedding." Tammy Lacewell was Chad's older sister. She had been out of school for a couple of years, working waitress at the Sellers restaurant. She was going to marry a local boy who worked with his father in home construction.

"All right, Clare," he said, "I'll ride along with you. Want me to meet you in town?"

"I'll pick you up. About an hour. O.K.?"

"O.K."

"It's all right, isn't it, if I go to Worthing with Chad?" Jilly asked.

"Well, I'm traumatized," Munday said. "My little girl who has always spent Sunday afternoon with me had rather go off with another man."

"You're really not going to cry, are you?" she teased, coming to put her arms around him.

For a brief moment Munday felt it would be great to do just that.

"We're going to go by Black Creek Point on the way to Worthing," Jilly said.

"Black Creek Point is not, not by any stretch of the imagination, on the way to Worthing."

She giggled. "You don't know the way Chad drives."

"He'd better damned well drive as if he has good sense," Munday said, "at least while he's carrying cargo that's precious to me."

"Oh, he's a very safe driver," Jilly said. "He just likes to take the long way around."

"Quite a long way."

"Actually, he wants to go out on the point to look at a boat," she said. "He and his father are thinking about buying a small shrimper. There's one advertised in the paper this week."

After digging and sifting ashes, Munday felt grungy. He showered, put on clean civvies. Jilly yelled a good-bye while he was still getting dressed. He was ready, hair still wet from the shower and brushed back tightly to his scalp, when Clare pulled into the drive and tapped the horn.

It was a nice day for a drive, bright, warm enough to activate the air conditioner, green as green in the tobacco and pine tree lands of the western part of the county and the more prosperous farm lands between sandy, coastal Clarendon and the capital city. They didn't talk much about the purpose of the trip. There just wasn't much to say. A mystery without the smallest handle to grab onto has little interest. All they knew was at least four people, three of them identified as being on the shallow side of adulthood, had died, most probably in some violent manner, and parts of the victims had been distributed about eastern Clarendon County in novel and differing ways.

Neither on the way to the state medical offices nor on the way back, after an all-you-can-gobble meal at the hot bar of a steak house, did either of them mention the incidents leading both of them, at least at some moment in time, to consider the not easily credible possibility that Lori Stamps and Julie Adams had told the truth, that Hillary Aycock could be counted along with unknown objects of human sacrifice or ritual murder as a victim of something so repulsively evil not even modern teen-agers running completely out of control could conceive it.

19

After the ten-hour round trip drive on I-40 and Clarendon County's bumpy, narrow river road, Clare needed a bath more than she needed an evening meal. Munday heard his chair calling him. When Clare dropped him off at the cottage the sun was in the process of traversing the last inch toward its watery repose. A bank of wispy cloud radiated crimson and orange. Windows had been left open. It was comfortably cool in the house without the air conditioner. Munday popped a beer, turned on the television to the news channel, answered the call of the chair that was, indeed, the exclusive domain of the master of the house. Elaine bought the chair at auction for ten dollars. It was a durable product of a Depression era furniture maker made more for comfort than for looks. It had not been reupholstered since Elaine chose blue velvet from the fabric outlet store in Worthing two years before she had decided rich was better than Fortier Beach. The cushion was soft, feather-filled. The contours of the seat and back molded themselves to Munday's shape over the years. The local news had not been on five minutes before Munday was asleep.

The telephone woke him. He let it ring four times more while he gathered his soul back into his body, reached out, growled, "Munday."

"Chief Munday?"

He didn't recognize the voice immediately.

"Speaking."

"Sorry to break into your Sunday evening, but it's rather important I see you in my office as quickly as possible."

"Who the hell is this?" Munday asked, still a bit groggy.

"Sorry. It's Adcock Burns."

"Adcock? Hey, I'm sorry I barked at you. What's going on?"

"Summerton police are holding a friend of yours. A school teacher. Sarah Eve Baugh?"

"Evie? Jumpin' Jesus," Munday said. "What's the charge?"

"She asked that you be called. I'm told she places great importance on seeing you, even before she sees an attorney."

"Why is she being held?"

"Not on the telephone, chief. How soon can you get over here?"

"Twenty minutes."

It took only fifteen. He used the blinkers in the bubble gum machine atop the car and urged Old Number One up to fifty-five on the three lane beach road. Lights were on in the main corridor of the courthouse. The door to Adcock Burns' office was standing open. Burns and Munday's counterpart in Summerton, Chief Ralph Barker, were drinking coffee out of Styrofoam cups. Barker rose and extended his hand, saying, "Sorry to roust you out of your den at this time of evening on Sunday."

"What's the story?" Munday asked. "You've got Evie Baugh in jail?"

"That is affirmative," Barker said. He had done twenty as a Marine, was in his tenth year as Summerton police chief. He looked younger than Munday, slim, fit, his silver-white hair cropped close to his skull.

"Sit down, Dan. Have some coffee," Burns said.

"I'll pass," Munday said. "You wanta tell me why Evie's in custody?"

Ralph Barker's voice lowered to the level of locker room smut. "Seems she had an itch and tried to get it scratched by a teenage boy."

"But that's only one charge, chief," Adcock Burns said.

"Just what is the charge?" Munday asked. His first impulse had been to blurt out disbelief in defense of Evie, but before he could speak he remembered. Evie had, by her own admission, been attracted to a young boy at least once before.

Parker laughed. "Be hard to get a jury to call it rape, wouldn't it? She's not bad at all for a woman of forty." He winked at Munday. "I can't figure out what's wrong with that young stud. When I was seventeen or so I'd have given my left leg to be molested by someone like her."

"The charge will be something akin to contributing to the delinquency of a minor," Burns said, "but the matter is more serious than that, Dan."

"Well, by God, I think it's pretty serious that you're about to ruin the reputation of a good woman and a good teacher," Munday said.

"The boy says the Baugh woman has been trying to get him to join a satanic cult," Barker said. "Says she's a devil-worshipping witch or something and she offered to lay some on him if he'd join up."

Munday's heart bumped. The unbelievable kept resurfacing. It just wouldn't go away.

"Dan, I called you because Miss Baugh said she wanted your advice before she selected an attorney," Burns said.

"Who's the kid?" Munday asked.

"Glenn Schul," Barker said. "His father is—"

"I know," Munday said. "His father is the mayor." The

Schul family was Old Summerton. "That makes it an us against them situation. Home folks, natives, against the damyankee outsider."

"I would not call that an accurate assessment of the situation," Burns said.

Munday's brain was churning. The same players kept coming back onto the stage. Glenn Schul had been the sneak-out boyfriend of little Hillary Aycock. Lori Stamps and Julie Adams maintained Hillary had been involved with the satanic cult. In the unlikely event the two runaways had been telling even a smattering of the truth, Glenn Schul, as Hillary's sexual partner, would have been in a position to know something about Hillary's involvement.

But Evie?

Hell.

It was Evie who gave him a quick seminar in satanism.

"I tried to smooth things over, Dan," Barker said. "If the woman had just been willing to keep her big mouth shut it would have been a different story."

"You'd better explain that," Munday said.

"When the Baugh woman accused the Schul boy of attempted rape—"

"Hold on just a damned minute," Munday said. "Evie said the boy tried to rape her?"

"That was her story," Parker said.

"But you choose to believe the boy's story, is that it?"

"Dan, he's a good kid. His parents are pillars of the community. He's never been in any kind of trouble. He's a B student."

"And a star on the football team," Munday said. "And all that makes his word more reliable than that of a Yankee woman."

"He came to us to tell us about what the Baugh woman

had done before she got around to calling in her attempted rape story. It looks to me as if she got to thinking and decided that she'd better throw up some smoke just in case."

"And, hell, she's only an outsider," Munday said.

"You're beginning to crowd me just a little, Dan," Parker said.

"And you're not crowding Evie? Look, I know Evie Baugh, and if I had answered the complaint I would have believed her, even if she was accusing the mayor's son."

"That's what makes horse races and court trials," Burns said. "We're not trying to railroad the woman, Dan. But serious charges have been made, and it's my job to see that those charges are answered."

"What about Evie's charges?"

"We'll look into them."

"But you'll file against her and not against the boy?"

"It looks that way," Burns said. "In the meantime, Dan, we don't want to have to hold the woman. She's in with a couple of coke heads."

"There's this little legal concept called bail," Dan said. "It's usually made available except in big time drug or murder cases."

"I imagine that's one of the reasons she wanted to see you," Burns said. "Why don't you go on down? I've told them to release her into your custody. We'll keep you posted on what we decide. It's Sunday evening, after all. I'd like to join my wife and children in church before the services are over."

"Adcock, you fellows had better think this situation through before you file any charges. I'd hate to see you set yourself up for the damnedest false arrest suit since Pilate put the cuffs on Jesus Christ."

"You and your friend will be among the first to know," Burns said.

Summerton shared jail space with the county. A Sheriff's Department matron escorted Evie into the waiting room. She was wearing a faded, old robe which, from experience, Munday knew she favored for comfort.

"Hey, Evie," Munday said.

"You can sign for her at the desk," the matron said.

"Sign for me?" Evie asked. Her eyes were swollen, but her face was set rigidly.

"I'm buying you," Munday said. "Special today on slightly used schoolteachers."

She waited, head high, eyes glaring at the matron, until Munday had signed the custody papers.

"Let's go home," he said, taking her arm.

She huddled against the door of Old Number One, as far away from Munday as she could get. He sensed it was not the time for questions, waited for her to speak. When she did he couldn't tell whether her voice was quivering with anger or shame.

"They wouldn't even let me—let me—get dressed," she said.

"It's all right now," he said.

"No," she flared, "it is damned well not all right."

"Take it easy," he soothed. "Just take it easy. We'll be at your place in a minute. We'll fix you a big cup of hot chocolate or something."

"Goddamnit, Dan, they're saying I tried to get that pimply faced little bastard into bed."

"Way I remember him, he's not so little," Munday said, trying for humor but realizing his error immediately. "I know, kid, I know. Look, let's not talk about it right now." He was turning onto the short street containing Evie's waterfront home and two other houses. He pulled into her drive. She sat as if she did not have the energy or the will to move until he walked around the car and opened the door, allowed him to steer her up onto the porch and up the stairs. He turned on lights, went to the kitchen to heat milk and mix in hot chocolate powder. She was standing at a window overlooking the yacht basin, arms clasped defensively in front of her generous breasts.

"Wanta sit down?" he asked.

She moved woodenly, sat stiffly. He handed her the mug of hot chocolate.

"Any time you're ready," he said, "but if you don't feel like talking about it, it will wait for morning."

"It'll be all over the county by morning."

"Yes," he said.

"I *can't* go back to Pennsylvania," she said, as if it were given she'd have to go somewhere.

"No one's saying you have to leave."

"Ha," she snorted.

He knew she was right. Whatever the outcome, whether or not Adcock Burns filed charges against her, she was finished as a schoolteacher in Clarendon County, tenure or no tenure.

"I guess I'm gonna have to ask," Munday said. "How did the Schul boy happen to be in your house?"

"He's been doing yard work for me," she said. "I thought he was a cut above. He honored the work ethic even though his family is well off. He did a good, neat job on the yard and he's making B's in my class."

"Was he here doing yard work? On Sunday?"

"No," she said. She tossed her head, said, "Oh, damn, damn, damn," reached for the cup of hot chocolate, missed, spilled it down the arm of the chair onto her robe. Munday leaped to his feet and got a roll of paper towels from the kitchen, began mopping up the spill. She stood up and re-

245

moved the robe. She was wearing a shortie nightgown with matching panties. Her breasts showed nipple-tents surrounded by dark moons.

"That's good enough," she said. "Let the new owners worry about the rug."

Munday was on his knees, working on the dark stain on the tan carpet. He got most of it off, took the sodden towels to the kitchen. She was standing in front of the window again when he came back into the living room.

"You were telling me how Schul happened to be here," he said.

"He mowed the lawn Saturday afternoon, and I wasn't at home to pay him. I told him I'd give it to him at school on Monday, but he decided to come by for it this afternoon."

"When?"

"About four o'clock."

"And?"

"I told him to come in. He did. I went into the bedroom to get the money from my purse. I was bending over the bed, getting the money from my wallet, when he came up behind me and put his arms around me. He very definitely had things on his mind, because I could feel him as he pressed against me. I told him to stop it."

"What did you say?"

"I said, Glenn, please take your hands off me and get out of my bedroom."

"Sounds very polite," Munday said. "Apparently he didn't take his hands off you."

"No. He tried to squeeze my breasts. I said, Glenn, so far no real harm has been done. If you get out of here right now there'll be nothing else said about this. He just laughed and said something about how he knew I wanted it. I stomped his toe, but I was wearing my house slippers and it hurt me more than him. I just went limp and he couldn't hold onto me. I slid down onto the floor and he turned me loose. I came up facing him and pushed backward. He hit me."

"Where?"

"In the stomach."

"Bruises?"

"I don't think so. I was moving away at the time."

"How many times did he hit you?"

"Just once. My legs were pressed against the bed. He pushed me backward and put his weight on me. I tried to knee him in the groin, but he was too strong. So I started screaming at the top of my lungs. He tried to make me stop by holding his hand over my mouth and I bit his fingers. That's when he got up and ran out of the house."

"Did you call the police immediately?"

"No. I was in shock, I suppose. I couldn't believe it could happen to me. My stomach hurt where he had hit me."

"How long did you wait before you decided to call the police?"

"I'd say about half an hour, maybe forty-five minutes."

"Just long enough for the Schul boy to tell his version of the story to Ralph Barker."

"I had just hung up the telephone when Chief Barker knocked on the door," Evie said. "I thought, at first, he had certainly responded quickly to my call. Then he looked at me as if I were five-day-old fish or something and said that I was under arrest."

"You were in your night clothes and the robe?"

"Yes. Sunday afternoon is my lazy time. I was going to make myself a sandwich and be a couch potato right up through *Masterpiece Theatre*."

"Evie, were you dressed the same way when the Schul kid was in the house?"

She looked at him for a long moment, eyes squinted. "It *is* my house. I had not invited company, either Glenn Schul or the police. Don't I have a right to dress as I please in my own home?"

"A shortie nightgown in the middle of Sunday afternoon?"

"Yes, damn it."

"Evie, if they decide to press charges and do a background check on you, what will show up on your record from your home in Pennsylvania?"

She flushed red. "I had hoped you had forgotten that."

"Is it on record there?"

"I don't have a rap sheet, as they say on the police shows. No. Not on record, except in the newspapers. My husband saw to it his grounds for the divorce were well publicized."

"So they could come up with the fact that you, ah, that you—"

"Seduced a minor once before," she said. "If they can find their way to the local library and know how to use a microfilm machine they could come up with that information."

"Did you ever do anything, anything at all to make this punk kid think that you were available to him?"

Her cheek twitched, as if a sharp pain had hit her. She rose, walked to the window to stand with her back to him, her mature figure outlined against the blackness. When she turned there were tears on her cheek. "Did you really have to ask?" she whispered.

"They'll ask far worse questions than that," Munday said.

"But you, not you—"

"Did you ever mention anything at all about a satanic cult to Schul?"

She was still staring at him as if he were a total stranger. "We had a class discussion when the rumor got around school that Lori Stamps and Julie Adams had been threatened by satanists. As I recall, Glenn had very little to say. I don't think he asked a single question."

"All right, Evie," Munday said, rising from the sofa. "I'm going to stay on this. I might even get Ralph Barker to agree to let me talk with the boy."

"Do you think I gave him reason to assume I was available?" Her voice sounded old, and bitter, and just slightly accusatory. Munday's male defense system was alerted.

"No, I don't," he said, but because he was, suddenly, on his guard against feminine attack, there was little conviction in his voice. He kept remembering how she'd said, "I guess it was a way of committing marital suicide."

"I'm so tired," Evie said, letting her shoulders slump. "I'm going to bed now, Dan."

Dan nodded. "I'll check with you tomorrow."

"I'll be here. I won't be going to school."

"It's best if you do," he said. "It will be best if you go on about your duties as if nothing has happened. To stay at home will be seen by some as an admission of guilt."

"If you, of all people, could entertain even a remote possibility of my guilt, what can others think?" she asked. "Goodnight, Dan."

"Don't let the bastards grind you down," Munday said, but the comment sank without a trace.

Jilly's convertible was in its place under the cottage, as it had been all day. Munday had left a lamp burning in the living room. He'd missed *60 Minutes* and it was too early for *Masterpiece Theatre*. He made himself a peanut butter and honey sandwich and played with the remote control, left the set on the Discovery channel. He often wished he could sleep as quickly and as deeply in bed as he did in his chair in front of the T.V. Television was instant lullaby.

When he awoke again the wind had changed into the

northwest, foretelling a change in weather, and was blowing in through the street side windows. The curtains were puffing out from the wall, ends whipping in the breeze. There was a feel of nighttime chill in the air. He checked the VCR clock. It was ten-seventeen. He'd slept through *Masterpiece Theatre*.

There was an ominous feeling of emptiness in the house. The voices coming from the television set were hollow and distant. He walked out onto the front porch. Old Number One and the Le Baron were at home by themselves between the pilings. A car came down the street, but passed by with a hiss of tires and mutter of engine. He went inside. He had to look up the Lacewell number in the telephone book.

"Mrs. Lacewell, this is Dan Munday."

"Yes, Mr. Munday, I was just about to call you."

"Same reason I'm calling you?" he asked, a little tendril of alarm beginning to crawl up his spine. "I called to see if Jilly and Chad had gotten back from Worthing."

"No, they haven't," Mrs. Lacewell said. "And they said they were going to try to be back in time to go to the beach for a while before dark."

Munday fought back a mixture of anger and pure fear. "Did Chad have a lot of shopping to do?"

"He was going to buy a navy blazer and a pair of gray slacks, that's all."

"Well, I'm sure they'll be along," Munday said. "If they come here first I'll have them call, Mrs. Lacewell."

"Thank you. Please do."

Munday didn't put the phone back in the cradle. He made the disconnect with one finger, waited for a tone, dialed the Clarendon Sheriff's Department. He knew the duty man slightly. He identified himself and asked if there'd been any accidents on the river road.

"Nope, it's been a quiet day, Chief," the dispatcher said. "You got a problem?"

Munday decided quickly he did not have a problem, not yet. He could not bring himself to say, "Yeah, look, my daughter and her boyfriend left for Worthing before noon and they're way overdue." The daughter of Chief of Police Dan Munday did not go missing. Jilly, solid Jilly, Jillian Jane Munday, all-American daughter, was dependable, loyal, trustworthy, true, and she never, never did anything to make her father pace the floor and think bloody, frightening, blood-pressure raising thoughts.

His faith in Jilly and his natural optimism kept him pacing until the new day had officially begun. It was twelve-o-six on a chill, damp spring night when Munday called C.S.D. once more and said, "Look, this is Dan Munday. I'd like to ask you if you can do some checking around for me."

He, himself, called the Summerton and Worthing hospitals. Worthing police told the dispatcher at C.S.D. there'd been no accident involving a Camaro and two teenagers. The highway patrol reported negative on having seen or apprehended said Camaro.

At one-thirty, just after the northwest wind had blown in a stinging, slanting, hard-pelting shower, Chad's parents parked behind Jilly's convertible under the cottage and ran up the stairs in the almost horizontal rain. Chad's mother had been weeping.

"Something's happened," she said, her voice thick with emotion. "I just know something terrible has happened. Where is my son, Mr. Munday?"

Munday would not permit himself to believe anything bad, much less terrible, had happened. He stifled an urge to say, "Your son? That little fruit picker is out with my daughter until almost two in the morning and you're worried about *him?*" He confined those sentiments to himself and said aloud, "Hey, there's bound to be an explanation."

For the actions of teenagers there was always an explanation.

20

Monday. Northeast wind. Cloudy skies. After a brief period of premature summer the early morning temperature of sixty degrees seemed severe by contrast. Dan Munday was sleeping in his chair. The voice of a hefty blond woman in a purple dress came from the television set. She stood in front of a weather map with the symbols and curves of a low pressure system pumping Canadian air into the southeast. Clarendon County would not see the sun on that Monday, but rain, if any, would be in the form of light showers.

Clare Thomas parked her C.S.D. black and white behind the Le Baron and mounted the stairs to the front porch. She saw Munday in his chair, head slumped to one side, mouth slightly open. She tried the door. It was unlocked. She stood looking down at him for a long time. She did not see a man slightly past his prime, a man who had let himself go about twenty pounds above his best weight. She saw a lover, a big man, a man of physical substance, a man strong enough to match the vitality of a girl too sturdily built to look good in a bikini. There were sun lines at the corner of Munday's closed eyes, and in his slack face an endearing hint of the boy he had once been. He needed a haircut. A grayish stubble of beard showed against his sun-browned cheeks and chin. He had loosened the top buttons of his shirt. The hair on his chest was still the chestnut color of his youth.

The weather girl on television finished her smiling forecast of a gloomy day and was replaced on the screen by a young man with a toothy smile. The lead story of the newscast caused Clare's head to swivel toward the sound.

"Here in the T.V. Four area a massive search is underway for two missing Clarendon County teens. The daughter of Fortier Beach Police Chief Dan Munday, sixteen-year-old Jillian Jane Munday, and her sixteen-year-old boyfriend, Chad Lacewell, also of Fortier Beach, were last seen by their families before noon yesterday when they left Fortier Beach to go shopping in Worthing. Chief Deputy Lance Carver, of the Clarendon County Sheriff's Department, would not rule out the possibility of foul play."

Clare reached down and punched the off button. She was not surprised the story had been broken so early. A retired small town newspaper reporter living in Summerton sat by his police band scanner at odd hours of the day and night in order to flesh out his Social Security income by calling in news tips to the Worthing media. Nor was she surprised there had been no delay in sending out the alerts to all law enforcement agencies. Usually Lance Carver would have delayed to give the situation a chance to resolve itself. Clarendon County was not a place where fatal things happened to teenagers, except in the rare auto crash.

Two things had bearing on Lance's decision in the small hours of the morning to bring all the resources of the state's police system to bear. First, and most important to a law officer, one of the missing teens was of their own. There are two sure ways to stir up the hive of law enforcement: Kill or seriously injure a cop, or do harm to a member of a cop's family.

The second thing that caused Lance Carver to send out all points bulletins on the missing boy and girl and to request maximum effort by the Highway Patrol, the law enforcement arms in the neighboring counties, and in the Grand Strand area south of the border was the knowledge that three or more unidentified young people had died, most probably of violence, in Clarendon County in recent months.

Police officers in Clarendon were not under siege, were not engaged day and night in the undeclared and deadly war with the barbarians which was gutting the cities of the nation. The evil plague of the Twentieth Century had tainted Clarendon, but to a far lesser extent. It was not a lack of compassion but an innate practicality and a traditional sense of values that led Lance Carver to feel it was fortunate violent death in Clarendon was usually meted out to competitors by the businessmen who imported illegal substances from southern areas by car, plane, and boat. Lance felt all along if they ever found a handle to the mystery of "dem bones, dem bones, dem dry bones" the remains would turn out to be those of drug trade entrepreneurs.

Lance had known Dan Munday since they were both young and new at enforcing the laws of Clarendon County and Fortier Beach. He hoped Munday's daughter wasn't quite the paragon of virginal perfection she seemed to be. It was not a mean thought nor was it a stupid hope. Better to learn the kids had done something teenish and inane, like running away to get married, than to find they had stumbled into deep stuff, had been inadvertently tossed into the middle of a situation where no casual witnesses were to be tolerated.

So it was that the wheels were turning slowly. Every law officer in half a dozen counties was keeping an eye out for Chad Lacewell's Camaro. Soon the modern machines of the law enforcement network would be cranking out likenesses of short-haired, pretty Jilly Munday and of the boyishly handsome Chad Lacewell. To that end Deputy Clare Thomas had come to the home of one of the missing teens, to obtain a recent picture of Jilly before moving on to the Lacewell house for a photographic image of the boy.

She leaned forward, put her hand gently on Munday's shoulder. He awoke with a start. His hand darted out for the 9 mm automatic in its leather holster on the table beside his chair before he was aware enough to recognize Clare.

"Hey," she said.

He brushed back his hair. "Anything?"

She shook her head. "I came to get a picture of Jilly."

"Yeah. O.K." He stood, grimaced as he turned his neck to dislodge a crick. He had just spent the longest night of his life in the hours between midnight and—he glanced at the glowing numerals on the digital clock of the VCR—seven a.m. He went to his bedroom, took an eight-by-ten portrait of Jilly from its frame on his bedside table, came back to hand it to Clare.

"I'm going over to the Lacewells," she said.

"Give me a minute and I'll go with you."

He splashed water into his face, brushed his teeth, buttoned his shirt, relieved himself. Clare was waiting in the black and white. A small, chilly rain misted the windshield as she drove up the beach. Chad Lacewell's father gave them a picture of the boy. The mother, they were told, was under a doctor's care, had been given a sedative.

"Mr. Lacewell," Clare asked, "where would Chad have bought the clothing items he needed?"

"Probably Belks or the men's store just up the mall from Belks," Lacewell said.

"Would he have paid cash?"

"No. I gave him my credit card."

"I'm asking," Clare said, "because I'm going over to Worthing to see if anyone remembers seeing Jilly and Chad in the mall."

"We appreciate your efforts," Lacewell said.

"I think they'll turn up," Clare said with a smile. "They are two very nice kids. We simply will not allow anything to happen to them, because the good ones are so rare these days."

A little flare of panic erupted in Munday's stomach. Evie had said, about Hillary Aycock, "The good ones are so rare." He felt as if he were clinging to the world with only two bent and broken fingernails while a grinning gargoyle of evil pounded at his fingers with a studded, steel mallet.

"Yeah, hang in there," he told Lacewell.

In the car Clare said, "Wanta go to Worthing with me?"

"Yes."

Munday sat in the car while Clare took the photographs into the courthouse. By the time she came back the machines were sending out the images to other machines in police stations all over two states.

"Gene Justice is with Lance," Clare said. "He said to tell you the S.B.I. is taking out all stops, that they are with you all the way."

"Good man, Justice," Munday said.

"We're all going to feel silly as hell when those kids show up with shit-eating grins on their faces saying that they decided to go to Worthing by way of Disney World."

Munday forced a half-smile, but he could tell by the hard look in Clare's eyes she didn't believe it any more than he.

The drive to Worthing and talking to the clerks in the men's department at Belks and the men's store a few doors away consumed the morning. None of the store workers remembered having seen two teens answering the proper description. No purchase had been made on Lacewell's credit card.

Munday had not eaten breakfast. He was not hungry until

he stood in line at the cafeteria behind Clare and smelled kitchen aromas. He chose turkey and dressing, asparagus, field peas, and cornbread. He ate hurriedly, eager to be off and away—to anywhere. Clare sensed his unease, finished her own meal quickly.

"Dan," she said, as they drove through the tiny, beading drops of another small rain, "what, exactly, did Jilly and Chad say about their plans?"

As a policeman, he knew the value of going over old ground. "They said Chad needed to buy something to wear to a wedding, that they were going to the mall in Worthing."

"Which doesn't open on Sunday until after church hours," Clare said. "But they left rather early in the morning."

"Or at least we assume they left shortly after we did," Munday said.

"Chad's mother said they told her they were going to get back as quickly as possible so that they could spend some time on the beach. She said that Jilly left her skim board there, in the garage."

"Jumpin' Jesus," Munday said.

"What?"

"I just remembered. Chad said something about going by Black Water Point on the way to Worthing to look at a small shrimp boat."

"Where on Black Water Point?"

"There's a convenience store about two miles up the road," Munday said. "Stop and I'll call Lacewell. Jilly said Chad and his dad had been thinking about buying a boat, so Lacewell probably knows where they were going."

The pay phone was outside. Munday misdialed his credit card number and had to start over. Finally he had Lacewell on the phone. He identified himself.

"The kids said they were going to go by Black Water Point

on the way to Worthing," he said. "I told them the Point wasn't on the way to Worthing, and they said they were going to look at a boat you and Chad had been talking about buying."

"We had discussed it, rather idly, I fear," Lacewell said.

"You didn't know they were planning to go to the Point?"

"No. Chad didn't say anything about it."

"Do you know how he knew there was a boat for sale?"

"No. Not really."

"What in the hell does 'not really' mean?" Munday asked in irritation.

"He had been checking the classified ads in the *Summerton Sun*," Lacewell said. "A couple of weeks ago he mentioned one boat, but it was a forty-footer, much too big for what we intended."

"And he hadn't talked to you about a boat lately?"

"No. No. Not really."

Munday slammed the telephone back onto the hook. Inside the convenience store there was a stack of the most recent issue of the Summerton weekly paper beside the cash register. He gave the clerk a quarter, threw the front section of the paper into a waste can, opened the back section to the classifieds. He found an ad for a twenty-five foot Harker's Island built boat rigged for shrimping under *Miscellaneous For Sale*. The only address given was Black Water Point, but there was a telephone number.

Having seen Munday's problem with dialing—he couldn't stand back far enough from the telephone to see the numbers because his arms were too short—Clare made the call. The boat for sale was not directly on Black Water Point, but was at a private home a few miles up the creek. One turned off the highway onto a dirt road at a red mailbox with the name Feltzer on the side.

"Y'jest folly the road three miles through the hoigh woods to the water," the boat owner told Clare.

"Mr. Feltzer, did two young people, a boy and girl, come to look at your boat yesterday?"

"Nary a soul set foot on this here place yestiddy," Feltzer said.

"How did he sound?" Munday asked.

"Old. Down home. Sounds as if he might be among those who migrated south from the Outer Banks."

"Do you think he was telling the truth about not having seen the kids?"

She shrugged. "He didn't hesitate."

"Let's go," Munday said.

Black Water Creek wound its way inland from the Waterway at Beaker's Inlet past a triangle of high pine lands before entering a huge expanse of saline marsh and swampy, softwood bays. At the junction of creek and Waterway the small community of Black Water Point existed because of the easy access to the Atlantic through Beaker's Inlet. Half a dozen large shrimp boats made the Point their home port, tying up at rickety docks on the bank of the creek. Away from the Waterway, settlement thinned. Few areas along the creek were high enough or solid enough to allow habitation. One narrow, asphalt road ran from the little community at the junction of the Waterway and the creek to Highway 17.

The rain stopped, but the air was heavy with chill moisture. The narrow road branching off from Highway 17 gleamed wet-black and the tires of the black and white ripped through standing puddles.

"There's the red mailbox," Munday said, pointing.

Clare slowed, turned into the mouth of a sandy dirt road.

"Hold it," Munday said. She stopped.

"What is it?"

Munday pointed to the red mailbox. FELTZER was painted on the side in black letters. It was a large sized box, but not even its capacity could contain a mass of material. The lid would not close all the way. Munday got out of the car. The box was stuffed with mail and newspapers. Clare came to stand by his side. He checked the address on a couple of sodden newspapers and a few pieces of mail, most of which was of that variety which is called, perhaps too mildly, junk mail. It was all addressed to Robert Feltzer at a rural route number, Black Water Point.

"I don't know what puzzles me more," Clare said, "whether it's why the mail carrier keeps putting it in the box to get soaked or why a man who answered his telephone just an hour ago hasn't picked up his mail in weeks."

Munday nodded.

"Should we do him a good deed and take it to him?"

"Taking mail from someone else's box is a federal offense, Deputy," Munday said, trying for lightness to cover the feeling of dread expanding in him like some poisonous fungus.

There had not been enough rain to completely wash away all traces of automotive passage on the dirt road, but enough to obscure any tire marks and to disallow any guess about when a vehicle had last turned off the asphalt. For more than a mile the road ran straight eastward over well packed sand. After that the vegetation began to change from slash and longleaf pines to bays and softwoods. White sand gave way to dark, boggy soil. There were deep, water-filled ruts in the dirt road. A canopy of vegetation closed in overhead to form a tunnel, further dimming the muted light filtering down from the leaden sky. The track skirted a black water swamp, curved north, then back to the east to turn northward yet again at a point on a curve where a huge water oak had fallen victim to the last northeaster. Clare had to steer very close to the rank, green, roadside brush to clear the branches of the big tree.

The condition of the road deteriorated immediately. Brush attacked the paint job on the sides of the black and white. The ruts were deep. The suspension of the car was put to the test as it bounced over potholes. Clare had taken note of the odometer reading as she left the asphalt.

"He said three miles," she said, as the fourth mile rolled onto the instrument.

"We're getting close to water," Munday said.

"The way it looks, we'll be swimming soon," Clare agreed.

The road sloped downward to a muddy trickle of water.

"Whoa," Clare said, coming to a stop.

"The land rises on the other side," Munday said.

"Dan, that's running water."

"The ruts continue on the other side. Look."

"Are you prepared to walk home?"

"All right," he said. "I'll check it out."

He pulled off his shoes and socks, got out of the car, stepped on a sharp twig and winced. He found a stick and felt his way into the black, slowly moving water. The bottom was solid, and the water was no more than three inches deep at the lowest point. He waded across and motioned Clare to follow. The black and white splashed through and stopped beside him. He let the heater dry his feet as Clare drove up a slight rise to ground high enough to support a few pine trees among the low country softwoods.

Spreading water oaks half hid a tin-roofed country house and a sagging barn. Tall grass mixed with weeds gave the place a look of desolation, but smoke was coming from a tin stove pipe on one of the small outbuildings. There was no vehicle in sight. Tall grass had been worn down in parallel tracks leading toward the rusting, black-molded barn. Beyond the house, a structure typical of rural Clarendon County, they caught a glimpse of openness, of the saline marsh along Black Water Creek.

"Well, let's see if Mr. Feltzer is home," Clare said.

She eased the black and white along the track pressed into the tall grass, past one of the ancient water oaks, stopped fifty feet from the front porch of the house, killed the engine. She proved she had not forgotten her training by picking up the mike and calling C.S.D. to report she would be out of her vehicle at the home of one John Feltzer approximately six miles north of Black Water Point. Munday was getting out of the car as the dispatcher gave his ten-four to Clare's call.

The wind was blowing from the direction of the smoke house—for that, evidentially, was what it was—between the house and the barn. It carried a smell familiar to both Munday and Clare, both of them being farm bred types.

"Little late in the year to be curing hams," Clare said.

"Maybe he's smoking fish." When he had first moved to Clarendon County a beer joint just inside the city limits in Summerton served cold beer with a smoked spot. It had been a quick and delicious snack.

"Not fish," Clare said.

"No signs of life," Munday said, as he stretched and yawned.

As if to belie his statement a fat, black dog, a Lab mix, sauntered out of the wide door of the barn and barked lazily.

"Try the house first?" Clare asked.

"Mr. Feltzer," Munday bellowed. "Yo, Mr. Feltzer. Anybody home?"

Silence. Munday thought he caught a motion out of the corner of his eye, as if one of the curtains in the front windows opening onto the porch had moved. Rain began to fall again

263

in a fine mist. The wind shifted and a rusting weathervane on the front top ridge of the barn moved with an agonized squeal of metal.

"Anybody home?" Munday called out again. The dog started barking again down by the barn. Munday turned to look, stood in profile to the house.

Clare walked toward the porch. Munday turned to follow, saw the faded and peeling front door move. It opened just a crack. "Clare," he said.

He was going to say, "Hold up for a minute."

He had time to say only, "Clare—"

The scabrous door opened suddenly, revealing a blackness within the house. A dark bulk was there. It winked at him, rapidly, and the blinking of light was accompanied by a burst of sound and a solid, wet, plop of force and shock that knocked his legs out from under him. As he fell heavily he saw Clare jerk backward, and go limp, and begin to melt. When he hit the ground old training took over as he rolled into the long grass, reaching for his weapon. He left a trail of blood behind him. He did not feel pain, not then.

The winking came again and high velocity rounds mowed the high grass near his head. It was an automatic weapon. Familiar sound. Probably an AR-16. Clare on the ground, melted, broken, and fire in his hip. He loosed two quick rounds from his 9 mm, aiming at the black bulk in the dark opening. The winking of the automatic weapon ceased. He rolled again, crawled in frantic haste to put one of the big water oaks between him and the open door. Waves of pain. Faintness. He put his hand back and felt blood, lots of it. He twisted. The high velocity, small caliber round had entered his buttock just behind his left hip socket and ripped a tunnel through soft flesh to leave an exit wound which felt to his exploring fingers like the Grand Canyon. He heard himself panting and moaning softly, forced his lips closed, lifted his head. Clare lay on her back. Blood was oozing from at least three wounds, one of them dead center in her right breast, another at the vee of her ribs, the last at heart center. She was stiller than death, her eyes open, not reacting as they were sprinkled by the fine, soft rain.

The shock of knowing she was dead, combined with the trauma of his wound, glazed his eyes. Through a red haze he heard a door slam, lifted his head with a great effort, saw a man in bib overalls moving slowly and cautiously along the north wall of the house. He was a tall man, a lanky man, and he held an assault rifle in his hands as if he knew what to do with it. He wore a visored redneck cap and the lower part of his face was hidden by a wild, black beard. Munday waited. The low hanging limbs of the water oak prevented a clear shot. It was a pistol against an automatic rifle. He would have only one chance, and his vision kept blurring. He gripped his automatic hard in his hand and waited, whispering subvocally, "Yes, come on. Come on, you mother. Come to me, you bearded bastard."

The bearded bastard halted at the corner of the house, peered cautiously around. "Hey, cop," he called.

Munday looked down the barrel of his 9 mm. One limb of the oak obscured the vital parts of the bearded bastard's body.

"Cop, you dead?"

"Not yet," Munday said to himself. "Not yet."

The pain in his ass, the shock of seeing Clare lying crumpled and bloody, had driven all but one thought from his mind. He lived for only one reason, to kill the man who stood at the corner of the house, assault rifle at the ready.

"Guess you're dead, huh?" the bearded man said. He stepped out. Munday's finger tensed on the trigger of his weapon. Two more steps. The limb no longer was in the way. Munday centered the sight on the man's chest and pulled once, twice. The first round knocked the tall, lanky man backward, the second knocked the assault rifle from his hands. He fell limply.

Munday forced himself to stand. He felt blood run all the way down his leg. It was pleasantly warm. He looked down. Blood stained the wet grass at his feet. It was a hundred yards from his nose to the ground, and it seemed that he was going to fall all the way down, down, down. He took painful steps toward Clare, sobbing, holding his left hand over the exit wound trying to stop the bleeding. He fell to his knees beside her and it was only then the totality of it hit him and he realized she was really gone.

A high velocity round from a military weapon does terrible things to human flesh. Her right breast was flattened like a deflated balloon. Blood oozed from exit wounds in her back. It was mixed with small, white, fleshy bits of her substance.

"You bastard," he said, turning his head to look toward the killer just in time to see the wink of the assault rifle. A round plopped into Clare's dead body. He threw himself to the left and rolled. The hail of death followed him. Heedless of pain, in spite of his weakness, he staggered to his feet and, bellowing in sheer rage, weaved his way directly into the muzzle of the winking rifle, 9 mm blasting once, twice, three, four times, the fourth bullet finding the bridge of the bearded man's nose. The man went over backward. His visored cap fell off. Munday stood over the body, looking down into a face not old, not young. Ordinary brown eyes, big, bushy eyebrows, the wild, scraggly beard. He put the muzzle of the pistol inches from the fallen man's forehead and pulled the trigger to kill the bastard again.

The smell of carrion was in the air. A lion's cage poorly cleaned. A slaughter house. A week old road kill.

The special at the Road Kill Café today is—

Some of the locals called John Sellers' restaurant the Choke and Puke. Old trucker's C.B. designation for a greasy spoon restaurant. Clare thought it was funny.

Clare.

He had to convince himself all over again she was dead. His vision was coming and going. If he didn't stop his bleeding he would be dead, too. He went to the black and white and found the first aid kit, stuffed gauze into the two holes in his ass, moaning and yelping with the pain. Only then did he reach for the radio, key the transmission switch. His voice was so weak he didn't recognize it. He couldn't remember the ten-codes.

"Officer down," he said, forcing his voice. "Officer needs help."

An eon or so later he remembered Jilly. He called her name. "Jilly. Hey, Jilly." He pulled himself to his feet by holding onto the car door and launched himself through a sea of crimson pain toward the house.

He saw Jilly there, in the living room. Although there was a rank smell the room was tidy, old-fashioned, but tidy. Faded window shades were pulled down. It was dim in the room, but there was Jilly's face. She was on a table beside a lamp. Munday felt for the light switch beside the door and the lamp illuminated both Jilly and Chad. They were pale. Their dull, filmed eyes stared unblinkingly at him. He heard someone making a sound like a dying cat. Still screaming, he fell to his knees in front of the table.

Jilly's head, and Chad's, were mounted on wooden bases. They made a set. Bookends. Munday recognized one of the books. He had an identical copy at home, a gift from the author who had written his name in it. It was *The Beachcomber's Handbook of Seafood Cookery*. Beside it was a book on southern-style barbecue and a thin volume with recipes for marinating steaks.

21

Lance Carver's Monday began with paperwork. Superior Court was in session so half a dozen of his deputies were tied up waiting to give their testimony to the Grand Jury or a trial jury. So far, True Bills had been returned in every case in which C.S.D. had participated. It was going to be a busy month with trials scheduled in no less than a dozen drug charges, two cases of assault, one rape, three breaking and entering, one instance of incest. Sometime during the month Larry Eubanks would face a judge to learn how he was to be punished for the murder of his mother.

Lance was in the process of revamping the duty roster to compensate for court time when Jug Watson came into his office. It was just ten-thirty on a gray, rainy morning.

"The Eubanks kid walked," Jug said without preamble.

"Damn," Lance said, letting his ballpoint pen fall.

"Fifteen years suspended. Five years probation. He is going to live with his aunt and uncle in Columbia."

Lance had not been notified of the time for Larry's appearance before the judge. He sighed. Although there were times when he rather regretted retirement was near that wet, gray Monday was not one of them. He remembered the smell in the Eubanks house, the icy chill of the room with the window air conditioner roaring, the white, wormy squirmings in the decaying flesh around the entry wound in the back of Ethel Eubanks' head.

"Where's Deputy Thomas?" Jug asked. "I think she'll be interested in hearing justice has been served."

"She's in Worthing, checking out the stores where Munday's kid and her boyfriend were going shopping."

"What kind of kids are we raising these days, Lance?" the sheriff asked, as he reached for a cigarette.

"Yeah," Lance said.

"Now you take this incest case on the docket this month," Jug said. "Single parent. Man taking care of his daughter by himself. Incest is a terrible thing but I've seen too many squeals where the kid was getting back at his or her mother or father out of sheer spite or plain deviltry. They threaten their parents. They say, you hit me and I'll tell my teacher I'm being abused. You go into one of those homes and there's nobody in charge. The kid is running things." He shrugged. "I donno."

"Yeah," Lance said, "listen to the knee-jerkers and you think three-quarters of the kids in America are victims of abuse."

"I notice things have been pretty quiet at the high school since we put a deputy in the halls."

"One minor fight since the kid was pushed through the plate glass, that's all," Lance said.

"Good. Good," Jug said, on the way out the door.

Lance completed the revised duty roster, read through a backlog of case reports, drank so much coffee his stomach went sour. He looked up and it was eleven-thirty. If you wanted even reasonably quick service at the Waterfront Café, you had to get there at or before eleven-forty-five. He buttoned his uniform jacket, put on his hat, was joined by three of the female deputies in administration. Usually they walked to the restaurant, but a fine, soft rain was falling so Lance drove and found a parking place near the front door. They had just placed their order—the special was meat loaf, green beans, fried okra, cornbread, and bread puddings—when the courthouse crowd began to pour in. Even if you hadn't known who they were, you could have spotted the lawyers. They gathered in gaggles, one with spectacles low on the nose, others with ties loose as if to give the impression they had been slaving over a hot witness all morning. One of them had a mass of gray, wiry hair cut stylishly. All were dressed in conservative blue and gray. Clerks in dresses and staff members from county offices gathered at different tables. A defendant sat stiffly with his concerned loved ones, a young man, looking ill at ease in suit and tie. The theory was that if you clean them up, shave off the beards, cut the pony tails, put men accustomed to jeans and tees into white shirts and vests the judge would be more lenient.

It was still raining when they finished lunch. The cold mist dampened Lance's jacket as he ran from the overhang in front of the restaurant to the car. Back in the office he pulled it off and, feeling just a bit guilty because it was, after all, late May, turned on one of the electric baseboard heaters to dispel the chill. He was feeling quite cozy and just a bit drowsy when he heard a knock on the door.

"Come," he said.

Gene Justice of the S.B.I. swept into the room and tossed a sheet of paper onto the desk in front of Lance. The paper showed upper and lower sets of teeth in opposition, upper on top, lower below. Lance looked up in question.

"Read the name and address," Justice said.

Lance read: "Clara Jean Feltzer, Box 34, R.R. 4, Black Water Point."

"You know how many copies of the chart from that jawbone we are even now in the process of sending out?" Justice asked. "Don't ask," he said quickly. "And where do we find the dentist who did the work?"

Lance could read. The dental chart was headed: Dr. Arlan P. Warren, Family Dentist, 455 Main Street, Summerton.

"There are several Feltzers out there around the point," Lance said.

"Doc Warren said her bill was paid by her husband, one John Feltzer. She was in his office last three years ago."

Lance punched his intercom, said, "Nancy, see if J. C. Barnes is home, please." He looked up at Justice. "J.C. lives in that end of the county. Knows all the people."

The intercom buzzed. "J.C.'s on the phone, Chief," the desk sergeant said.

"Yeah, J.C.," Lance said. "You know a John Feltzer, down at the Point?"

Lance could tell from the deputy's fuzzy voice he had been asleep. "Sorry to wake you," he said.

"No sweat," Barnes said. "John Feltzer. Yes. That would be old Robert Feltzer's younger brother. Lives up the creek from Robert's place."

"He had a wife named Clara Jean?"

"Had is right, chief," the deputy said. " 'Bout two, three years ago Clara Jean ran off with a young stud crewing on one of Robert Feltzer's shrimp boats."

"She didn't run far," Lance said.

"Something up, Chief?" Barnes asked.

"That jawbone Dan Munday and Clare Thomas found checks out by dental records to belong to Clara Jean Feltzer."

There was a musing silence from the other end of the line, then Barnes said, "Yes. You know, I don't doubt it, come to think of it. John Feltzer always was about ten degrees off true north. Looks like he killed his wife, huh?"

"Somebody did," Lance said. "You know how to get to his place?"

"Yeah, I think so."

"I hate to knock you out of your sleep, you pulling the night duty," Lance said, "but I'd appreciate it if you'll go in with us."

"No sweat," Barnes said.

Sometimes it is like that in police work. Real mysteries do not come along too often in a rural county like Clarendon which is one-third slash pine paper company land, one-third swamp and bay, not much farming, mostly seaside resort communities. There is, of course, the ever-present drug traffic, happy and belligerent drunks, winter-time burglary, family fights sometimes ending in knife or gun use, fender-benders and the occasional auto fatality, a rape or two. It leaves a fellow unprepared to play sleuth when something like the affair of the bones comes along. As a result, a check of the records would show an unsolved murder here and there back through the years. A shooting in a mobile home park with no apparent motive. Unsolved. A missing woman found decomposing in a pulpwood forest. Unsolved.

But ah, dem bones. Mystery solved because the answer is right under your nose.

"I'd like to go along," Gene Justice said.

"Sure thing."

Lance stooped, turned off the baseboard heater.

"Damn," said Justice, "that's why it's so hot in here?"

"My blood remembers the turgid, tropical atmosphere of Africa," said Lance Carver, with a grin.

"Bullshit," said the S.B.I. man, grinning back.

And into the midst of this significant conversation bursts Nancy, her eyes wide, mouth open.

"Chief," she blurted, "we've got an officer down."

Time is halted. Lance is pulling on his jacket in slow motion. Gene Justice's head is swiveling toward the watch sergeant, Nancy, with glacial slowness. And Lance has a sick feeling fate has played false with him, that the apparent luck at having identified the burned and blackened jawbone came too late.

Forty-five minutes later—Clarendon was a big county—C.S.D. 10, the Chief Deputy's car, turned off a narrow, wet-black asphalt road into a sandy track. Lance noted the overflowing mailbox, but did not stop to examine its contents. It was evident a car had preceded them. About a mile down the dirt road Deputy J. C. Barnes said, "Stop a minute, Chief." He got out of the car and walked around a huge water oak blown down by the last northeaster.

"That's the road to Robert Feltzer's place," Barnes said, as he got back into the car. "Looks like that tree has been hiding it since the last blow."

"His mailbox was full," Lance said.

Two C.S.D. black and whites, each carrying two fully armed deputies, followed the Chief Deputy's car down the black dirt road and across the ford of the little stream. The three cars fanned out as they came into the weed-grown clearing around the quaint, old country house and its crumbling outbuildings. Deputies ran, swerving and juking, toward the house, the smokehouse which still emitted a hint of smoke, the rusty-roofed barn.

Lance and Gene Justice found Clare Thomas' body. There was no time to mourn. A deputy took shelter momentarily behind the smokehouse, edged around, prepared to make a run for the porch of the house, glanced into the open smokehouse door, froze, backed away, his shotgun aimed at the door in readiness, calling, "Chief, hey, Chief."

Lance ran to the smokehouse, looked in. The smell was meaty, rich with smoke, honey, and salt. Hams, two of them, hanging on hooks. Not pork hams.

"Uhhhh," Lance moaned. He had to fight to keep his stomach down as he backed away.

Behind him he heard a crash as the front door of the house was forced.

"Chief," a deputy called from near the north corner of the house, "there's a dead one here. Shot several times. He smells like shit."

The two deputies who had slammed their way through the front door came scurrying out. One of them sat down weakly on the warped steps and put his head in his hands.

"Hey, Chief," the other said weakly, pointing toward the dark interior of the house. His mouth worked. He could not find words.

Later that day the rain stopped. A rare rainbow formed over the Black Water Creek marsh. S.B.I. forensic experts were flown down from Raleigh by helicopter. Coroner Clef Burns watched, listened, learned, and waited to help load rescue squad ambulances from three municipalities.

Chad Lacewell's Camaro was found in the creek behind John Feltzer's house, the top of it showing above the black water on low tide. In the drawer of a lamp table in John Feltzer's bedroom there were three driver's licenses that had belonged to a seventeen-year-old girl from Maryland, an eighteen-year-old boy from Kentucky, and a sixteen-year-old boy from New York. In the same drawer there were rings, watches, a bracelet, a set of dog tags stamped with a name and an army serial number. In the barn, which served as garage and butcher shop, was a late model Ford pick-up big-cab with a large tool box on the back. S.B.I. investigators found traces of blood and human hair in the tool box.

John Feltzer was dead. He would never confirm the assumptions made by Lance Carver and Gene Justice that he made occasional forays away from the old house on Black Water Creek. Hunting trips. Killing expeditions to replenish his stores. When deputies tracked down John's older brother, Robert, he told them it had been almost a month since he had left his house, that he had wondered why no one came to see the shrimp boat he had advertised by calling the Summerton newspaper. The old man told deputies he had not seen his brother in three years, not since they fought over the way John treated his young wife. He allowed that his brother, John, had never been quite under full sail since he got back from that there war, and that he got worse after Clara Jean run away with that there young stud off the shrimp boat.

Lance was back in his office with Gene Justice. It was almost ten o'clock. He was tired, and for the first time since his mother had died he felt as if he would like to put his head down on his desk and cry. He had suffered a personal loss with Clare Thomas' death. He did not know Jilly Munday that well, just through Dan and by sight. A pretty little girl. One of the good ones, from what he knew about her. And she was dead because of an unpredictable series of unconnected events. The desire of a young boy to own a boat. The mutual attraction that had made Jilly and Chad a pair. A windstorm that blew down an oak tree and blocked the road to Robert Feltzer's house, forcing Chad Lacewell to drive his Camaro down a black dirt road and into the den of one of society's predators, one of the products of the Twentieth Century's plague, a creation of the pressures, the tensions, the crowding, the media's fascination with the plague of violence, the devaluation of the system of punishment for criminal acts, of permissiveness, and war, and human madness, and the tendency to pity the perpetrator more than the victim.

The two kids drove into the jaws of a carnivore and the world was diminished by their loss.

"The sonofabitch had a great collection of cookbooks," Gene Justice said musingly.

Lance nodded. The S.B.I. forensic people had taken cooked bits of flesh and hair from a microwave oven. There were tasty looking pot pies in the freezer. A deputy had shot and killed the black Lab when he saw the bones he had been chewing.

The intercom buzzed. It was Summerton Hospital on the line. Dan Munday had recovered from the anesthesia and was asking for Lance. Lance said, "I'll be there directly."

"I doubt if we'll ever identify all of them," Justice said. "The sonofabitch was sly. My guess is that most of them were runaways, hitchhikers. The soldier whose dog tags we found was a deserter."

At the John Feltzer house deputies and S.B.I. men were working under floodlights, digging into old flowerbeds and the manure-rich dirt of the barnyard.

"If that Lacewell kid had waited just one more day to go looking for a boat—"

Lance wasn't listening. He was back in the old house remembering the dimness and the slaughterhouse smell. He was standing in the doorway of a bedroom. Looking at Dan Munday as he knelt beside a bed.

Munday had reassembled them on the faded chenille bedspread. He had carried legs and arms from the butcher shop in the barn, honey and salt covered parts from the smokehouse. The heads were still mounted on wooden bases. He looked up at Lance with a pained expression on his face.

"I think it's fitting," Munday said, "that they lie here together, because she'll never know the consummation of her feelings. He took that away from them, didn't he?"

A number ten washtub was beside the bed. Lance swallowed hard and turned away when he saw its contents. The slaughterhouse smell wafted upward from the half-full galvanized tub.

"The trouble is," Dan Munday said, reaching down to touch a purplish, bulging mass that moved sluggishly under his fingers, "I can't tell which ones are hers and which ones are his."

22

Munday spent a lot of time on the front porch that June. He lay on a lounger on his stomach and stared at grains of sand tracked in from the beach. Now and then the Kid or one of the other Fortier Beach policemen dropped by to see if he needed to restock his supply of frozen dinners. At first they brought beer, paying tribute to that old male-perpetuated myth that alcohol can help a man forget. At first the beer disappeared, but then the refrigerator was full of beer, so they stopped bringing it.

Late in the day, after the beach was mostly clear of people, Munday would limp down to sit on the lower step of the walkway and watch the sandpipers dance before the foamy, reaching ripples of surf. He dreaded going into the house. The silence of it was a shriek in his mind, the emptiness a load too heavy to bear.

They told him Elaine attended the funeral services for Jilly, that she came to his hospital room to stand in the door and look at him as he slept. He could imagine her standing there, eyes squinted in hate, for she made it clear with one terrible telephone call after he came home from the hospital she blamed him for Jilly's death. He listened without comment. He was tempted to make Elaine's day by telling her she was one hundred percent right, he was to blame, if he had been half the policeman he pretended to be—

But what the hell, it was over.

He lost not only the surplus twenty pounds that caused too much of Munday to hang over his belt, but ten pounds in addition to that. He was at his football playing weight of twenty-five years past. He didn't give a damn about that, either.

They patched the exit hole in his buttock the way punctured inner tubes used to be repaired, with a swatch of skin transplanted from the other side of his rear. He had one hell of a dimple there. A fist-sized depression ached when he sat on it. He kept postponing going back to work, although the commissioners were getting a little antsy, making it quite clear to him the little town of Fortier Beach couldn't afford to have its police chief on sick leave forever.

The answering machine tape was full. He didn't bother to check it. He dozed away the evenings in his chair, the television set muttering on a randomly selected channel to keep him company. He answered the door only reluctantly because he did not want to have to face the pity of the Kid and the others.

Summer came pouring up from the tropics, conveyed by the giant heat pump known as the Bermuda High. Driven inside by sweat running into his eyes, Munday prowled the house, pacing, favoring his left leg. When the doorbell rang he growled, moved slowly—giving whoever it was plenty of time to leave—to open the door.

"Hey, Dan," Lance Carver said. Sweat was already beading on Lance's *café au lait* forehead. He didn't wait for an invitation, but pushed past Munday. "Lemme in out of this bake oven," he said.

Munday closed the door, stood staring at the game show on the television.

"I'm going up to the restaurant and have some shrimp,"

Lance said. "Put your shoes on and come along."

"I don't think so, Lance. Thanks."

"Don't give me any stuff, Dan. Just get your shoes. I've got a couple of things you need to know and I'm not going to talk in this bear's den. Hell, it smells almost as bad as John Feltzer's place."

He drew the comparison deliberately. He felt it was time for Munday to emerge from the hole he had dug, crawled into, and pulled in after himself. The Munday he knew from the old days would not have retired from the world, even when the world imploded on him. The Munday he saw in the bedroom of the Feltzer house, the mad Munday who could not figure out which heart, lungs, kidneys, belonged to the daughter he was trying to reconstruct, haunted him. He had in his pocket and in his head two items that, he felt, might just bring back the Munday who had been a good cop.

Munday flinched mentally at the reference, but managed to hide the flood of remorse and pain. He pushed his bare feet into a pair of loafers, brushed back his silver-sprinkled chestnut hair, followed Lance down to the black and white. Neither of them spoke until they were seated in a secluded booth at the back of Sellers Harbor Fine Seafood. Lance reached into his jacket pocket and handed Munday a letter. The envelope was lavender, and smaller than business size.

"It's addressed to you," Munday said, reading Lance's name written in a feminine hand.

"Read it."

There was a smell of lavender to match the color of the envelope and the one sheet of stationery inside. The date was ten days past.

Dear Chief Deputy Carver,

I left Summerton so hurriedly I didn't have time to

thank you for having saved what was left of my reputation, not to mention my self-respect. What you did will
forever be one of the few pleasant memories I have of
that quaint little village on the Blue River. Thank you
again, and God bless you.

Evie Baugh

There was no return address. The envelope was post-
marked Jacksonville, Florida.

Munday's first reaction was pain. He told himself he was
being paranoid to think the phrase about pleasant memories
was aimed at him. In Evie's time of desperate need he had
been lacking. He had questioned her as a cop, when he
should have been giving her the unqualified support of a
friend. He had failed Evie, too. His ineptness had killed
Clare, his lack of foresight had killed Jilly and Chad; and he
could not even bring himself to believe in a woman who had
been his lover.

"I thought you might be curious," Lance said.

"Yes, I appreciate it."

"What I did, I brought that Schul kid in on the pretext of
having him record his statement and I put the screws to him.
Hell, I'm so close to retirement I can risk having all the polit-
ical weight in Clarendon County thrown at me. I told the
little bastard I knew he was lying, that he was as guilty as sin
of making improper advances to a nice lady and if he didn't
withdraw the accusations he made I was going to kick his
white ass up between his shoulders."

"Lance, that is damned fine police work," Munday said,
feeling a chuckle almost ready to break through the sludge
clogging his mind.

"He confessed, and begged me not to tell his dad. I told
him all he had to do was withdraw the charges he made

against Miss Baugh and he could tell his dad whatever he chose."

Oddly, relief was temporary. Guilt was heavier. He should have told Evie he believed her instead of grilling her as if he suspected she was lying.

"I tried to convince her to stick it out here," Lance said, "but she said—and she was right—that she'd never live down being hauled in to jail in her shortie gown and a ratty old robe."

"Lance, anyone ever tell you that you're a good man?"

"My wife does, two or three times a week," Lance said with a wide, white grin.

"Sheeeeit," Munday said.

"No brag, just fact."

"Sure," Munday said.

They both ordered shrimp, potato salad, and slaw. Hush puppies came automatically. The waitress delivered coffee while they waited. It was, after all, a civilized Southern café.

"You heard that the judge gave Larry Eubanks fifteen suspended, five probation?" Lance asked.

"Yes. The Kid told me."

"Now get this," Lance said. "I had a call the other day from South Carolina Social Services in Columbia. This dear little sweet voiced social worker was inquiring for information regarding one Larry Eubanks, a minor, who had applied to the welfare office for money because he was an orphan. She said there was only one question. I asked her how I could help and she said, well, on his application it is stated that his mother died as the result of homicide. Is there any way to verify that?"

Munday shook his head. In the modern world it seemed wonders would never cease.

"I told her it was a matter of record in Clarendon County

Superior Court the Eubanks kid shot and killed his mother."
He grinned at Munday. "I was curious enough to ask her if
that would have any bearing on his application for welfare
payments. Know what she said?"

"Was she a blond?" Munday asked.

"Probably. She said, in that sweet, upper-crust little voice,
well, if he's not in prison doesn't that mean the court found
him to be innocent?"

"Didn't it?" Munday asked, raising his eyebrows.

"That's what I told her," Lance said. "I said, lady, I guess
you're right."

"Think he's going to get the money?"

"What do you think?" Lance asked cynically.

Actually, wonders never *do* cease. Just as Munday was finishing his large plate of Australian shrimp he looked up into
green eyes framed by cornsilk hair, into a smile that flattened
a big, full upper lip into a thing of awe and beauty.

"Hello, Chief Munday," Toni Aycock said.

"Toni," Munday said. "You're looking very good."

"Thank you," she said.

Munday said, "Lance, do you know Toni?"

"Miss Aycock," Lance said. "How are things upstate?"

"Not good," Toni said. "Mr. Munday, would you like to
buy an unemployed girl a drink?"

"Sure thing," Munday said, sliding over to allow Toni to
sit beside him.

"I hate to rush things," Lance said, "but I've got to get
back to the office."

"That drink will have to wait," Munday said. "I'm riding
with him."

"I can take you where you want to go," Toni said.

"I'll leave you in good hands," Lance said, exiting before
Munday could protest.

Toni ordered a margarita. Munday took a refill on his coffee.

"An unemployed lady?" he asked. "Last time I saw you, you were top salesman—lady."

"The market went to hell in a handbasket," Toni said, "and this dizzy little blonde came into the office and very quickly secured a favored position with her plush little body."

"It's a cruel world," Munday said.

"To the cruel world," Toni said, lifting her glass.

"Cheers," Munday said, with his cup raised.

"Mr. Munday, I was shocked when I heard—"

"Yep," he said.

"I couldn't believe it. Not in silly, peaceful old Clarendon."

"Believe it," he said. He needed to change the subject. "I haven't seen your parents lately. They holding up?"

"They still can't accept it," she said.

"I can understand that."

"I think if they knew, really, why she did it—"

Munday felt a familiar sinking inside. Another failure. He had told this pretty young woman with the cornsilk hair he would answer that question for her.

She touched his hand. "Please don't think that I'm faulting you."

He shrugged.

She looked away, lifted her glass, drained it. "Can we get out of here?"

"All right," he said.

She drove him home. He had not realized how rank the house was. It stank of stale, dirty laundry, unwashed dishes. "What a bear's den," she said.

"I haven't felt much like cleaning up."

"Show me where things are," she said, putting her purse aside.

"Hey, you don't have to."

"Kitchen first, you slob. Come on, get with the program."

Food had hardened on plates. She attacked them with a scouring pad. She put Munday to work loading the dishwasher, wiped her hands, went into the living room and put a CD on Jilly's machine. Patsy Cline.

I go out walking, after midnight—

One of Jilly's favorite songs. He tried to shut it out. Toni was back, giving orders, being bossy.

"What do you get when you play a country western song backward?" Toni asked.

"A headache?"

"You get back your wife, your girlfriend, your dog, your pick-up truck—"

She had the washer and the dishwasher running. After a while the first load of clean laundry went into the dryer. In spite of the air conditioner there was a sheen of perspiration on her face as she ran the vacuum in the living room.

"You're going to make someone a good wife someday," Munday said.

"I tried that," she said.

"Welcome to the club."

"Loser's club?"

"Whatever," he said.

When she decided to take a break he opened two beers and handed her one.

"I can remember when you'd have arrested me for this," she said. He was standing beside her chair.

"You've come a long way, baby."

"Two steps forward, three back," she said.

"Listen," he said, "both of us can't go moping around feeling sorry for ourselves."

"I thought of it first."

He chuckled, put his hand on her shoulder. "Little girl need some sympathy?"

"Just a ton or so," she said, putting her hand atop his.

He thought, as he felt his libido surge, *"Well, aren't you a prize, you horny old bastard?"*

She stood, looked up at him. "Do you ever feel you just need something to hang onto, someone to hold, someone to keep you from falling off the world?"

He swallowed.

Her eyes were wide, her lips parted. "Dan, we've both lost something, but I suspect you're hurting just a bit more than I am right at the moment, so if you want something to hang onto—"

She came into his arms. He put his nose into her fragrant, cornsilk hair and felt his chest constrict, his throat close. When he could no longer hold back the huge, racking, male sobs she wept with him. When they came together in his freshly made bed their eyes were red and swollen and their emotions rubbed so near the pith that the surge and detonation of consummation left them weak and panting. She laughed.

"I've always heard it said older men make good lovers," she said.

"Well, we try harder."

She lay with her head in the hollow of his shoulder. A moon peered in the window, glowing softly on her rounded whiteness.

"You're crazy, you know," he said.

"It's going around."

"Are you going to stay?"

"Want me to?"

"God, yes."

"O.K."

She slept, making a sound like a bee. He watched the

moon throw shadows on her face, touched her flat, full, upper lip with his fingertip. She stirred. Loneliness assailed him, but the guilt that tried to follow was overbalanced by the smell of her, by the pleasure of the feel of her against him, by the knowledge there was in her a wealth of human kindness and tenderness, enough to make her want to reach down a slim, pretty hand to save the life of a drowning old man of forty-five.

"Hey," he said.

"Ummm." She burrowed closer to him, throwing one full, warm leg over his middle.

"Hey, Toni?"

"What?"

"Know what you get when you put a blond in the freezer?"

"Ummmf."

"A frosted flake."

She hit him in the stomach. "If you're going to wake me out of a nice, sound sleep, you'd better either have a better joke than that or have something interesting on your feeble male mind."

"This interesting?" he asked, moving his hand gently.

"Ummm," she said. "Very, very, very."